THE TATE REVENGE

A NOVEL

To Mrs. Pike,
Enjoy the book!
W Rayf

THE TATE REVENGE

A NOVEL BY
WILLIAM RAWLINGS JR

HARBOR
HOUSE

AUGUSTA

THE TATE REVENGE
By William Rawlings Jr.
A Harbor House Book/2005

Copyright 2005 by William Rawlings Jr.

For information address:
     HARBOR HOUSE
     111 TENTH STREET
     AUGUSTA, GEORGIA 30901

Library of Congress Cataloging-in-Publication Data

Rawlings, William, 1948-
  The Tate revenge : a novel / William Rawlings, Jr.
    p. cm.
  "A Harbor House Book"--T.p. verso.
  ISBN 1-891799-33-9 (alk. paper)
  1. Southern States--Fiction. I. Title.
  PS3618.A96T38 2005
  813'.6--dc22

             2005015129

Printed in the United States of America

10 9 8 7 6 5 4 3 2 1

To the memory of
William Rawlings Sr., MD
1918-2004
He had an interesting life

SPECIAL DEDICATION

I want to thank Tammara Bryan, PhD, for her support of The American Heart Association and her inspiration in the writing of this book.

ACKNOWLEDGMENTS

Any book is rarely a work done alone. There are many people to whom I owe a debt of gratitude for their help, encouragement and inspiration. As with my previous books, many thanks go to the team at Harbor House Publishing, including especially Randall and Anne Floyd, Carrie McCullough, and others.

Special thanks are due two accomplished writers, Bill Harris and Steve Berry. I appreciate their encouragement, insight and advice. I am immensely grateful to Steve for the time that he has devoted to showing me fine points in the craft of writing.

Several friends have been kind enough to read the manuscript of *The Tate Revenge* during its creation and afterwards, and have offered invaluable criticism and support. These include Larry Walker of Perry, Ken and Diane Saladin, Anne Nevin, Becky Burgess, Tommye Cashin, and others.

Without the support of my long-suffering wife and daughters, finding the time that it takes to create a novel would not be possible. Many others have been most kind in their enthusiastic support, especially John and Carole Barton. I am grateful to St. John Flynn for having me as his guest on Georgia Public Radio's Cover to Cover. I appreciate the many bookstore owners and staff who have allow me to do book signings, and the many libraries and civic organizations that I have had the pleasure of addressing over the past year. I must thank my brother Judge Tom Rawlings who, in a fine "throw me in the briarpatch" moment, agreed to go to Paris with me to make certain that I had accurately described those scenes that take place in the City of Light. Finally, a special word of thanks to Kate Allgood, who made the word flesh.

Finally, for me, no work of creativity would be possible without the influence of my muse, the lovely Laura Ann Ashley.

Part I:

Oh how they cling and wrangle, some who claim
For preacher and monk the honored name!
For, quarreling, each to his view they cling.
Such folk see only one side of a thing.

-From the Buddhist *Parable of*
The Blind Men and the Elephant

CHAPTER
One

Paris
Saturday, April 10, 2004

THE PART OF THE JOB that I should have loved the most had become the part of my work I loved the least. Tour guides are supposed to be enthusiastic, eager people. At times like this I couldn't have cared less. I still missed Colette.

It was one of those rare perfect spring days in Paris. The mass of the Eiffel Tower loomed above me, gleaming warmly in the fading light of the clear, chilly April afternoon. To my right, a sea of bright tulips lined the green expanse of the Champs de Mars as the sun glinted off the dome of the École Militaire in the distance. To my left, lovers strolled along the Seine, huddling close for warmth. Behind me, in an irregular queue, stood six American divorcées who had signed on for the exclusive one-week "April in Paris" offering of Madeleine Tours. They were all mine for the evening for the "Nighttime in the City of Lights" segment.

As we waited for tickets to the lifts I surveyed my charges. Directly behind me stood Erica Frank — early forties, blond. All considered not a bad client except for her obvious expectation that the services of the guide should include more than a simple tour of the highlights of Paris.

Next to Erica stood three pudgy middle-aged ladies from Atlanta, all of whom had lost their husbands to younger women. They came to Paris to spend their alimony checks while secretly hoping to meet some mysterious stranger without a criminal record. Beneath it all they had to know their chances here were about as dismal as those at home, but I couldn't fault them for trying.

Bringing up the rear were Mary Pearson and Amy Clarke, a mother and daughter whose marriages had fallen apart simultaneously, and for whom a week in Paris was a brief respite from the world at home that had collapsed around them.

Erica was pressing her case. "Nate, tonight after the tour, I thought maybe we could — " She was interrupted by a commotion from the direction of the river.

Turning at the sound of a muffled scream, we saw a woman holding her hands over her mouth while her companion pointed in our direction.

After a moment Erica pulled the collar of her white kid leather coat around her neck and began once more. "Look, this is my first time in Paris, and since you live here, it would be nice if we could — " She stopped abruptly when she sensed me staring at her shoulder.

It appeared suddenly in the periphery of my vision as I listened to her proposition: a blotch of red, sharply defined on the stark white of her jacket. Following my eyes, she turned her head to the side to see another ragged splotch appear next to the first one. Something liquid and red.

We both looked up. Hanging limply in the iron lattice-work of the tower above us was the body of a dark-haired woman, her fall from the top broken by the struts and girders that supported the massive structure.

Erica Frank screamed.

CHAPTER
Two

I ARRIVED BACK AT MY FLAT on the rue des Capucines shortly after midnight. Trudging up four flights of creaking stairs I silently cursed the concierge, Madame Bouchard, who cut the power to the ancient and noisy lift every evening at eight. As if baby-sitting tourists for six hours was not enough punishment.

All considered, the rest of the evening had gone surprisingly well. Of course the standard start of the tour, watching the sunset from the Eiffel Tower, had been canceled.

The suicide — as I assumed that was the case — wasn't the best opening act for the pleasures of Paris by night. I'd managed to make up for it by taking them to a small open air café overlooking the Seine and plying them with *vin de table* until they were sufficiently mellow, all the while distracting them with amusing stories from my experiences as a tour guide in Paris. That was followed by an informal dinner at a left bank bistro (with more wine) and finally by an unfailingly romantic hour cruising the Seine on one of the many *bateaux mouches*.

At the tour's end the ladies from Atlanta, now emboldened by wine, set out on a self-directed search for French masculinity and, most likely, more disappointment. The mother and daughter headed back to their hotel room, leaving me alone with the increasingly persistent Erica, who was now in full predatory mode thanks to the alcohol. I managed to pry myself away after a single drink in the bar of her hotel accompanied by the declaration that, as tempting as her offers might be, company management strictly forbade relationships between tour guides and clients. That was mostly true, deleting only the part that I was co-owner of the company and could change the rules whenever I wanted.

My apartment was dark, illuminated only by the yellow glow of the street lamps reflecting off the ceiling from the boulevard below. It was cold, thanks again to Madame Bouchard who cut back the central heating nightly at eleven. I turned on a lamp and pressed the message button on the answering machine. There were two early afternoon messages from my assistant Michelle, but it was nothing that couldn't wait until the morning. The machine beeped for a third message and I heard, in English this time, "Nate? Are you there? Please pick up if you are! I need to talk with you!"

A pause. "Nate, it's very important that I — " Another pause. "Oh. I've… I've got to go now." There was a click followed by the sound of a dial tone. I looked at the time stamp displayed on the panel. 3:27 PM. The voice seemed familiar. Or was it? If she didn't bother to leave her name it couldn't be that important. I erased the messages and went to bed.

The mechanical groaning of the lift awoke me at seven. Street sounds mixed with soft sunlight filtered thought the tall windows. I was contemplating getting up when I heard a sharp rapping at my door accompanied by the harsh voice of Madame Bouchard, "Monsieur Finch? Are you there? You have visitors."

My first thought was that the ladies from Atlanta had gotten themselves arrested and that I was being summoned to try to talk their way out of police custody, but that didn't make sense. The one company rule that I never broke was giving out my home address. I yelled back, "I'll be there in a moment." I leapt out of bed, pulled on the faded robe that I'd left flung over a chair and padded barefoot to the door.

The venerable Madame stood before me in her dressing gown, her silver hair covered in a long tasseled nightcap. Two men stood behind her, both wearing ties and protected from the morning chill by long dark overcoats. I noted close-cropped hair and polished, but scuffed, shoes. Cops. "Monsieur Finch. These gentlemen are from the police and they say that they've come to question you about an incident. Now, I don't know what this is all about—"

The taller of the two men interrupted her. "Madame, we are here on a routine inquiry. We merely need to see if Monsieur Finch can help by providing us with some information. Please be assured that he is not a suspect in any crime," he paused, "at this time." He stepped forward and extended his hand. "Monsieur Nathan Finch?" I nodded. "I am Lieutenant Andrade of the Paris police. This is my associate, Sergeant Foch." I shook Andrade's hand. Sergeant Foch nodded. I stood in the doorway waiting. Andrade spoke, "May we come in? This may take a few minutes and it's a bit chilly out." It was more of a command than a request.

I opened the door and pointed them to the divan in what had at one time been a formal parlor. "It's early in the morning for a 'routine' matter, Lieutenant," I said. "How can I help you?"

"You are American," he replied, stating the obvious.

"I am."

"And we understand that you operate a tour company headquartered here in Paris. It that correct?"

"It is. We have two offices, one here and the other in Atlanta, Georgia, in the U.S. We specialize in Paris and other French destinations."

He nodded. I was beginning to get a hint of where this all was leading. At any given time we had an average of sixty clients on travel itineraries somewhere in Western Europe, most within a couple of hundred kilometers of Paris. On any given day at least one of those clients was likely to cause a problem. Several times a year this involved the police, usually with the vacationer being charged as drunk and disorderly, or as the victim of petty theft, but nothing to bring the police to my flat at seven in the morning. "Monsieur Finch, can you tell us your whereabouts yesterday afternoon at approximately five o'clock?"

"Of course," I replied. "I was at the Eiffel Tower." Both Andrade and Foch involuntarily stiffened.

"And your purpose there?" The tone of Andrade's voice had changed.

"I was leading a group of clients on a city tour."

"Then of course you are aware of the, er, incident, that occurred." Both officers watched closely for my response.

"You mean the jumper? The suicide? How could I not be? We were standing directly under where the body lodged. I suppose if it hadn't gotten caught in the metalwork it would have landed right on top of us."

Foch spoke for the first time. "You were alone?"

"No. You didn't listen. I said that I was there with a group of tourists. That's my business. I'm a certified Paris Tour Guide and I lead tours!"

"You called it a 'suicide'," Andrade said. "Why do you say that?"

I was beginning to get angry. "Hey! You barge in here and roust me out of bed to ask me questions about something that I know nothing about. If you need witnesses I've got six of them. Six lonely American women."

"I apologize," Andrade stopped me. "Let me be more direct. Did you know the woman who died yesterday?"

"No, of course not." *At least I don't think so*, I thought to myself. "Who was she?"

"We don't know," Foch answered. "We thought you might be able to help us. She carried no identification. No purse, no passport, nothing. The labels in her clothing would seem to indicate that she was American."

I stood up. "Officers, there are hundreds of tour services in Paris. Yes, our clientele is chiefly from the States, but I would have heard by now if we had anyone missing."

"Sit down, Monsieur Finch," Andrade's voice was cold. "We have a reason for being here. You say that you didn't know the victim, but she seems to have known you." My stomach fluttered. "Your phone number was found on a slip of paper in her coat pocket. Not your business number, Monsieur Finch, your private number here at this flat."

I had no idea what he was talking about. I told him as much.

"We checked the records and found that a call was placed from a phone booth near the Place de la Résistance to this number at about half past three yesterday afternoon. An hour and a half later our young lady — I believe you Americans would refer to her as 'Jane Doe' — was dead.

Just why, Monsieur Finch, did she have your private number?"

I was beginning to worry. "There was a call yesterday afternoon. They left a message but they didn't leave a name. It was a woman, an American judging from the accent, but I don't think I recognized her voice."

"Do you think you might be able to identify the body?"

I cringed. "If necessary, yes."

Foch was carrying a leather portfolio that I hadn't noticed before. He laid it on the coffee table in front of me and flipped it open. A large glossy photo of a face, obviously taken in the morgue, was on top. A wave of nausea swept over me. The long dark hair framed the finely sculpted face of Rebecca Tate, whose last words to me two years earlier were, "I love you."

CHAPTER
Three

BY NINE, I WAS AT the 7th Arrondissement Police Head-
quarters, located on rue Fabert in a near-subterranean building carved out of the green expanse of the Esplanade des
Invalides. It could have been a typical urban police station
in any American city. The waiting area next to the entrance
held a diverse group of Sunday morning supplicants: nervous women with too much makeup, two bedraggled-look-
ing men with bandaged foreheads, and others who were
obviously trying to recover from a hard night of drinking. I
announced my presence to the Sergeant at the desk and sat
on a sagging couch next to a young dark-skinned mother
who whispered into a cell phone in Arabic-accented French
while her fretting infant pawed at her left breast.

Earlier at my flat, Andrade and Foch saw the shock on
my face when I realized that I had known the dead woman.
We spoke there for a few minutes more, Foch having me
repeat in detail my whereabouts and my activities the preceding afternoon. After a whispered conference, Andrade

20

stepped out of earshot to make a couple of phone calls and then announced that we should continue the interview at his "office." Before they left, they asked for a list of persons who could confirm my alibi. I gave them Erica Frank's name and hotel telephone number.

I sat and waited silently, thinking of Rebecca Whitford Tate of Atlanta, Georgia. She'd been twenty-eight when I'd last seen her. The owner of Tate Interiors, LLC — Importers of Fine European Antiques. 'Becky' to her friends. The beautiful Becky with stunning brown eyes and a smile that made me weak in my knees. The Becky who I held close in my arms as we leaned against the ramparts at Le Mont St. Michel. The only woman who, given the time and opportunity, might have made me forget Colette. Why had she called? What was she doing in Paris? Had she been in trouble? Why would she want to kill herself — or had it been a terrible accident? If I had been at home to answer the phone could I have stopped her? Waves of guilt crested and crashed in my head.

After half an hour, Foch appeared in the lobby and directed me to follow him. He led me through a maze of narrow hallways with offices on either side, finally arriving at a door labeled "Homicide Section." The thought of murder had not occurred to me. I wanted to ask but thought better of it. I was ushered into to a windowless interview room with a table, an ashtray and three metal straight-back chairs. A video camera was affixed to the ceiling in one corner, and a microphone was suspended over the table. "We'll be with you presently. You may smoke," Foch said and left, the door clicking shut as he closed it. I got up and tried the handle. It was locked.

Another half an hour passed. I stared at the gray walls and studied the pattern on the ceiling tiles. A ventilation grill hissed softly with the flow of forced air into the room.

I tried to use my cell phone to call my office but I couldn't get a good signal through the thick masonry walls of the building. The door opened and Andrade entered followed by Foch. They didn't smile. Andrade spoke. "You can relax, Monsieur Finch. You are definitely not a suspect. Your alibis for yesterday check out. I presume that by now you realize that we suspect that Mademoiselle Tate's death was not an accident and not a suicide. We appreciate your assistance, and this early in the investigation we need every scrap of information that might be of help." Andrade sat down in the chair across the table. Foch leaned, arms akimbo, against the wall just behind me.

"Are you implying that Becky was murdered, Lieutenant?" I asked.

"Suffice it to say that we're still working on hypotheses."

"For god's sake, what happened? There must be witnesses. The Eiffel Tower on a Saturday afternoon...."

"Let us conduct this interview, Monsieur Finch. If it seems appropriate, we will give you a few details," Andrade replied. He reached in his shirt pocket and took out a pack of unfiltered Gauloises. "Do you mind if I smoke?"

"I do," I replied. Ignoring me, he lit his cigarette and flipped open a folder.

"All right," Andrade began, "Let me tell you some of what we've discovered and ask you a few questions." He took a color copy of the photo page of a passport from the folder and placed it in front of me. "Is this the woman that you know as Rebecca Tate?"

I studied the photo. It was the same passport that I'd seen before. "It is," I replied. "Where did you find it?"

"We canvassed the hotels, starting with the area nearest Place de la Résistance from where Mme. Tate called you. The proprietor of a small hotel on rue de Gros Caillou recognized the name, and identified the morgue photos as those of a woman who'd checked in six days ago. She'd left her passport and a few pieces of jewelry in the hotel safe. So I think now we are sure who she is."

"But what was she doing here in Paris? Why?" I began.

"Your command of the French language seems perfect, Monsieur Finch, but in case you didn't understand me a moment ago, *we* are conducting this interview." I said nothing. Andrade took several drags on his cigarette while he shuffled through the papers in the folder. He consulted a sheaf of computer generated forms held together with a paper clip. I couldn't quite read the heading at the top. "Now, you have lived here in Paris for, what, several years now?"

"That's correct."

"And it seems…" he paused as he scanned the forms, "that your residence permit and your work permit are both current and up to date." He studied another sheet, a copy of the declaration page of my passport. "Surprising." His mouth turned down on the sides. "You actually look like your passport photo, Monsieur Finch. Thirty-two years old, brown hair, brown eyes, one hundred eighty-three centimeters in height, weight approximately eighty kilos, scars, what's this? You have a small scar on the right side of your face?" He looked up. I pointed to the short white streak on my right cheek. I acquired it at age seven in a fall from a farm tractor. "Well, that's enough of that. You seem to be who you say you are." *As if there was ever any doubt*, I thought to myself.

"So, tell us how you knew Mme. Tate."

"We were lovers."

Andrade pursed his lips. "Your documents show that you are married to a French citizen," he ran his finger over one of the forms, "here it is, née Colette Dominique St. Jacques, whose address is, what's this? Atlanta, Georgia?" He gave me a hard look. "Your wife lives in the States."

"Ex-wife. We're divorced."

"I see. We have no record of that." He scribbled a note on a pad and drew a star by it.

"We were married in the U.S. and got divorced in the U.S.," I replied. "There's no reason why you should have a record of it."

"Oh." He glanced at Foch who was standing behind me. I couldn't read the expression on his face. "And how long have you been divorced, Monsieur Finch?"

"About a year and a half."

"So Mme. Tate was your mistress while you were married to your wife?" Andrade smiled smugly.

"No, Lt. Andrade, it was not like that. My wife and I were living apart. She got involved with someone. She told me that she wanted a divorce. That's when I met Becky. It's a long story, but it was over two years ago."

"So, you said that you've had no contact with Mme. Tate for these two past years?"

"That's correct."

"Did you still have feelings for her? Did you still care about her?"

I hesitated before I answered. "Yes, probably."

"And you swear that you have no idea then why someone might want her dead?"

"No, Lieutenant, I don't, and I'm getting tired of this game!" I found myself raising my voice. "I've been answering your questions all morning and I still don't have any idea what happened to her. Are you investigating a suicide, or an accident, or what?"

Andrade stubbed out his cigarette and glanced up at Foch. He flicked out another one from the pack, tapped it on his watch face to pack the tobacco, and lit it with his lighter. The room was quiet except for the hissing of the air from the ventilation duct. "We *think*, Monsieur Finch, that Mme. Tate was meeting someone at the Eiffel Tower. We *think*, Monsieur Finch, that someone picked her up and tossed her over the rail of the third level observation platform. The drop is nearly three hundred meters, the equivalent of a ninety-story building. We *think*, Monsieur Finch, that someone wanted Rebecca Tate dead and that someone planned her murder in advance. We want to know why, and right now you're our only link."

CHAPTER
Four

ANDRADE WANTED TO KNOW every detail of my brief relationship with Rebecca Tate. Reduced to the bare facts, it all seemed simple enough, almost inconsequential. Two adults — one married, the other not — had met casually. Circumstances intervened. One thing led to another. Neat, trite little terms that could never in an eternity begin to describe Becky's smile, the way she laughed, her perfume, the way she touched me...

We'd met in late January 2002. She was in France on an extended buying trip for her antique import business. A friend of hers, Julia, had booked a week in Paris with Madeleine Tours. They met unexpectedly in a shop at the Louvre des Antiquaires just after I'd finished a guided tour of the nearby museum. Julie introduced us. We were both from Georgia and were both graduates of Emory. An invitation to join Julia and Becky for dinner followed. Becky said she'd be in the city for two more weeks. I gave her my phone number and told her to call if I could be of assistance.

following day Colette called with the news. It was a bolt out of the blue. She wanted a divorce. She'd met someone else and fallen in love with him. Becky called an hour later to ask if I was familiar with an antique fair held the following weekend in Orléans. Numbly, I said I was guiding a group there and asked her to come along as my guest. We had dinner. We drank wine. I poured my heart out. We slept together. I felt horribly guilty.

The following three months were a blur. I'd flown to Atlanta desperately trying to change Colette's mind until she told me the terrible truth. I needed a friend. I needed someone to talk to. I called Becky at her shop. We met and ended up spending the weekend together. Her business took her back and forth to Paris every couple of weeks supervising the loading and shipping of her antiques. I traveled back and forth to Atlanta meeting with divorce attorneys and accountants. Whenever our paths crossed we were together.

By late April, I realized that I was either falling in love or, more likely, rebounding from the shock of losing Colette. It was too much, too soon. I told Becky that we needed to break it off. I told her that I needed some emotional breathing room. She told me that she loved me. I told her that I'd call. I never saw her again.

Andrade sat quietly while I talked, nursing his cigarette and making occasional notes on his pad. When I finished speaking he looked at Foch and raised his eyebrows. "You have any more questions for Monsieur Finch?" Foch shook his head. They both left the room, now blue with smoke, leaving me alone with my memories.

Andrade returned ten minutes later. "You're free to go, Monsieur Finch. Thank you for your cooperation. I doubt if we'll need to talk with you again, but we'll contact you if we do." He'd reached the conclusion that I had nothing to add to the investigation. I walked out of the station into the sunlight of a clear blue sky and the smells and sounds of Paris on a Sunday midday.

I decided to take the Metro. The La Tour Maubourg stop was just down from the precinct house and went directly to the Opéra station, just a short walk from the flat. I lived on the fifth floor of a building constructed in the 1870's following Baron Haussman's grand renovation of Paris under Napoleon III. The units were originally designed to be sold to wealthy aristocracy living outside of the city who desired an appropriate *pied à terre* for their lengthy visits to the capital. The flat belonged to Colette who had inherited it from her grandmother. I had the right to stay there. It was part of the divorce settlement.

An arched passageway flanked by carved stone and protected by massive wrought iron gates led to the building's cobblestone courtyard. The concierge's apartment was on the ground floor just behind the gates. Madame Bouchard and, prior to his death, her husband had served since the late 1940's as concierges and gatekeepers. The courtyard was designed to be of such a size that a carriage with a four-horse team could easily turn around after discreetly depositing its aristocratic passengers safely out of the view of the commoners on the street. The original stables on the ground floor level now housed the Mercedes and Bentleys of the wealthy residents, many of whom were elderly widows.

Next to Madame Bouchard's apartment was a small flat for the handyman who kept the antique lift functional and his wife, who served as a part-time cleaning lady for several of the tenants.

Colette's *Grandmère* Isabel lived in an apartment until her death in 2001. She was a formidable woman who became Collete's surrogate mother after her parents' death. Colette had been raised in what was now my home, playing as a child in the courtyard, and attending the convent school nearby. We made it *our* home when we were in Paris. To describe the flat as a mere apartment would have been an understatement. It was one of four similar units on each level. The ceilings were nearly four meters high, with huge windows that opened onto balconies overlooking the tree-lined Boulevard des Capucines. There were three bedrooms, a huge kitchen, formal rooms and a small separate bedroom and bath for a live-in maid. It had become my prison, a dark lonely reminder of all that I'd lost.

Madame Bouchard lay in wait for me as I walked through the gate. "Monsieur Finch." She paused as if to gather her words. "During all the years that the dear Madame St. Jacques lived here we had no problems. Even when you and my precious Colette were here, all was the same. Now," she paused, "in one single day we have two separate sets of officials here seeking you. I realize that I am merely an employee here."

"Excuse me, Madame," I interrupted her. "What did you say? Two separate sets of *who*?"

"I don't know who. Police, I presume. But the point is that the residents of this building are French citizens with taste, culture and breeding. I realize that you are American, and we are eternally grateful for your assistance during the last War."

"Did you say *two sets* of officials?" I interrupted again.

She seemed a bit thrown off by my interruption of her reprimand. "Yes. Yes. This morning, early, the ones I showed to your door and the two that came just after you left."

I was puzzled. "Who were they? Where are they?"

"Oh, they left. I suppose they got tired of waiting."

"What did they look like? Did they leave a name, a card, a phone number?"

Madame Bouchard seemed a bit taken aback. "Monsieur Finch, it is not my place to interrogate the guests of our residents. It is my place, however, to maintain civility and decorum. We simply cannot have the police showing up on a quiet Sunday to question you. It's wrong. It's not done!"

"Again, what did they look like? Were they police?"

Madame Bouchard pursed her lips and stared upwards for a moment. "Well, there were two men — but I told you that. They didn't leave a card, but they said they were from... from somewhere — some government agency, I didn't quite catch it. I think they were from the police. One of them was a short white man, muscular looking under his suit and carrying a briefcase. The other one, the one that did all the talking, was black and he had an accent."

"What kind of accent?"

"I don't know. A foreign accent." Madame Bouchard considered anyone not born and reared within a hundred kilometers of Paris to be "foreign." The fact that one of the men was black made it more likely that he was an immigrant from one of the current or former French colonies.

"Was he from France or elsewhere in the world?" I tried to get her to narrow it down further.

"Oh definitely not France! Perhaps Africa, perhaps the Caribbean. Who knows? All these foreigners look and sound alike to me."

"But they said they were from a French government agency, correct?"

"Oh, I don't know, but that's not the point, they — "

I decided that I'd try a different line of questioning. "Did they wait? What happened?"

"I told them that they could wait here in the courtyard, but the tall one said that they'd prefer to wait next to your door so that they wouldn't miss you when you came in."

That didn't make sense, I thought. If I entered the courtyard it wasn't likely that I'd be going anywhere other than my apartment. "So, how long did they wait?"

"I'm not sure. I went to the eleven o'clock Mass and they were gone when I returned."

"Thank you, Madame. I appreciate your concern and I will try to avoid such problems in the future." I nodded politely and bounded up the four flights of stairs to the flat.

I was reaching in my pocket for my keys when Madame Géricault, whose doorway was opposite mine on the fifth level, stuck her head out and chirped, "Good day, Monsieur Finch. I enjoyed meeting your friends. They are such nice men." The elderly Madame was getting a bit senile, but her words grabbed me.

"My friends?"

"Yes, the two nice gentlemen that were waiting for you in your flat. They said that they were visiting here in Paris and you'd told them they could come by and wait until you got home. I suppose they got tired, though, and left."

"Madame Géricault, did you say *in my flat*? They were inside?"

"Oh, yes. The shorter of the two, I didn't get his name, was just trying the keys when I opened the door to get a breath of fresh air. He was having a bit of trouble getting the key you'd given them to fit, but the tall one named Vincent talked with me while he got it to work. And then they both came over and said that they were waiting for you and I offered them tea, but they said they'd just wait on the inside for you."

I had given no one a key. "Did you see them leave?"

"Yes, about an hour ago. I was watching through my curtain and they waved at me."

I thanked her and cautiously opened the door to my apartment. It was quiet. Systematically, I walked through every room, opening drawers and cabinets, peering into wardrobes. Nothing had been disturbed. The Boudin sketch hung in its place on the parlor wall. The dust-covered tea service of heavy coin silver sat untouched on the sideboard. Nothing was missing. I assumed that everything had been searched, and whoever did it were definitely professionals.

They had to be police, I concluded. In France, the rules governing entry and search are less stringent than those in the United States. Getting me down to the precinct station for questioning was nothing more than a ruse to search my apartment. But why go to such trouble? It just didn't fit. I fished Andrade's card out of my pocket and punched in his direct number. I was very angry.

He answered on the second ring. "Andrade here."

"This is Nate Finch. Look, Andrade, I don't appreciate your having my apartment searched. If you didn't believe me, you'd have been welcome to have a look around. I have nothing to hide. You may be within your rights, but I am definitely going to report this to…"

Andrade broke in, his voice tense. "Monsieur Finch! I have no idea what you're talking about."

CHAPTER
Five

AN HOUR AND A HALF LATER I SAT listening as Andrade finished interviewing Madame Géricault. It was evident that she could offer little help. Neither she nor Madame Bouchard had come up with new information. Both agreed that two individuals dressed in nondescript suits came to the building looking for me. One was a short muscular white man whom neither woman heard speak. The other, a tall black man, spoke grammatically correct but heavily accented French. They were probably in the apartment for about an hour. Beyond these facts, neither woman agreed on anything else.

Instead of Foch, Andrade brought with him this time a short, thin, wiry police technician introduced only as "René." He explained that he "just wanted an expert to have a look at things." René reminded me of a Jack Russell terrier. He moved quickly and precisely over the apartment, a lingering glance here, a muted "Hmm" there.

While the lieutenant interviewed the elderly ladies, René examined my door lock with a huge magnifying lens. Digging in his satchel, he produced a large ultraviolet light that he methodically passed over door handles, cabinet pulls and trafficked areas of carpet, carefully peering at each irregular splotch that it revealed. I watched him with curious fascination for a while, then stepped across the way to sit in while Andrade questioned the forgetful Madame G. He was just finishing as René appeared at the door.

"Definitely a professional job, Lieutenant." Corsican accent. "Front door lock picked — minimal scratches. Whoever did it knew what he was doing. Strange thing is, nothing seems to have been disturbed otherwise. Looks like they just came in and sat down. Of course, all this is informal. If you want me to bring the van and a team over — "

Andrade pursed his lips. "Not just yet." Reaching in his shirt pocket for a cigarette he said, "Let's step outside and have a bit of conversation. Just the three of us." He nodded in my direction.

We stood on the landing next to the elevator. Andrade picked a bit of tobacco from his lip and gestured with his smoke. "All right, what do we know? A woman dies under mysterious circumstances and the only hint of identification found on her body is Monsieur Finch's telephone number. Shortly after he leaves to go for a police interview, two unknown men representing themselves to be policemen or government agents of some sort show up, pick his lock, and wait quietly for him in his apartment. Then they leave, which implies that they weren't in fact waiting for him. But there is no evidence of burglary, or in fact of any crime being committed, with the possible exception of unauthorized entry into a private residence, of course." He paused in thought. René and I stood silently, waiting for his conclusion.

"So," he continued, "the facts would imply that…" The ringing of his cell phone interrupted him. With a pained look he glanced at the number on the screen and flipped open the phone. He answered only with his name "Andrade," and listened while the other party talked. Almost immediately his facial expression changed to a look between anger and disgust. "Oh! I see. So it was all legitimate, eh? And just when is this type of case in their jurisdiction?" A pause. "If they want — " The voice at the other end seemed to cut him off. He listened quietly now, occasionally frowning, as the disembodied voice droned on. With a resigned look he said, "As you wish, sir. I'll take care of it." He flipped the phone shut with unnecessary force.

We both stared at him, waiting. Andrade lit another cigarette from the butt of the first. I spoke, "Well?" He took a deep drag and blew a double smoke ring. I spoke again, a question this time, "I presume that call had to do with this case?"

"Well, yes." He hesitated, evidently deciding how to sound diplomatic. "You know, not that it matters, but I studied Medieval Literature at the Sorbonne. Unfortunately, the market for such an education is — at best — limited. So I end up with this job." He shrugged his shoulders. "To quote your great English bishop, Richard de Bury, 'the right hand knoweth not what the left hand doeth.'"

René gave a frustrated look. He snapped, "Which means?" then catching himself quickly added, "With all due respect, sir."

"It means that we are off the case. According to the Captain, who got his orders from the Director, this case should have been handled by the Criminal Investigation Division."

"Those arrogant pigs!" René spit. "What the hell do they know about homicide? They are a bunch of overblown

35

security guards with their high tech toys who wouldn't know — "

"René! Enough." Andrade spoke firmly. Turning to me he continued, "According to my superiors, this case is going to be handled by another jurisdiction. My office's involvement was, well, how should I put it, a bit of an overlap. The gentlemen who were here earlier today were apparently not aware that you were being interviewed on the very case they came to investigate, and in any event, I'm told it won't be necessary for you to go through the whole process again."

René started to speak but a look from Andrade silenced him. Turning to me the Lieutenant said, "So, Monsieur Finch, with our thanks for your help, we'll bid you *adieu*."

They left. I was glad to be rid of them. I felt disgusted and used by the whole series of events. Dragged into something that didn't concern me. Having old memories painfully reawakened. Considered — albeit briefly — as somehow involved in a friend's death, then dropped as if nothing had happened when it became clear that I was not.

I realized that I was hungry. It was close to four in the afternoon and I hadn't eaten all day. I spoke to Madame Géricault to thank her for looking out for things and went back in the flat to find some food. I rummaged in the refrigerator, finally settling on beer and a package of frozen lasagna, which I popped in the microwave. Paris might be the gourmet capital of the world, but I wasn't in a mood to go out.

While it was heating I called my office and spoke to Michelle. In the travel business weekends are usually the busiest times. We had groups arriving and departing from both major Paris airports. She demanded to know where I'd been and why I had not returned her calls. I started to tell her, then thought better of it and made some lame excuse about being a little under the weather. She saw right through it. "So, it's a woman, then. Nate, it's about time you started getting out more. You can't spend the rest of your life pining away for Colette. Face it, she's never coming back."

"Yeah. I know."

"Which reminds, me, I met a girl the other — "

"Hey, I'll handle my own arrangements." I thought it best not to mention Becky Tate. She had been the one woman that Michelle approved of, and my breaking it off was still a sore point.

"While I've got you on the phone, can you get up those budget summaries for the accountant?" Michelle asked. "They were due ten days ago."

"Sure. I'd completely forgotten." I was lying. I just hadn't been in a mood to spend several hours in front of the computer typing in numbers. I hated it, but it was the sort of thing that I simply couldn't delegate to anyone else. "I'll have them for you in the morning."

I retrieved the lasagna from the microwave and spooned it onto a plate. Pouring my beer into a glass I headed for what Colette and I had called the "children's room," the place that was going to be the nursery for our first-born. After the divorce I'd stripped it bare of furnishings and turned it into an office.

The three new pieces of furniture that I had brought in now seemed lost in the huge room. In one corner a large modern desk held a computer with a flat panel monitor, a printer and a telephone. In the center of the room a library-sized work table was piled with various reports and trade magazines. The third piece was a high-backed leather task chair on wheels that I used to shuttle back and forth across the polished oak floor between the other two. I set the plate of lasagna and the beer on the table while I pressed the button on the CPU and waited for the computer to boot up.

Sitting in the chair at the table, I washed down half the lasagna with the beer and rolled over to the desk to start work. I reached under the desk to slide out the shelf that held the keyboard. It was then that I realized that there was a problem.

CHAPTER
Six

I AM LEFT-HANDED. Or more correctly at one time I was left handed, and now I am ambidextrous. As a child I attended a small rural school not far from my parents' farm. I spent my first three years under the tutelage of the feared "Miss Bradley," a harsh septuagenarian spinster who believed in an absolute standard of discipline and order. Mornings began with a prayer and a pledge of allegiance to the flag — in that order. Children must not speak unless spoken to. There was but one way to solve a problem in math, and cursive writing must never stray outside the thin blue lines on the tablet.

Left-handers in Miss Bradley's world were, at best, a bit different. They violated some unwritten tenet of the natural order of things. With effort, however, this aberration could be corrected. So, while other students quietly scribbled away at their desks, the equally deviant Mary Kate Johnson and I were forced to stand at the blackboard and practice our right-handed script with our left hands

39

firmly tucked in our pockets. This went on week after week until Miss Bradley was satisfied that we had successfully suppressed whatever sinister urges we might have to write with the "wrong hand." The net result of all this was that I did my schoolwork using my right hand and my homework using my left. Only by careful attention to the subtle left or right slant of my script could one determine which hand I'd used.

The benefit of this perverse retraining became evident only when I was in college and took a class in accounting. I spent hours on the computer entering data into forms and spreadsheets. I discovered that I could operate the mouse left-handed while entering numbers with my right hand, a distinct advantage that saved me much time.

One of the jobs that had fallen to me by default as co-owner of Madeleine Tours was doing the quarterly budget estimates. I was the only one who had a sufficient "feel" for the business to handle it. It meant several hours of drudgery pouring over the preliminary figures for the pro-ceeding quarter, reviewing actual and projected bookings, plus going over a long list of known or estimated fixed and variable expenses. Michelle emailed the basic files to my home computer, and I would usually spend a couple of hours looking at the numbers and making notes. Based on this information I had to formulate some guess as to our projected income and cash flow needs, a wildly speculative process at best. As if this were not punishment enough, I then had to enter it all on a spreadsheet which in turn I emailed to the accountant's office.

It was on the basis of these illusionary numbers that I would receive a dozen or more phone calls over the quar-ter stating with pride that "You're ahead of projections," or with dire concern that, "You're falling behind." I generally ignored them all.

I rarely used my home computer for anything else, and as well I could remember, hadn't even been in my sparsely furnished home office in weeks. I slid the shelf holding the keyboard out from under the desktop. As usual I reached for the mouse with my left hand and realized that it was not there. Looking down quickly, I saw the mouse on the right side of the keyboard. I hadn't put it there.

Puzzled, I thought about the situation. No one else had been in my home office so far as I knew. The housekeeper who changed the sheets, did the laundry and lackadaisically dusted once a week had strict instructions not to enter this one room. There were a few visitors, but no one with any reason or opportunity to be in my office. If the computer mouse was not where I left it, my second set of "official" visitors had to be responsible. But the apartment didn't appear to have been searched otherwise — even René, the crime scene tech, agreed on that. So why had it been moved?

I surveyed the room. The piles of paperwork on the table appeared untouched. I kneeled down and squinted across the table. The fine thin layer of accumulated dust was undisturbed except where I'd sat and finished my meal. Turning my attention to the computer, I entered my password and brought up the email program. Clicking on "Send/Receive" I downloaded two dozen-odd unread emails including the financial files from Michelle sandwiched between layers of spam and pornographic solicitations. Calling up my spreadsheet program, I randomly checked several archived business documents. Nothing appeared to have been disturbed.

If someone wanted to see what was on my computer, they would have to know my password. And then, or logically so it seemed to me, they would have checked my email. But I'd told no one my password and my email had not been downloaded. Perhaps I was wrong. Perhaps for whatever reason I'd moved the mouse and forgotten that I'd done so. Then a thought struck me.

On the shelf in the pantry I found a flashlight that I kept for those rare power outages that sometimes strike even major European cities. The computer CPU sat on the floor under the desk on the left side. Dropping to my knees, I beamed the light carefully at the accumulated dust on the case. Toward the rear on the shiny hardwood floor I could see the pattern of a palm print in the dust. This, together with other random disturbances indicated someone had reached behind the CPU to access a communication port on the rear panel. Sitting on the floor under the desk, I pulled the case around and beamed the light on the rear. An absence of dust on the USB plug for the printer cable indicated that someone had tampered with it. Someone, for whatever reason, had accessed my computer.

I found Andrade's card and called him at his office. After six rings I was connected to a recorded message. I hung up. I tried a cell phone number. He answered on the second ring, "Andrade."

I explained to him what I'd found, and what I thought had happened. I could almost see the amused look on his face when he said, "Now, let me get this straight. You say that you think someone has accessed your computer files because you think that someone moved your mouse?"

"No! That's not exactly what I said." I explained it to him again. He seemed to take it a bit more seriously this time.

"I'll call you back." I gave him my number.

Twenty minutes passed. Michelle called with a minor problem. One of the hotels we used in Rouen had had a fire and we'd need to relocate a group of twelve for three nights the following week. I told her to handle it. The phone rang again. It was Andrade.

"I've checked on things. The two detectives who entered your flat did so without official permission and will no doubt be reprimanded for violating procedure. They say they simply sat and waited for you, and then left when they had a more urgent call and you'd not yet returned. They deny touching your computer." Before I could speak, he continued, "But let me assure you Monsieur Finch, you are not a suspect and should not be hearing from the police again on this matter. Perhaps I should apologize, perhaps not, but we thank you for your cooperation." The line went dead.

I decided he was lying, probably trying to cover for the other detectives. And in the end, what did it matter? Nothing had been taken, and no practical harm appeared to have been done. It would be best to let this go and get on with other more important things. Three hours later I finished entering the last set of numbers. Typing a quick cover note, I attached the files and emailed them to the accountant.

I grabbed another beer out of the 'fridge, found the remote and flicked on the TV for a quick news summary from ITN. I was trying to decide whether or not to go out for a bite to eat when the phone rang. It had not been a good day and I was not in a mood for any more hassles. I started to let the machine pick up but thought better of it and lifted the receiver. A familiar voice addressed me in French. "Nate! For God's sake what is going on over there?" I could hear a child crying in the background.

"Hello, Colette. How have you been?" I replied in English.

"Fine, of course, but..." she paused to hush the child and continued, "I get this call from some crazy woman named Tate — Kate Tate or Claire Tate or something like that. She was hysterical, screaming into the phone. She wanted to know what happened to her sister. She wanted to

43

know if you were with her. Nate, I don't know this person and I don't know your relationship to her but I want you to keep your girlfriends out of my life."

I felt like I'd been punched in the gut. "As if you ever let your relationships interfere with our marriage." I replied again in English.

She continued in French. "That's not the point, Nate. We are just finishing a nice Sunday dinner when Carl answers the phone and this woman is sobbing and crying. Apparently she was calling to get your phone number. I have no idea who she is, but wasn't that the woman you were seeing when we got divorced named Tate? I am your ex-wife now and you can keep your lovers' quarrels away from me."

"She's dead, Colette."

"I have a new life and…" She stopped suddenly as if the translation had taken a few seconds to register. "Dead?"

"Yes, apparently murdered here in Paris. I don't know the details."

There was a long silence. "Are you involved in this, Nate?"

"Of course not. I haven't seen her in two years."

"Oh." Another pause. "So I need not be concerned." I said nothing, waiting for her to continue. "Sorry I bothered you, then. *Au revoir.*" The line clicked dead.

I sat down. Michelle was right. Anything Colette and I may have had disappeared long ago in a sea of betrayal. She was married to another man now. She had a son named Carl, Jr. But we were still business partners. The phone rang again. I picked it up. "I forgot to tell you one thing, Nate. I gave her your phone number." Colette hung up.

CHAPTER
Seven

HENRY JAMES AND ERNEST HEMINGWAY came to Paris to write. Mary Cassatt came to paint. Isadora Duncan came to dance. I can't say that I arrived in Paris with such lofty aspirations. I was born and raised on a farm in Treutlen County, Georgia, the fourth son and a "change of life surprise" to my parents who eked out a living from the sandy soil of the northern Coastal Plain.

Our farm was, and still is, located about halfway between the crossroads known as Blackville and the dusty little town of Soperton where I attended high school. My parents are farmers because their parents had been farmers, as had their grandparents. They graduated from high school at seventeen, married at eighteen, and by the time they were twenty-two had three sons, conveniently born a year apart. My father, being an only child, inherited some 240 acres of gently rolling fields that produced a middling yield of corn, soybeans and cotton. My mother was the youngest daughter of the next-door neighbors, which in that part of the world meant that she lived a couple of miles down the road. They attended school together from the first grade on, and there was little doubt that one day they they'd be married and raise a family to follow in their parents' footsteps. For a wedding present, my mother's father gave the young couple 220 acres adjacent to my father's land, creating a farm large enough that, with hard work, could support a couple and their children in a reasonable but simple style.

In 1971, shortly after my mother's forty-second birthday, she discovered that she was pregnant. She had missed a few periods and had experienced a bit of morning nausea, but like many women who were accustomed to self-reliance and hardened by poor access to medical care, she kept her symptoms to herself, attributing them to "the change." A vague swelling of her abdomen and the necessity of multiple nighttime visits to the bathroom finally forced her to the doctor, who on Pearl Harbor Day of that year diagnosed her problem as a late second-trimester pregnancy. I was born on the Ides of March a bit more than three months later.

My parents and siblings dearly loved me but my presence was definitely unplanned. Although my father was relatively unschooled, he was not uneducated. He was, and is, an avid reader with an abiding interest in southern history. Accordingly, my older three brothers were named Robert Edward Lee Finch, Thomas Jonathan Jackson Finch, and James Ewell Brown Stuart Finch, which apparently represented his ranking of the pantheon of Southern Heroes. I was duly christened Nathan Bedford Forrest Finch, and given the nickname of "Nate," to accompany my older brother's appellations of Robert, "Stonewall" and "Jeb."

By the time I was old enough to attend school all of my brothers had graduated from college with degrees in Agricultural Engineering and returned home to join my father in the family farming operation. While I was learning to read and write from Miss Bradley, they were using their education to convert the fields that formerly grew low-profit mechanized row crops to meet the growing national demand for sweet Vidalia onions. By the time I reached the third grade, we were one of the largest growers in the county, producing nearly three thousand tons a year.

It was a wrenching but necessary transition. The farm economy, formerly based on regional and statewide sales, had become a national and international market. The local cost of production no longer set the market price. A series of hailstorms in Iowa could send the price of corn soaring in Georgia, just as an unexpectedly wet spring in the mid-West could send the price of wheat through the floor. Small farmers like my father were whipped about like a small boat on an open sea, sometimes fortunate but more often than not losers in the international commodity markets that now controlled the prices of farm products.

It had started in the depths of the Great Depression when one farmer in rural Toombs County began to get a higher price at the Vidalia Farmers' Market for seemingly ordinary looking onions grown in the local yellow soil. They were said to be "sweeter" and somehow "juicer," as if those were terms that one would ever normally use to describe onions.

The magic was a geologic accident resulting from the unique characteristics of the sandy, acidic soil deposited on the ancient seabed eons ago in what was now a twenty-county area in southeast Georgia. Over the following years the fame of "those Vidalia onions" spread, at first locally, then statewide, and by the 1970's across the nation. First available only in the local Piggly Wiggly supermarkets, the distinctive taste of this locally grown vegetable was soon a staple in the trendiest New York restaurants.

Thanks to my older brothers, we were on the cutting edge. Finch's Finest® Vidalia Onions became (and still is) one of the best-known national brands. When my father was in charge, a good year would see a yield of more than a hundred bushels of corn per acre sold for a bit more than two dollars a bushel. Now an acre of the same fields might produce fifteen thousand pounds of plump yellow onions, selling at retail for up to a dollar a pound.

The changes on the farm were neither easy nor cheap. While my brothers were growing up, my father managed to run the farm with the aid of a couple of black men who lived with their families in modest tenant houses a short way down the road from ours. With row crop production the three of them worked long days side by side as equals in the fields, plowing, planting, spraying and harvesting. Onion production is very labor intensive.

In almost no time we exhausted the local labor pool and began to hire seasonal workers for the planting and harvesting seasons. They were mainly Mexican migrants, following the crops from the south to the north and as much a part of the agricultural cycle as bees are in pollination and the production of honey. They would arrive in swarms of beat up cars and recycled panel trucks, setting up house-keeping in whatever local lodging we could find.

My mother was horrified. She declared that no human beings should have to live that way and immediately demanded that my father provide "decent housing." He responded by setting up a small village of used but clean mobile homes. The workers loved it. The next year they returned with their families and pleaded with my father and brothers to give them full time work. It was a mutually beneficial arrangement and they readily agreed. My father paid better than average wages. He provided good housing, took care of the sick and injured, and generally respected his new employees for the hard and dedicated workers that they were.

From my perspective, it was a great arrangement. I had readily available playmates, a rarity in this area of large farms and remote farmhouses. They spoke a different language, but I seemed to catch on quickly. It never really occurred to me that this was a "foreign" tongue, it was just the way we kids talked as we ran across the fields playing war games or cowboys and Indians.

My great epiphany as to my language skills occurred when I was seven. It is a somewhat complicated tale that requires me to begin by describing my parents. My father is a relatively short man, about five-foot-seven in his stocking feet. He was, and is, handsome in a rugged sort of way with thick brown hair and a thin, muscular physique honed by years of hard work. My mother, on the other hand, is what is politely described in the South as "big-boned," meaning that she was significantly overweight but carries it well. She's tall, towering over my father by at least four inches. She inherited her mother's characteristics of carrot-colored red hair and pale white skin that freckled easily in the south Georgia sun. She was a good woman, a hard-working wife and a caring mother but was not, by any stretch of the imagination, comely.

As an unintended addition of insult to injury, my mother's parents elected to grace their children with distinctive names. I never met my maternal grandparents Gordon and Alaphea. They both died long before I was born. They were said to be "good country people," but were uneducated. My mother was the youngest of three girls. The oldest was named Virzilia, evidently a name her mother had seen in some dime novel in the 1930's. The middle child was saddled with Vulva Mae, which clearly reflected my grandparents' lack of anatomic Latin. She changed it to Noël the day after her eighteenth birthday. For the third child my grandparents borrowed from each of their names to create the chimeric Gordaphea. Her mother once said she chose it because it "sounded pretty." This was quickly shortened to the nickname of "Phea."

Consuela, the wife of Gilberto Guerrero and mother of my friends Pépe and Tat, helped my mother prepare the midday meal that fed the dozens of workers during the planting and harvesting seasons. They lived on the farm year-round, and when things were quieter, she helped my mother with routine chores around the house. I liked Consuela. She smelled of coconut soap and would slip me cookies behind my mother's back. Her command of English was limited, but she and my mother seemed to enjoy one another's company and understood each other on some matronly level.

I noticed one strange thing, however. Every time my father would say my mother's name, Consuela would giggle. Sometimes I'd hear the field workers referring to "*la Señora Gordaphea*" or "*la Señora Phea*" which would inevitably produce mirthful grins. I once asked one of them in my broken Spanish why he always smiled at my mother's name. He replied, "Sometimes we name children for how we'd like them to be. I have a brother named Jésus." I said I didn't know what he meant. He wouldn't say any more.

Months passed. I began to understand almost everything the workers were saying. I knew the names of their wives and their girlfriends. I heard what happened in the backseats of cars parked on lonely dirt roads, never quite comprehending why all that seemed so important to these men in their twenties. My older brothers began to call on me as the *de facto* in-house translator to explain some fine point of this or that to men whose English skills were nonexistent.

Then one day it struck me. *"La Señora Gordaphea,"* — Mrs. Gordaphea — could also mean *"la señora gorda fea"* — the fat ugly lady. At first I was a little angry and amused at the same time, but at that very moment a whole new world opened to me, far away from the endless rows of green onion shoots poking their heads out of the yellow sandy soil. By the time I finished high school I had mastered Spanish and French and was working on Italian. I scored in the 1500's on the SAT and received a full academic scholarship to Emory University in Atlanta. Only later did I discover it was a scholarship reserved for "culturally deprived students from rural areas of Georgia."

CHAPTER
Eight

THE MOVE TO ATLANTA was indeed a culture shock. Despite the fact I had grown up on a farm in what was essentially the middle of nowhere, I foolishly considered myself quite well prepared for the transition. I had been at or near the top of my class in every subject in high school. I had been to Washington, DC, and New York on my Senior Trip. I could read and speak — or so I thought — passable French and Spanish. It never occurred to me it was a dubious accomplishment to do well in a high school where the highest goal of most students was merely to graduate. Or that having visited the big city didn't mean I could match the sophistication of my new classmates who actually lived there.

The most degrading embarrassment came from two instructors in the Department of Romance Languages. I signed up for French and Spanish; having aced the written placement exams allowed me to skip the introductory level courses in both subjects. On the first day of my Intermediate Spanish class, the instructor asked each student to stand up and say a bit about themselves in Spanish. *No problem*, I thought, until I saw the expression on her face as I spoke. After class, she curtly informed me that while I had basic knowledge to continue at the intermediate level, I had "the accent and vocabulary of a Veracruz gutter rat." So much for having learned Spanish from field workers.

I didn't fare any better in French class. The instructor opined that my underlying Southern drawl might make it impossible for me to ever learn to pronounce French words properly. He went so far as to suggest I should consider majoring in Southern Literature. "You'd probably do well reading Faulkner, or *Gone with the Wind* or something like that." Furious, I decided I'd prove them both wrong.

For the next month I spent every spare moment in the Language Lab. Correcting my Spanish was less of a problem. I sat for hours with earphones on my head, repeating endless strings of phrases and working with interactive computer simulations. The instructor termed my improvement "remarkable."

French, however, was an uphill battle. After several weeks of frustrating efforts the graduate student in charge of the Lab said, "Look, Nate, you've really got a long way to go. You didn't grow up with diphthongs and carets and agues. If you really intend to stick this out you need some one-on-one work with someone who knows the language. I think I've got just the person. There's this first year student from Paris whose English pronunciation is just about as bad as your French. She's like you — she knows the academic part and can read and write well — it's just that she needs to work on the speaking part. Maybe you two could help each other out. Her name's Colette St. Jacques. Want me to line something up?" Thus I met my future wife.

We had very little in common. She was a vivacious bundle of energy who managed to butcher even the most common English words. I was the awkward farm boy out of his league in the city. The fact that we were both in a foreign situation drew us together. Our meetings in the Language Lab soon became dinners, which led to weekends watching a French movie on Friday night and an American one on Saturday afternoon. We dated other people, but kept coming back to each other. By the end of my freshman year we were sleeping together. My instructors said my French accent was "nearly perfect."

I may have been able to speak the language, but I had never been to France. This was something Colette said must be remedied. Without the scholarship my parents never could have afforded to send me to Emory, much less to spring for a ticket to Europe. Even though my tuition was paid, I knew my apartment and other expenses were a burden. I helped out when I could with odd jobs to make money, but keeping my head above water in an intensely academic environment didn't leave me much free time.

Near the end of my sophomore year Colette invited me to visit her in France during the summer. She was an only child, having been orphaned as a toddler when her parents were killed in an avalanche while skiing. She'd been raised in Paris by her grandmother who insisted she attend college in the United States. She said we could stay for a few days in Paris, and then spend time traveling around the country. I told her I couldn't go. Besides not being able to afford it, I needed to earn money over the summer to help pay my living expenses.

Colette came up with the bright idea we'd organize a student tour of France. She called around until she found a tour wholesaler who'd give us one free round-trip air fare for each ten paying tickets we sold. She then called a friend who she'd known in school, whose parents operated a small hotel on the outskirts of Paris. I watched her in awe. She managed to negotiate a deal to rent a block of rooms at a guaranteed price of less than half the going rate. "All we've got to do now is sell the package."

She sat down and began to scribble with an indelible marker on a blank sheet of typing paper. Five minutes later she held it up for me to see. "What do you think?" On the top was a roughly drawn Eiffel Tower next to the headline *Cheap Student Tour to France, July 1st through July 10th.* Below that she'd written next to neat little bullet points *Includes: Hotel with Daily Breakfast, Guided Tour of Paris, All Transfers, Introductions to French Students.* At the bottom in big letters was the name *Madeleine Tours,* followed by my apartment phone number.

"It looks great, I think," I said, "But Colette, just who or what is Madeleine Tours?"

"Oh, Madeleine was the name of my school in Paris. It was run by the nuns from *l'Église de Ste.Marie Madeleine.* As for Madeleine Tours, that's us." She grinned.

"Do you have any idea what you're doing?"

"No. But I like the concept. We'll work out the details later." We spent the afternoon making photocopies on fluorescent orange paper and posted them all over campus. The first twenty spots filled within two weeks. We started a waiting list, which soon grew to over fifty names. We scheduled a second trip. By the end of the summer we'd been back and forth to France four times and cleared more than four thousand dollars in profits. We started planning a skiing trip for mid-semester break.

Colette, in addition to being one of the most beautiful women I've ever known, is a natural born salesperson. She is thin, with close cropped black hair and darting dark eyes that never miss anything. She has an almost magical way of instantly sizing up a potential client's wants and needs. To the horny college jock she would present Paris as full of lithesome females whose one desire in life was to meet young single American men. To the sorority sisters of Tri-Delta or AΔΠ, Paris became the ultimate source of designer fashion — at a discount, of course.

The following summer, we hired four other students who were fluent in French and did a total of twelve departures between June and August. We made a profit of more than twenty thousand dollars. By September of my senior year I had come to two firm conclusions. First, I enjoyed the travel business and wanted to make a career of it. Secondly, I knew I was hopelessly in love with Colette and wanted to spend the rest of my life with her. We were married on the Sunday following graduation the next June. Within weeks we had opened offices of Madeleine Tours in both Paris and Atlanta.

The next five years were ones of heady success. The student tour business remained strong, but we began to expand to a larger and more upscale market. We hired more staff on both sides of the Atlantic. By our fifth wedding anniversary in 1999 we were one of the largest French travel specialist agencies in the Southeast with an annual sales volume of over twenty million dollars.

Our marriage was doing equally well, or so I thought. We purchased a small but comfortable house near Emory, and commuted back and forth between Atlanta and Paris several times a month. A sort of natural division of labor developed. The lovely Colette with her natural allure and charming French accent became the primary force behind marketing and sales. I was the practical guy, the one who made things work, who handled problems and took care of the day-to-day nuts and bolts of running an international tour company. While Colette was giving sales presentations, I would be making sure our hotel of choice in Reims maintained its rooms properly, or we had reserved sufficient space on Paris to Atlanta flights to meet our anticipated sales needs. We had, and still have, a great manager for our Atlanta office and had hired and trained an equally competent person for the same position in Paris.

In mid-2001 several things happened. In June, Colette's grandmother died unexpectedly. She had been my wife's only close living relative. Even though she was elderly and her eventual death was not unanticipated, Colette was devastated. Perhaps it was the suddenness of it all. She became depressed and starting seeing a therapist. I tried to spend as much time with her as possible, and within a couple of months she seemed better.

The events of September 11th in New York caused massive cancellations of our fall travel bookings. In no time I had dozens of hotels, bus companies and other suppliers screaming at me for our having to cancel reservations with them. Shortly thereafter our Paris office manager quit in frustration, requiring my presence in the city for weeks at a time running the office as we searched for her replacement. Cash flow fell to a trickle. We laid off a half-dozen employees while we struggled to keep the company afloat.

By December things were beginning to look up. Our Spring and Summer bookings were beginning to rebound. Both Colette and I were worried, but we thought we could see the light at the end of the tunnel. We spent Christmas together in the flat on the rue des Capucines, which had become our home in Paris. She seemed distant, somewhat distracted. Our lovemaking was passionless and mechanical. I asked her what was wrong. She replied simply, "Nothing. I've just got a lot on my mind."

One month later Colette called to say she wanted a divorce. She said she still cared about me but she no longer loved me. She was in love with someone named Carl and she wanted to be with him. I pleaded, I begged, I cried, all to no avail. She told me she didn't want to see me right then, and not to come to Atlanta to try to change her mind.

I wandered about in a trance for a week. I didn't sleep. I didn't eat. My calls to Colette went unanswered. The Atlanta office said she'd told them she didn't want to talk to me. Finally, I booked a flight home and was waiting on our doorstep when she drove up.

It was the 3rd of February and very cold. Colette was wrapped in a long black overcoat and was wearing a Russian style hat trimmed in white fur. She acknowledged my presence with a nod, but her dark eyes looked right through me. "Colette," I began. "Please. Please let's talk. Let's try to work this out. I love you. I don't want to lose you."

She stood on our front porch, her hands thrust deep in her coat pockets. Her face was expressionless. She didn't speak. She had that look that she'd always wear when we'd talked about having a baby, about raising a family. It was something I'd wanted so very much right then, and something she said she wanted someday. The someday that seemed would now never come.

I continued, "Tell me what I can do to make things right"

"Nate," She began, and then paused as if she didn't know what to say. "I can't lie to you any more. There's a part of me that will always love you but — " She stopped.

"Talk to me!"

"I'm pregnant. It's not yours." She unlocked the door and walked in the house, slamming it in my face.

CHAPTER
Nine

THE DIVORCE SHOULD HAVE BEEN simple enough, and would have been if I'd let it. The facts were straightforward. Young couple, married nearly eight years, no children. Wife had an affair and demanded a divorce. Limited joint assets consisting of a profitable travel company and a small amount of equity in an older three bedroom, two bathroom house in a good section of Atlanta. Manageable liabilities including short term business debt and a mortgage on the marital residence.

The first divorce lawyer I spoke to said, "Piece of cake," and offered to represent me for a thousand dollars "if you two can get the property settlement details worked out." He said he'd get in touch with Colette's attorney. The next day he called back with the recommendation that we should sell everything and split the proceeds, or that I could buy out my wife's half of the business.

I told him I had few problems with that. First, I was angry at Colette and was not going to let go of things that easily. Second, the business we'd built was both highly profitable and uniquely dependent on both of our skills. I told him I couldn't afford to buy her out and that I wasn't about to throw away my career and ten years worth of hard work. He said the price of his services just went up, and suggested we try mediation.

We did. I got to meet Carl. He seemed like a nice enough fellow. Perhaps we actually might have been friends had he not chosen to slither into my wife's bed. He was an orthopedist in his late forties, divorced with two grown children by his first marriage. He was tall and with graying blond hair and would seemed like he would be more at home playing tennis at the country club than wielding a bone saw in an operative suite. He'd met Colette when she'd given a presentation to the local medical society. He said, "I'm sorry," and held out his hand, which I ignored. The mediation went nowhere.

Six months and nearly twenty thousand dollars in legal fees later, we were divorced. In the end, little changed. Colette and I agreed to "amicably" manage the company as before, each having fifty percent ownership and each taking half of the profits. I would continue to manage the French end of the business. I could stay in the Paris apartment but had to sign away any claim on its ownership. We agreed to meet at least monthly to discuss business. I secretly believed one day she'd come to her senses and want me back. Carl, Jr. was born two days after we signed the papers. Eighteen months later nothing had changed.

∞

ON MONDAY MORNING I was back in the office. The day passed quickly with no more than the usual emergencies and problems. Everyone wanted to hear the details of what happened at the Eiffel Tower on Saturday evening. I thought it best not to mention my being questioned by the police, and let Michelle continue to pick at me about my whereabouts on Sunday. The accountant called with half a dozen unnecessary questions about my cost projections. Colette called and spoke with Françoise, our receptionist and part-time booking agent, about a group scheduled to arrive the following weekend. Before I could ask, Françoise pointedly told me Colette had specifically said she didn't need to speak with me.

Tuesday and Wednesday were equally routine. I sulked, or at least the staff told me I did. I couldn't get Becky's death out of my mind. Our relationship lasted for only a few months two years earlier, but despite my best efforts my mind kept replaying scenes like excerpts from an old movie. The Monday papers had devoted a short item to her death, but did not give her name, "pending notification of relatives." My decision to keep the truth to myself was unsuccessful. Late Wednesday afternoon Michelle rushed into my office waving a sheet she'd torn from the morning's copy of *Le Parisien*. "Nate, the girl that was killed last weekend — it was your friend, Becky! It's all here in — "

"I know," I said simply.

"But why... why didn't you tell us? That's why you've been in such a mood. She so was so special. I know she was in love with you! I could see it by looking in her eyes."

"Michelle!" I said abruptly. "I know. I know all about it. She's gone and there's nothing we can do about it, so let's — "

"Did you find out what happened? Was it a suicide, or an accident, or what?"

"I don't know, and I don't want to talk about it, okay?" I gave her a hard, expressionless look.

"I'm sorry, Nate," Michelle replied, slightly offended at my tone. "You cared about her whether you choose to admit it or not." She turned and walked out of my office. No one mentioned the subject again.

By Thursday, the news focused on impending strikes (or "work actions" to use the polite local term) by museum guards and garbage collectors. The tragic death of one unknown American tourist had fallen from the consciousness of the great Parisian masses.

⁌

THE OFFICE OF MADELEINE TOURS is located near the Arc de Triomphe in a nineteenth century building on the Avenue de Friedland. On most days, weather permitting, I walk the two kilometers from the flat to the office. I usually pick up a croissant from the baker's on the way for breakfast, and most evenings I eat alone at one of half a dozen small restaurants near my route. The spring weather had warmed to a point of near balminess by the time I left the office Wednesday evening. Deciding to take my time getting home, I set off on a different route down the Champs Élysée.

I bought a newspaper, stopped at one of the many sidewalk cafes and ordered an espresso. I didn't pay much attention to him the first time he walked by. Just another tall black man strolling slowly down the boulevard on a perfect evening. The second time he walked past I noticed he was looking at me. I raised my eyes and he looked away. I continued to sip my coffee and read the paper. As I looked for the waiter to order a second cup, I saw him again, this time across the broad boulevard talking with a shorter, muscular white man. They stared my way, and seeing me staring back, averted their eyes and started walking away at a rapid pace.

Dropping my newspaper and tossing a ten euro note on the table, I waded out in the rush hour traffic of the Champs Élysée heading toward the pair. The short man looked over his shoulder and spotted me. He said something to his companion and they broke into a half run. I watched them as they turned the corner onto the rue de Colisée past the colorful displays of the Disney Store.

Dodging in front of honking taxis and saved by squealing brakes, I reached the other side and sprinted toward the corner, arriving just in time to see my quarry at a full run in the fading twilight. I barely caught a glimpse of them as they veered right against oncoming traffic into the rue de Ponthieu. Breathless, I reached the corner and paused for a moment to peer down the long narrow street. In the distance I could see two figures darting through pools of yellow light under widely spaced lampposts. I ran after them.

At the Avenue Matignon I paused again to survey the landscape. A couple of hundred meters to my right was the crowded Champs Élysée. If they'd taken that route I'd lost them. To my left were apartment buildings separated by a maze of residential streets. Straight ahead and on the right was the weekly *marché aux timbres*, a small forest of tents and booths selling stamps and other postal collectibles. I plunged straight ahead.

Running from one booth to the next, I scanned the customers in the fading light. Nothing. At the end of the short street lay the walls of the Élysée Palace, home of the French president, and beyond it a fenced park that bordered the American Embassy compound. I could see a guard slowly patrolling the perimeter of the Palace. I approached him and introduced myself as an American citizen. I lied and told him I'd seen two men snatch a purse from an elderly lady and had chased them in this direction. Had he seen anything? "I'm afraid not, Monsieur," he replied with a slight tinge of sarcasm. "It's been as quiet as a pro-American rally on the streets of Baghdad." I caught a taxi back to my apartment.

CHAPTER
Ten

I WAS ALMOST ASLEEP when I heard a sharp rapping at my door. I rolled over and focused my eyes on the green digits of my bedside clock. 11:22 PM. No one had called, and I couldn't think of any legitimate reason why I'd have an unannounced visitor this time of night. Switching on the bedroom light, I slipped on a pair of jeans and a sweatshirt. I walked to the unlighted foyer and pulled back a curtain from a parlor window, trying to see who was at my door. A shadow moved on the darkened landing. The visitor knocked again, more loudly this time. I started to switch on the light by the door, but for some reason thought better of it and called, "Who's there?"

A female voice replied in English. Southern accent. "I'm sorry, I don't speak French. Is this Nate Finch's apartment?"

"Yes. Who are you and what do you want?"

"I'm a friend. I need to talk to you about my sister."

"And just who is your sister?" I said, flipping on the entry light and easing open the door. She didn't have to answer. In the dim light it was obvious: The long dark hair, the finely sculpted facial features, the brown eyes and the lips were those of Rebecca Tate.

She stuck out her hand. "I'm Clair Tate. I know we've never met, but I've got to talk with you about Becky. Please let me come in." She was shivering even though the evening was warm. I stepped back and held the door widely open.

"Are you the one who called my ex-wife the other night?"

"Yes, I'm sorry. We had just gotten a call from the Embassy saying Becky had been killed in some kind of an accident, but then they said it might be more than that and started asking all kinds of questions about what she was doing in Paris and who she was meeting and did I have some kind of information about the business."

It was clear she was upset. I waved my hands, "Hold on! Calm down. Just give me minute to wake up and we'll talk, but first, what the hell are you doing here this time of night and how did you get in? The good Madame locks the gate at eleven. And if you wanted to talk with me, why didn't you call?"

"I did. I called several times, but I kept getting your answering machine. The message is in French. I didn't know if it was you or not, so I found your address in the phone book and came by to see you. The old guard dog downstairs wouldn't let me in. I tried to explain to her what I wanted, but she kept saying, "*No parlez anglais.*" I wrote your name on a piece of paper and pointed at my watch to show her I wanted to wait. She scowled and kept saying something about *gendarmes* and *inspecteurs* and pointed at me and at the street. From the tone of her voice I think she was telling me to get lost. About that time her phone

65

rang and she went back in to answer it. When she was out of sight I sneaked in and hid in the backseat of someone's Mercedes in the garage until the lights went off in her apartment."

"There are twenty flats in this building. How did you find mine?"

"The directory by the entrance. It still says 'M.& M. Nathan Finch.'"

"Oh." For whatever reason I hadn't changed it. I wasn't sure I wanted to talk to this person. I didn't want to dredge up old memories. I didn't want to get involved. "So what did you need to talk to me about?'

Clair didn't answer directly. She looked around the room. "This is just like she told me it was." Turning to me she said, "She loved you, you know."

"I don't know," I lied. "We were involved briefly two years ago. I was going through a bad time."

"She told me. She told me all about it — about you, about Colette and about what happened."

"I don't think she ever got over you, Nate. And now... now," She began to sob. I walked in the kitchen and grabbed a handful of paper napkins, which I handed to her.

"You need a drink. Brandy okay?" She nodded and I poured three fingers of Rémy Martin. She gulped it down in one swallow. She put the glass down and sat bundled up on the divan, her arms clutched tightly around her and her legs folded up under her skirt. I studied her for a moment. She was definitely Becky's sister, though a little taller, fuller lips, more beautiful perhaps. I felt like I was looking at a ghost.

She was silent for a while and then began, "They said it wasn't an accident, Nate. They think someone murdered my sister." I started to speak, but held my tongue. She continued. "We got the news Sunday. I guess you know my father's dead, and my mother is not in good health. I got a flight that night from Atlanta and got here Monday morning. They were waiting for me at the airport."

"Who?"

"The American Embassy people. They pulled me aside as I was going through Immigration and grilled me for two hours. They wanted to know if I had been involved with what Becky was doing. They wanted to know if I'd been in on the deal, too. I told them I didn't know what they were talking about. They asked me if I realized my sister might be involved in an international smuggling operation. I told them they were crazy, that she imported and sold European antiques. They accused me of lying. They kept asking the same questions over and over. Nate, I just don't know what's going on." She started sobbing again. I poured her another brandy.

"So what happened?" I asked.

"Nothing! That's just it. It's like they got tired of badgering me and just said 'okay, you're free to go,' as if nothing had ever happened. They even gave me a ride to my hotel. I spent most of the day Monday talking with the police — just routine things — they didn't seem interested in why Becky was in Paris but kept asking if she had any enemies or if anyone would have a reason to want her dead. The strange thing was, though, they wouldn't tell me exactly how she died, just that she fell from the Eiffel Tower. They kept saying her death was probably not an accident and they'd let me know if or when they found out something more. They won't release her body. She'd wanted to be cremated, Nate, and," she paused to dab at a tear, "I guess I'll be flying home with her ashes later this week. I've still got to pick up her things from the police and sign some more paperwork on Friday."

"Clair, I cared about Becky, I really did, but I don't know what I can do to help you. I haven't seen or talked with her in nearly two years. It's late. Let me call a taxi to take you back to your hotel."

She seemed alarmed. "But Nate, I haven't told you why I'm here. I didn't tell them the truth. There was something going on. Becky and I were close, but there were some things she held back from me. She told about a deal she was working on, but I didn't pay that much attention — it wasn't that important at the time. I remember she said she had a chance to make a really big commission on the sale of some old paintings. She mentioned the name 'Slosh' or something like that."

I told her the name didn't ring any bells.

Clair continued, "She'd been working on this for the last four or five months. It was all hush-hush. She's not usually that way, and I sort of got the impression there might be a problem with French export laws or something like that. Anyway, I think she'd gotten suspicious of it. She said she was going to call you and get some advice before she agreed to anything. I just want to know what *really* happened, Nate. I thought maybe she'd talked with you, or told you something."

I started not to say anything but decided I should be honest. "She did call. She left a message on my answering machine a few hours before she died on Saturday."

Clair sat up suddenly. "What did she say?!"

"Nothing, really. In fact, she didn't even leave her name. The police found my phone number in her pocket and traced a call to this phone from a phone booth not far from the Eiffel Tower."

"Then the police have talked with you, too."

"Yes, and apparently they've decided I don't have much to add to the picture."

The brandy seemed to have calmed her down. Clair sat silently for a moment and then said, "What I'm afraid of is I may never know how or why she died."

"Maybe not. But why didn't you tell them everything you know?"

She hesitated. "I don't know." She nervously twirled her hair with her finger. "I guess I didn't want to. All I know is my sister is dead, and after what happened to my father, if there was something illegal going on it might be best for it never to come to light."

I started to ask what she meant about her father but instead said, "I'm calling a cab. You shouldn't be out on the streets alone. I'll ride with you to be sure you get there safely." Fifteen minutes later we were in a taxi heading to her hotel on the *rive gauche*.

Clair's hotel was a small three-star commercial establishment on the rue Dupuytran near the Sorbonne. Half a dozen drunken Japanese businessmen were crowded around the entrance evidently trying to get directions from the doorman to some brothel that specialized in servicing visitors from the Far East. They spoke no French and he spoke no Japanese, so the conversation was going back and forth in broken English. They began to hoot at Clair as she opened the door to step out of the taxi. I said, "I think I'd better walk you in," and opened the door on my side to get out. The hooting immediately stopped and the businessmen politely nodded their heads at me like a set of staggering bobble-dolls.

The hotel lobby was small and crowded. A few overstuffed leather sofas and a collection of waxy looking rubber plants added touches of color. A scuffed marble reception desk was on one side, and on the other a small passageway led to a dimly lit, smoke-filled bar. Clair thanked me and was walking toward the lifts when she suddenly stopped, stared into the bar and then turned to walk back over to me. "Nate,

69

see that man sitting at the table by the door in the bar? He looks like one of the men in the airport on Monday."

I looked toward the bar. The man was in his late thirties or early forties and wore a tight fitting knit shirt that revealed his muscular physique. His table had a clear view of the lobby. He seemed to be watching us intently. I hadn't gotten that good a look but I thought I recognized him as the one of the men that I'd chased on the Champs Élysée earlier in the evening. "Was he one of the guys who questioned you at the airport?"

"No, but I think I saw him there talking to someone from the Embassy. In fact, I think saw him sitting here in the lobby yesterday. Maybe he's a guest in the hotel."

"Let's find out." I headed toward the bar. I was even more certain I'd seen him somewhere before. He continued to stare into the lobby, calmly returning my gaze.

I walked to his table and addressed him in French. "You look familiar, monsieur. Have we met before?"

He looked at me disdainfully, took a drag on his cigarette and stubbed it out forcefully in the ashtray. He replied with a harsh Australian accent, "I don't speak yer fuckin' frog language, mate, but I don't see no good reason for you to be talkin' to me. So how's about gettin' outta me way? I'm waitin' on a chick."

It had to be a mistake. "Sorry," I replied in English. "I thought you were someone I knew."

"No harm done then." Just at that moment a bleached blond with heavy make-up entered the lobby and headed toward the bar. He stood up and grinned, "Maeve, babe. How ya been?" They disappeared arm-in-arm into the smoky haze.

Clair had watched the scene from the lobby. "I guess I was wrong," she said.

"Yeah," I agreed, but I wasn't so sure.

CHAPTER
Eleven

I DIDN'T THINK I'd hear from Clair again. I was wrong. She didn't call on Thursday so I presumed she was successfully wading through the slough of local and European Union paperwork that inevitably accompanied the death of a foreigner in France. I did hear from Colette. We talked business on the phone at least twice a week. She didn't bring up Becky's death or Clair's phone call. Neither did I.

On Friday afternoon shortly after four, Michelle buzzed my office and said, "There's a Clair Tate on line four. She sounds upset. Are you here?"

"I guess so," I replied. I owed it to her sister.

"Nate, I need your help. I'm scared. They won't release Becky's remains, and the American Embassy people called and said they want to see me. They say it's important. They said they'll have me 'detained' if I don't cooperate — whatever that means. Nate, they know I came to see you the other night. I think I'm being followed. You've got to tell me what to do!"

"Clair, listen. I don't know how to say this without sounding cold, but I really don't want to get involved, okay? Becky and I were close, but I last saw her two years ago. I have no idea what she was involved in, and quite frankly, I don't want to know. If you need an attorney, I can refer you, but let's leave me out of all this. Please?"

I could hear sobbing on the other end of the line. "I think they believe you may already be involved. I think they're watching you too, Nate." She paused. I could hear snuffling while she dried her tears.

"I'm not and if they are they'll eventually figure that out. I'm sorry I can't help you." I hung the phone up feeling very guilty.

To have someone tell you you're being watched is probably the easiest way in the world to induce paranoia in an otherwise sane individual. I left work at five and started home at a leisurely pace on the rue du Faubourg St. Honoré, a delightful street lined with antique shops and trendy boutiques that wends its way down the hill toward the Élysée Palace. Every hundred meters or so I'd stop to look in a shop window and watch the passers-by in the reflection. No familiar faces. No mysterious strangers lurking in the shadows. I relaxed and stopped at one of my favorite small restaurants near St. Michael's Church for an early supper of *cheval rôti* and with a glass of good bordeaux.

It was nearly dark when I finished. The wine relaxed me. It had been a long week. All the tour groups had assigned guides so I didn't really have anything to do for the weekend. I decided to stroll over toward the Jardin des Tuileries and walk along the Seine. I had just turned on the rue de Rivoli when a woman dressed in a short black miniskirt with a red silk blouse hissed at me. "Monsieur! Looking for some friendly company?" The oldest profession still thrives in the City of Lights.

"No. Thanks." The truth was I could use some company, I thought.

I crossed the boulevard through heavy early evening traffic and headed down a flight of steps into the park. I cut through the formal plantings of widely spaced trees heading toward the Quai des Tuileries. Two hookers paced in the half light under a street lamp. They eyed me for a moment and apparently decided I wasn't interested. I was on the wide central walkway when behind me I heard the high-pitched whine of an approaching motorbike. Out of curiosity, I turned to look. It was a large off-road machine driven by a leather-clad man wearing a black helmet with a tinted facemask. A similarly helmeted passenger sat behind him. My first thought was that motorbikes were not allowed in parks. My almost instantaneous second thought was that the passenger was holding a long barreled object and seemed to be pointing it in my direction.

The bike was forty meters away when I realized it was heading straight for me. I turned and sprinted toward the open ground of the park. The pyramid in the courtyard of the Louvre glowed in the distance. With fluid ease the driver corrected his course and came directly toward me. I was prey trapped on open ground in the sights of a more agile predator. The bike was now twenty meters away; I realized I couldn't outrun it. I leapt in the opposite direction, but the driver calmly redirected his course while his passenger corrected his aim. I saw motion out of the corner of my eye. Glancing away for an instant I saw one of the hookers sprinting toward me while reaching in her oversized purse.

I reached a sycamore tree and tried to shield myself behind its trunk. The motorbike rider's silenced gun flashed twice. I heard no sound except the bullets slamming into the wood just above my head. The driver came to a stop as his passenger raised his gun and took more careful aim this time.

The woman was nearly on me. She, too, was holding a weapon — a large-framed automatic. She raised her pistol in my direction and screamed in English, "Get down!" I hit the dirt. She fired at the riders. They ducked, but apparently she'd missed as they did a quick one-eighty dirt-spewing turn, and disappeared in the direction from which they'd come. The whole incident had lasted less than thirty seconds.

I lay on the ground not moving. The hooker rushed over. "You okay?" She spoke American English, no accent. In the dim light I could see she was blond, wearing fishnet stockings below a skirt slit up to her thigh with a low cut blouse above. She took off her spike-heeled shoes and tossed them toward a tree.

"Those goddamn high heels almost got you killed," she said with disgust. "How do they expect me to — " She stopped suddenly. "Oh, the hell with it. Let's go! The *gendarmes* will be here any minute. Just act like we're friends — close friends." She pulled me up, linked her arm in mine, laid her head on my shoulder and started walking me down the central path toward the Place de la Concorde as if nothing had ever happened.

"Who the hell are you?" She smelled of lavender. I couldn't see her face. I was trembling.

"Just shut up and walk. Smile. Act like I promised you a two-for-one special for ten euros. My partner should be waiting for us straight ahead." In the distance I could hear the distinct wailing of police sirens. Like two lovers we sauntered past the fountain toward the huge black and gold gates that framed the entrance to the massive plaza. A nondescript blue sedan with a "Taxi Parisien" dome on top sat idling, lights off, near the front of L'Orangerie. Its headlights flashed twice.

We were in a more brightly lit area now, but the woman — whoever she was — kept her left arm linked tightly in my right, with her right hand thrust in her bag clutching her gun. Without seeming obvious, she scanned the area. I still hadn't gotten a good look at her face. "Okay. You get in the cab first and I'll follow."

"And if I don't? I still don't know who you are."

"Cool it, Mr. Finch. I'm the one who saved your sweet ass tonight. Trust me on this one."

We reached the cab. Someone was in the back seat, her "partner" I assumed. She shoved me in and, taking a quick look around, jumped in after me as we sped off toward the Champs Élysée. For the first time I got a clear look at her face. It was the woman who'd met the Australian in the bar of Clair's hotel.

"You're, you're… Maeve."

"Yeah, that's me. Can it for the moment. We've got lots to talk about."

CHAPTER
Twelve

SPEEDING OUT OF THE PLACE DE LA CONCORDE, we headed west along the Seine. It was not until we were in the tunnel under the Place de l'Alma that I realized we were following the same basic route taken by Princess Diana on that fateful night in August nearly seven years earlier. I hunkered down shaking in the middle of the back seat while "Maeve," or whatever her name was, made several calls on her cell phone. Sitting to my left her "partner" scanned the streets behind and beside us, his hand nervously flitting in and out of his jacket where I presumed he holstered a weapon. He looked to be about my age, mid-thirties, with short reddish hair and a certain ex-military look about him. The driver, obviously not French but very familiar with Paris traffic, turned onto the Avenue de Versailles and headed away from the river toward the southeast.

After almost ten minutes of near silence I had regained enough of my composure to say, "I guess I should thank you. But I'd feel a lot better if you'd tell me who you are."

"Maeve" was still on the phone. Her partner answered. "You're welcome, of course, Mr. Finch. We're FBI assigned to the American Embassy here in Paris. I'm Special Agent Kelly, and our friend in costume there who saved your life is Special Agent Kazinsky." She held her thumb over the microphone of her cell phone and said simply, "Lora. Not Maeve. Lora," and then continued her conversation. Momentarily she flipped the phone shut and said, "Okay. We're clear to use the house at Chaville. Steed's meeting us there."

"Good," Kelly replied. The driver nodded, saying nothing. He obviously knew the route.

"How about telling me just what the hell is going on?" I asked.

"You need to know," Agent Kelly replied. "One of our senior agents is going to meet us and try to answer your questions. It may or may not be obvious, but we hadn't planned on what happened a few minutes ago."

We crossed the Seine at Pont de Sévres and continued southeast on the N-10, bypassing the town center and turning off on a secondary road toward the village of Chaville. Here the land was flat, with former farming areas giving way to large housing developments. I was unfamiliar with the area and couldn't exactly follow where we were going in the darkness. Eventually we turned off the road onto a long gravel drive lined by Lombardy poplars and running for half a kilometer between plowed fields. The open land became dense forest. After another couple of hundred meters the drive ended in the courtyard of a smallish stone country house, probably at one time the summer cottage of a Paris family.

The housekeeper, a nondescript French woman in her sixties, met us at the door. She appeared to be expecting us. The house could be described as cozy. Despite the relative warmth of the evening a small fire smoldered in the hearth of the large downstairs room. A steep staircase led up to what I presumed were bedrooms. Down a small hall I could see a table in a large dining room beyond which a door opened into a kitchen. "Where are we?" I asked.

Kazinsky replied, "This house is actually on a moderate-sized farm that has been owned by an agency of the US government for more than fifty years. It was a gift after the war from a grateful French family. As far as the French government knows, it's owned by an absentee landlord in the States. One of the embassy officers is assigned to oversee it, but for a number of reasons, your government doesn't 'officially' have anything to do with it. Over the years it's been used it as a safe house for defectors from the Eastern Block, for interrogations, and for various other activities we would like to keep away from prying eyes." I didn't want to ask what she meant. "Want a drink?"

"I could use one."

"Calvados okay? I've kind of developed a taste for it over here." I nodded. She poured me a stiff dose of the fiery apple brandy named for the region in Normandy that surrounds Caen.

I sat quietly, sipping my drink and waiting. There wasn't a lot else I could do. Kelly and Kazinsky disappeared toward the kitchen, leaving me alone with my thoughts. Things had happened so rapidly, I really hadn't had much of a chance to sort them out. The more I thought about it all, though, the more suspicious it became. It was a pleasant spring evening. I'd been taking an unplanned and rather random evening stroll. I'd checked to see if I was being followed and detected no one. I was walking through the park when two guys on a motorbike start shooting at me. Suddenly out of nowhere an American FBI agent appeared and saved my life, after which I ended up in this secret government safe house. This whole episode was beginning to sound like a plot from a cheap spy novel. The more I thought about it, the more I realized it all had to be a set-up. I couldn't decide if I should be angry or suspicious. My thoughts were interrupted by the sound of a vehicle on the gravel of the front drive.

The housekeeper opened the door to welcome two men, one of whom I recognized as the short muscular Australian in the bar of Clair's hotel. The other man, apparently his driver, headed toward the kitchen with the older woman. The man stuck out his hand. The accent had disappeared. "Mr. Finch. I'm Special Agent Steed. Sorry to have to meet you under these circumstances, but I think when we've brought you up to speed you'll understand better what's been going on."

"I see you've lost your accent."

"Yes. My French is not too bad, but I didn't want to blow my cover right then and there. Quite honestly, we thought we probably wouldn't be seeing you again. Looks like the picture's changed now, and you've become part of it."

There was something I didn't like about the guy. The anger won out over the suspicion. I stood up and moved closer to his personal space. "I want to know just what you're up to. I'm walking along, minding my own business when two guys I've never seen before try to kill me. You, in turn, jerk me out of the park and bring me here. I think you staged this whole damned thing."

He raised his hands, showing his palms. "Hey! You know you may be right." He paused. "But then, you may be wrong." He walked over and sat down in an overstuffed chintz covered armchair. "Just say the word anytime you want to leave, Mr. Finch. We'll have you back at your place in no time. But if I were you I think you'd want to hear us

out. Agent Kazinsky tells me those bullets were very real."
He did have a point.

Kelly and Kazinsky entered from the kitchen. Kelly was munching on a ham-stuffed croissant. Kazinsky fingered a bottle of water, unscrewing the top periodically and taking little sips. She'd removed the blond wig to reveal her natural dark brown hair. She wore jeans and a modest blouse instead of the hooker outfit and had found some shoes for her bare feet. They sat down on a sofa and indicated I should sit opposite in a chair.

Steed began, "Mr. Finch, you seem to have sort of blundered into an ongoing investigation that involves several agencies of the American government on both sides of the Atlantic. I know you're not eager to get involved, and quite frankly, we're not eager to have to deal with another player. But — for whatever reason — the people we're watching are also watching you, and they have apparently decided you represent a risk to their operation. I say 'apparently' because, to be honest, we don't know. They seem to want you silenced and chose to set up what would probably be considered a botched mugging. Another routine statistic. That wouldn't draw attention to their other plans."

"Whoa! Who are these people? What 'other plans' are you talking about?" I asked.

"I don't have permission to tell you that right now. It's Friday night, it's late, and like the rest of America the government slows down on the weekend, even here in France. I need to consult my people in Washington, but right now our concern is keeping you out of harm's way. I'm trying to get permission to get a team together for Monday morning."

"So what do you expect me to do? Stay here? Hide, locked up in my flat like some sort of hunted animal?"

"I wouldn't suggest the latter. Both your office and your place on the rue des Capucines are being watched."

"How do you know that?"

"We're watching the watchers."

I stood up. "The hell with all this! I'd feel better back in Paris."

The three agents looked at one another. "I'm afraid we can't allow that, Mr. Finch."

"And just why not?"

"Two reasons. First and foremost, our overall charge includes protecting the life and safety of American citizens. If you want my opinion, you'd be dead before Monday if you return to Paris. Second, we don't know what you really know. On a somewhat superficial level we're working with the Paris police. We know what you told Lieutenant Andrade, but we're not sure we believe you."

"Screw you! Call your driver. I'm going home." I got up and headed for the door.

CHAPTER
Thirteen

I DIDN'T GO BACK TO PARIS. I don't know what Steed and the others would have done if I tried. After much back and forth, I agreed to join one of our tour groups in the city of Blois, a couple of hours drive south on the Loire River. To do so would not have been unusual for me. Several times a year I join a tour just to get some feedback from our clients. Most of our guides are freelancers, and my being able to pop in unannounced is one of the conditions in their contracts. It keeps them on their toes and allows me to do a bit of quality control. Kelly and Kazinsky insisted on driving me there, presumably to be sure I'd not renege on my promise to avoid Paris. It was the weekend anyway, and no one would have missed me. The truth be told, I was really scared.

I arrived back in Paris early Monday after spending the weekend with the tour group. On Sunday night we'd stayed at a hotel in Orléans after touring the *châteaux* of Chambord and Chenonceau. The tour leader did a great job, the clients were happy, and I had avoided Steed's pronouncement of certain death. The group was departing for the States and took the tour bus directly to Charles de Gaulle airport. I caught an early train to Paris from the Orléans station and arrived at the American Embassy without event.

I told the guard at the gate who I was and that I had an appointment at the Embassy. He consulted a list and, finding my name on it, immediately told me to wait in the foyer. It may have been my paranoia, but it seemed he wanted to get me off the street. Steed had told me to arrive promptly at ten, and they'd give me all the details. I'd called my office to tell them I'd be in later in the day. I had no idea where this whole thing was leading.

Kazinsky appeared within five minutes. Long gone was the Friday night Paris hooker. She was now dressed in a conservative blue skirt with matching jacket. Her embassy ID badge, identifying her as a Department of State employee, hung around her neck. "I thought the FBI fell under the Department of Justice," I observed.

"We're working on a special project, so we're temporarily on another list. Helps maintain our cover, too."

"Oh." We got into an elevator.

Kazinsky led me to a large windowless conference room on the fourth floor. It could have been a boardroom anywhere in corporate America, with a long table seating at least thirty, a pull-down projection screen on one end, and a counter holding a sink and industrial-sized coffee maker on the other. An LCD projector suspended from the ceiling pointed at the screen. Five people were sitting at one end of the table. Judging from the half empty cups of coffee, the stacks of shuffled papers in front of them and the notes on their individual writing pads, they appeared to have been meeting for some time. Evidently I was not the first item on the agenda. They stood up when I entered the room. I recognized Steed and Kelly. A tall thin black man, introduced as Agent Brookins, had to be the other half of the team that had broken into my flat. His speech hinted at a Caribbean background — Haitian perhaps? A sixtyish grey-headed man in a dark suit was introduced as Deputy Commissioner Levin. The fifth person, a somewhat rumpled- looking man in his forties, was introduced simply as Dr. Berne "who works with the State Department on special projects like this one."

Levin began, "Mr. Finch, I'm glad you could be with us. Looks like we're waiting on one more person before we can get started. I trust your weekend was without event?"

"Copasetic," I said in a sarcastic tone of voice. At that moment the conference room door opened and a very tremulous Clair Tate was shown in. Her face brightened when she saw me. I started to speak but held my tongue. I smiled and nodded. Introductions were made all around once again.

Levin, who was seated at the head of the table, stood up. "Okay, We're all here. Ms. Tate, Mr. Finch, I want to say before we get started that I am sorry that you've both been dragged into this investigation. Ms. Tate, I know that you want to know as much as possible about what happened to your sister. Mr. Finch, I know you're here against your wishes. I understand that. I realize you both want to know what is going on, and how it affects you. We've got our Paris team here, and Dr. Berne and I flew over Saturday night from Washington. We're prepared to tell you about the entire investigation, but I must require that both of you agree not to divulge anything you're about to hear. Is that clear?"

I looked at Clair and raised my eyebrows. She shrugged. We both said we could keep secrets.

Levin continued. "I'm with the Department of State. Agent Steed is the FBI's head man here in Paris. Agents

Brookins, Kelly and Kazinsky are also with the FBI and are specialists in international crimes, especially those of a financial nature. Dr. Berne is actually one of the European art curators for the Smithsonian Institution. He helps us out occasionally with art theft and smuggling operations." I glanced at Clair. She seemed pale. "We met before you two arrived and we've decided it's best to lay out the entire investigation in chronological order. It makes it easier to understand how we all ended up here in this room." Levin nodded at Agent Kelly. "Mark, you want to start?

Kelly looked at his notes and began, "Ms. Tate, Mr. Finch, we've met before but I don't think I've told you exactly what I do. As the Commissioner said, I'm with the international crime unit and I'm normally based in Washington. As you may be aware, the U.S. government monitors many sorts of international communications. Following the attacks in New York in 2001, and especially since the formation of the Department of Homeland Security, there has been a real effort to share information between the various protective and enforcement divisions of government. We often get tips from the CIA or NSA or others, and we in turn refer information to other agencies if it's not something we're charged to investigate.

"Ms. Tate," he continued, pausing to phrase his words, "I'd like to express our profound sorrow at your sister's death. If we could have prevented it, or even had an inkling that any harm might come to her, we would have acted. We didn't, though, and her murder has made this investigation all the more complex."

Clair was clearly on the verge of tears. "Dammit! She was my sister, my friend, and one of the very few living relatives I have. I want to know what happened."

"Just give me a moment and I'll tell you everything we know." Clair bit her lower lip. Kelly continued, "As you can well imagine, over the years we have identified certain individuals and certain bank accounts associated with these individuals that are of interest to the U.S. government. We monitor the activity in these accounts. This takes place in the international arena, so our surveillance is not really subject to the same safeguards and legal niceties we have in the U.S. Roughly four months ago we received a referral from another agency that there had been a transfer of one point five million U.S. dollars from an account in Berlin to an account in Atlanta.

"Normally, a transaction of that size would not raise any suspicions, but the account from which the funds were transferred is one controlled by a former East German resident who is engaged in many international businesses, not all of them legitimate. Under provisions of the Patriot Act and other existing laws, we are allowed certain discreet investigations. Ms. Tate, this transfer was made directly into the account of Tate Interiors, LLC, your sister's company."

Clair clenched her fists and said, "She was in the business of importing antiques, Mr. Kelly. On occasion she'd find a piece in Europe and sell it to a buyer there without even bringing it to the States. That wouldn't have been unusual at all."

"You're absolutely right, but that's really not what raised our suspicions. When we looked at the Tate Interiors account, we saw that within twelve hours of the time that the wire transfer was received your sister wired an even one million dollars to the account of an antique dealer here in Paris, a certain Bertrand Lavalle who had a small shop near Sacré Coeur in Montmartre. Again, this might seem to be a normal transaction for someone in her business.

"I don't know what it was — a hunch, or something — that made me want to follow the money trail. And here's where strange things began happening. Almost immediately after the funds were credited to the Paris dealer's account, he wired the sum of nine hundred thousand dollars to a law firm in Berlin. It looks like he took a cut of ten percent. The law firm in turn wired this entire amount back to the *same exact account* from which the one point five million dollars had originally been transferred to Tate Interiors. It was unclear at that time — and still is — whether or not Rebecca Tate knew the source and ultimate destination of the funds that went through her account were one and the same."

I spoke, "But that doesn't make sense."

"Not at all! And that's what led us to open an investigation. On the surface it looked like whoever wired the funds was paying your sister half a million dollars for something. But what? And you have to assume the dealer here in Paris was involved since it looks like he took a tidy little commission for running some cash through his account."

"You're making something out of nothing! I'm sure there is a reasonable explanation," Clair injected.

"Let me finish, please, Ms. Tate. Somebody wanted your sister dead and we think that reason is directly related to these cash transfers." Kelly paused and looked at his notes. "At this point we brought in Agent Brookins who is with the FBI's Atlanta office. He speaks passable French and has worked on a number of international investigations. Tim, you want to take over here?"

"Sure. As Agent Kelly said, I'm headquartered in Atlanta. I checked around quietly and got nothing but good reports on Tate Interiors and your sister, Ms. Tate. We are aware of the problems your family has had, though, and when we began to dig deeper it became evident Rebecca was on the verge of bankruptcy. She — "

"What!" Clair sat up. "She never said anything about that!"

"I don't know what she told you, but things were not looking good. Since the crash of the stock market in 2000, the demand for upper end antiques has tanked. She had used up all her available credit. If she hadn't gotten the cash infusion, she'd have been out of business within months." He paused, waiting for Clair's reply. She said nothing.

"Anyway," he continued, "because of the unusual nature of these transactions we requested and received the court's permission to monitor your sister's email and telephone conversations."

I could hear Clair whisper, "You bastards!" Brookins either didn't hear her or chose to ignore it.

"I don't want to go into a lot of detail, but generally speaking, the actual content of the emails we monitored wasn't especially helpful. The attachments, though, were another matter. There was one in particular from the Parisian dealer Lavalle that consisted of a dozen or so high resolution photographs. We forwarded these on to Dr. Berne for his comments, and he found something very interesting about two of them. Let me show them to you." He opened a laptop computer sitting in front of him and pressed a few keys. Kazinsky got up and dimmed the lights. The LCD projector came to life, throwing an image of a painting on the screen at the end of the room. It was hard to guess the exact size, but it appeared to be small judging from the proportions of the frame. The image displayed an exquisite rendering of a vase of flowers, their vivid colors sharply contrasted against a darker background.

"Ms. Tate, Mr. Finch. Do either of you recognize this painting?

We shook our heads negatively.

"How about this one?" This time the screen was filled with an almost photorealistic portrait of a bearded man dressed in what I would guess to be formal seventeenth century Dutch or Flemish garb.

Clair looked at me and shook her head. I spoke for the both of us. "Neither of us has ever seen it."

"I'm not surprised. To our knowledge neither has anyone else. Not since 1944, anyway."

We sat in stunned silence.

CHAPTER
Fourteen

IT WAS DR. BERNE'S TURN NOW. Very much the ruffled academic type, he wore a tattered tweed jacket that clashed with his wrinkled pinstripe shirt, and a regimental stripe tie festooned with a faint series of random stains down its front. Shuffling his notes like a professor about to give a lecture he began, "I guess I'm a little out of place here, so I hope you'll forgive me if I'm not exactly sure how the game is played. I normally work in a very quiet office at the National Gallery in Washington. My field of expertise is Western European art from the fifteenth through the eighteenth centuries. That's a long way from a murder investigation.

"I'm often called upon by museums and private individuals to give an opinion about works of art from that period. I'm also on the Board of IFAR — that's the International Foundation for Art Research. One of our biggest concerns is the worldwide trade in stolen works of art, and my consulting role in that field has been the major reason for my interaction with the FBI. Every now and then, perhaps once in a lifetime, an incredible case comes along that makes your whole career and all your training worthwhile. This may be one of those times.

"I believe that for you to fully understand the significance of the photographs Agent Brookins just showed you, I need to show you several more." He motioned for Brookins to display the next image. A grainy black and white photo of a long gallery hung from floor to ceiling with paintings appeared on the screen. "This is a photograph taken here in Paris sometime in the early nineteen-thirties. It's a gallery in a private home, specifically the residence of Adolphe Schloss at 38 rue Henri-Martin in the 16th Arrondissement. Do you see the portrait of a man just here on the second row?" Using a laser pointer he focused a sharp red dot on one of the paintings. It appeared to be one of the two works whose photograph had been sent in the email from the Paris dealer.

After a moment he nodded at Brookins and the scene changed. "This is another photograph of the dining room in the Schloss residence taken at the same time." The wall above an ornate sideboard was covered with a series of smallish paintings depicting still life subjects, mainly flowers. "Do you recognize this one?" he asked, aiming the pointer's beam at what appeared to be the other work seen in the email photographs. "You'll have to admit both images seem on the surface to be the same as those contained in the photos Ms. Tate received.

"Now, let me show you two other photographs." He nodded and a higher resolution black and white image of the formally dressed man in Dutch clothing appeared. "And another." This time the photograph — again in black and white — was of the floral still life.

"Now these are good images. Professionally done. Where and when do you suppose they were taken?" Without waiting for an answer he continued, "Not far from where we are sitting at this very moment. They were taken by Nazi occupation forces in the Jeu de Paume Museum during the summer of 1943." He stopped as if he'd made a major point and waited for our reaction.

I decided I'd say nothing. Clair spoke, "So what are you saying Dr. Berne?"

"Don't you see? These two works were among those looted from France by the Germans during World War II. Don't you know your history?"

"Goddammit, Dr. Berne, the only thing I'm sure of at this moment is that my sister is dead, and I want to know why she was killed and who did it. As far as my knowledge of World War II goes, neither of my parents was even born."

"I'm sorry. I'm sorry. Forgive me, Ms. Tate." Berne was clearly embarrassed. "Sometimes you lose perspective. I know you've, you've…" He stopped, pulling nervously at his ear lobe and said, "Let me back up and give you a very brief overview of the situation and why the apparent discovery of these long lost works is so important." He looked at Clair for approval. She glared back at him stonily.

Brookins flipped off the projector and Kazinsky turned up the lights. Berne sat down and began, "Between 1938 and 1944, the Germans at one time or another controlled the entire continent of Europe from the Atlantic in the west to near Moscow in the east, and from the Baltic in the north to the Mediterranean in the south. One of the avowed goals of Hitler's government was to systematically collect the rarest and best examples of European art. These would eventually become the heart of a proposed *Führermuseum* to be constructed near Linz, in Austria. Every major army group had a unit attached to it whose job it was to collect, confiscate or otherwise acquire objects of art. That included not only paintings, but also furniture, tapestries, porcelains, and the like. Some of this was done under the guise of 'preservation' but much, if not most, of their methods simply boiled down to the outright state-sponsored theft. Particularly at risk were the collections of Jews and other 'undesirables' who were often sent to death camps without so much as any pretense of legality.

"At the start of the war, France was one of the leading art centers of the world. Her public and private art collections were without equal. While the French government was hiding behind its purportedly impregnable Maginot Line, Hitler's spies in the guise of academic researchers were quietly making a list of those works of art to be 'acquired' once the country had been conquered.

"When German troops rolled unopposed into Paris in June 1940, they were accompanied by the *Einsatzstab Reichsleiter Rosenberg* — the ERR — a special unit under the direction of Alfred Rosenberg, a Nazi Party ideologue and one of Hitler's cronies. He was executed, by the way, for crimes against humanity following the Nuremberg trials in 1946. The ERR set up shop in what was at the time the Jeu de Paume Museum and went about systematically looting the art treasures of France. The Museum became the central collecting point. Works of art were brought there, photographed, catalogued and held for transport to Germany." He stopped and looked at the rest of us seated at the table. "Are we clear thus far?"

Levin said, "We could all use the education. Go on."

"Okay. Well, special attention was paid to what was considered by the Nazi hierarchy to be the more 'classical' European works, especially Northern European art prior to the nineteenth century. And there was no better single collection of such works as those of Adolphe Schloss. He was a wealthy businessman who had amassed a magnificent assemblage of European early masters around the turn of the century.

Schloss died many years before the start of the war and left the paintings to his wife and children who kept them on display in the family home here in Paris. Acquiring it should have been easy. The Schloss family was Jewish, so the collection could simply be expropriated under existing German law. The problem was the family had moved the paintings to the South of France in 1939 and had gone into hiding in 1940. In 1943 the collaborationist Vichy government and the Gestapo found and arrested several family members and soon discovered where they'd hidden the collection. The works were taken to Paris, catalogued and photographed. A few of them were given to the Louvre, but most became a part of the Führerreserve and were shipped to Germany to be held for the proposed museum in Linz. On a practical basis, that was the last time the world saw them.

"It is assumed many of them were destroyed in the final days of the war. Perhaps they were looted by the Soviets as war booty. Who knows? Even though it's been more than sixty years, every so often one of the paintings will appear on the market. In the late seventies a work by Jan van de Capelle was found. In 1990 an important portrait by Frans Hals was confiscated by the police from an art show in Paris. More recently a long-lost Rembrandt was found — you get the idea. And then these two turn up." Berne stopped as if his lecture was complete, looking around to see if there were any questions.

I spoke. "Dr. Berne, we really appreciate the background, but are you saying the two paintings whose pictures we just saw were part of the Schloss collection?"

"Of course! I thought I made myself clear. The smaller of the two — it's titled *Still Life with Tulips* — is by Jan Brueghel the Younger and dates from the mid-seventeenth century. The other is by Frans Hals and is known as the *Portrait of a Haarlem Elder*. It's a guess, but I'd date it about 1620."

We sat silently for a moment staring at each other. Clair spoke. "Are you telling me my sister was purchasing these two paintings from a dealer here in Paris?"

"That appears to be the case, but it doesn't explain the strange money trail." Levin answered. "If she were simply buying them for resale, that would be one thing. From what we know, though, I would suspect both Rebecca and Monsieur Lavalle were part of an elaborate smuggling operation."

"Why don't you ask him — Lavalle?"

"We'd like to, but he was murdered in what was reported to be an armed robbery shortly after the funds were transferred out of his account. At the time it seemed to be a random act of violence, but now…" Levin's voice dropped off.

She said quietly, "I don't see how that —" She stopped, thinking, and then said, "She paid a million dollars for them. She had to be buying them for someone."

"Perhaps," Levin replied, "but tell me, Dr. Berne, what would these go for at auction on the open market?"

"Conservatively, with a clear title?" Levin nodded.

Berne pursed his lips and looked at the ceiling. "Hard to say. Works of this quality simply don't come on the market. A guess — maybe fifteen to twenty million dollars."

Clair leaned forward. "Fifteen to twenty million dollars for two paintings! That's ridiculous, Dr. Berne."

"No, not for two paintings, Ms. Tate. Fifteen to twenty million *each*."

CHAPTER
Fifteen

THE GROUP STARED QUIETLY at Berne while the magnitude of the numbers sank in. It was Levin who spoke first. "You see Ms. Tate, this does not appear to be your ordinary smuggling operation."

I interrupted him. "What's the French government's take on this?"

After an unusually long pause Levin replied, "We haven't told them the whole story. At least not yet. There are some sensitive international issues involved."

Clair stood up. "You mean to say my sister is murdered, and you, you... bureaucrats" — she spit the word out — "are holding back information that might help..."

"Ms. Tate!" It was Steed who spoke this time. He paused, looking to Levin for approval who nodded his assent. "Please, understand. It's not that simple." Clair sank back in her chair. The FBI agent continued, "Your sister's death is a horrible tragedy. But if we treat this as a routine murder investigation, there is a good chance it may never be solved. Let me lay out for you what we know, what we don't know, and why we want to handle things differently than we might with other cases.

"To begin with, we think the killer or killers have a source inside the Préfecture of Police. At this point in time they may know everything the Paris Police know. It is important the United States government is — on an 'official' basis at least — leaving the investigation to the local authorities. We did quietly manage to have primary jurisdiction transferred to the Criminal Investigation Division where we have some 'friends' who will work with us discreetly and off the record." Steed paused and took a sip of coffee. "Let me get back to what we think took place at the Eiffel Tower."

"I'm sorry," Clair said. "All I want to know is what happened, and all I want to see is Becky's killers brought to justice."

"We'll do our best," Steed replied. "I'll tell you what we know and what we've reconstructed as to the sequence of events that took place on Saturday. Becky had been in France for about two weeks before her death. She'd been doing what an international antique dealer would normally do, buying inventory and arranging to have it shipped to the States. She carried a tri-band cell phone that works both in the US and here in France on the GSM standard. We have the technology in place to monitor some — but not all — of her phone conversations. We'd also been intermittently tailing her when she was here in Paris.

"On Friday the ninth, the day before she was killed, we caught a snatch of conversation in which she seemed to be making arrangements to inspect something. For technical reasons, we didn't pick up on everything that was said, but she was talking with someone who spoke flawless American English. For reasons I'll explain later, that tipped us this might have something to do with the paintings from the Schloss collection. She was in a taxi at the time, and we had no way of following her. We know she returned to her hotel shortly after dark. We interviewed the taxi driver that dropped her off, but he wasn't very helpful. He said he'd picked her up on the Place de la Concorde near the obelisk for a short ride to her hotel. We suspect someone dropped her off there, but we have no idea where she'd spent the afternoon. I'll let Agent Kazinsky take over from here."

Kazinsky had found a bottle of water and had been nervously unscrewing the cap, taking a sip, and then replacing it. She began, "I was assigned to tail your sister on Saturday. Becky ate a late breakfast and left her hotel about ten. Instead of heading to the Saturday *marché aux puces* where she usually went on weekends, she took a taxi to the Musée d'Orsay. She seemed to be looking for someone. I couldn't risk getting too close, but I noticed a man whom I didn't recognize spoke to her and appeared to be asking for directions. He took out a small map — I think it was of central Paris. They talked for a few minutes. She pointed to an area on the map. He appeared to thank her and handed her something — it looked like a business card. Almost immediately she began to look around as if to see if she were being followed.

At that point, I realized something unusual was going on. I called for back-up, but before anyone could arrive Becky had managed to slip out of the museum mingled in with a busload of German tourists. I caught sight of her as she headed into the Metro station, but I lost her after that. The next thing we knew she was dead.

I observed, "Ms. Kazinsky, the Eiffel Tower is one of the most public places in Paris. There are guards and centrally monitored video cameras, not to mention the only rapid way up or down is by elevator. If someone were planning a murder that would be the last place you'd think of — it's just too public."

"Exactly! And that's why we think Becky arranged to meet someone there around five on Saturday afternoon when there were likely to be crowds of visitors. She must have feared her life might be in danger. We've been over the surveillance videos a dozen times. At roughly four-twenty, Becky purchased a lift ticket at the north pylon to take her to the third floor observation platform. There was a big crowd — you know, Mr. Finch. You were there. She took the elevator directly to the second level observation platform. To go to the top, she had to change lifts. From the video you can see very clearly she's nervous. She keeps looking around to make sure she's not being followed. She arrived on the third level platform at about four forty-five."

Kazinsky paused and took another sip of water. She consulted her notes and continued, "The surveillance video shows Becky getting off the elevator, looking about and apparently seeing someone she knows. She walks toward that person — or persons, we don't know — who are standing in what turns out to be a blind spot out of camera range. About ten minutes pass. The elevator comes and goes a couple of times letting off a dozen or so people and taking a dozen or so back down to the second level. Becky and whomever she's with remain out of view.

"The next thing that happens is recorded by a camera focused on the opposite side of the platform. You can observe a young blond-headed woman who appears to be engaged in a quiet conversation with a man who looks to be in his late twenties. She looks in the direction of where Becky was standing and nods her head. Almost immediately and without warning she reaches out and slaps the man she's been talking to. She then starts to climb up on the railing like she's going to jump. The man grabs at her.

She stops climbing, but continues to scream at him and wave her arms. A crowd starts to gather. She takes off her coat and then starts to unbutton her blouse. There is only one guard on the platform and he rushes over. By this time the woman has stripped down to a very revealing lace bra. There is no audio, but you can see him trying to calm down the woman. She seems to be arguing with him about something, but from what we found out later, she's yelling at him in German and he's yelling back in French. Neither one understands the other.

"Needless to say, the crowd's attention is totally diverted by all this chaos and noise. You can see the guard calling for assistance on his radio. At about that same time your sister is fighting for her life. The struggle apparently ends when she is physically tossed to her death over the rail of the platform. There is a nine second snatch of video from another camera that appears to show Becky's arm reaching out as if to escape before it is jerked back. She's off-camera for another six seconds and then you get a glimpse of a struggle — her head briefly appears with a male hand clamped over her mouth to keep her from calling for help.

"Unfortunately most of whatever happened took place out of camera range. No one admitted seeing anything because the crowd was focused on the half-naked screaming blond. Seconds thereafter, another camera shows the backs of three men entering the stairwell. They apparently walk down to the second level platform where they disappear into the crowd.

"Meanwhile, the German-speaking woman calms down just as suddenly as she started, jumps down from the rail and hurriedly pulls on her blouse. Her male friend, who has now found his voice, explains to the guard that it's all a lovers' quarrel. He's trying to talk their way out of being detained when the guard gets a call on his radio about the apparent jumper who's managed to make her move while he was otherwise occupied. While the guard is distracted, the couple uses the confusion to slip back on the same elevator that was bringing up reinforcements. Judging from the videos, by the time the lift reaches the second floor platform, the girl has stripped off her blond wig and emerges as a redhead. They, too, disappear into the crowd.

"Your sister's body careened off the roof of the second level observation platform and ended up lodging in the iron latticework a hundred feet or so above ground. We're not totally certain, but the autopsy results suggest her neck may have been broken before the fall. Her purse was missing and her pockets had been stripped clean." Kazinsky stopped and looked at Clair.

Steed spoke. "Apparently the only thing the killers missed was a slip of paper in her pocket with your phone number on it, Mr. Finch." The room was quiet. I felt seven pairs of eyes boring into me.

CHAPTER
Sixteen

EVERYONE WAITED FOR A RESPONSE. It struck me that they honestly thought I had some secret knowledge about Becky's death — that I knew more than I was willing to admit. "I've told you before; I haven't seen or talked with Becky in two years." Levin started to speak but I continued. "I have the very real impression you don't believe me. I'm telling the truth. That's all I can say."

"If that's the case, why would someone want to kill you, Mr. Finch?" Levin asked.

"I don't know." I paused. "But tell me this, why are you holding back information from the Paris police? And where are you going with your investigation?"

Steed answered, "If the Deputy Commissioner will allow me to speak for the group," he paused and Levin again nodded for him to continue, "I'll tell you what we think is going on, and why we think you are a part of it."

"In truth, all we have are theories, but this is the one we are working on. Ms. Tate," he said, looking at Clair, "your sister was a respected and fairly well known antique dealer. She was in financial trouble. We think that someone — and I'll have more to say about who in a moment — approached her and asked her to help smuggle two extremely valuable works of stolen art from France to the U.S.. We don't know the whys and wherefores, but certainly there are wealthy collectors who are willing to pay millions to have such paintings in their private collections.

She got half a million dollars. This was enough to allow her to buy her way out of debt, and we presume perhaps enough to make her look the other way as to the origin of the paintings. It may be that she had no idea the works were stolen. We may never know. "On Friday before her death she disappeared for several hours, we think to look at the paintings. Something must have happened to cause her concern. She may have recognized the works as stolen art. Who knows? We imagine she worried about it overnight. The next day she set up a meeting in one of the most public places in Paris. Maybe she wanted out of the deal. Assuming that you, Mr. Finch, are telling the truth, she called you — an old friend — for advice. Despite everything, she is killed."

"Okay," I replied, "so how does that drag me into all this?"

Steed looked around at the other agents. This was evidently a topic they'd been discussing. "When an American citizen is murdered in Paris, naturally the embassy is notified. The local police initially viewed you as a person of interest, but our sources tell us you've convinced them you're no more than an innocent bystander. When we heard the facts we were not so sure of that, hence our supposedly surreptitious visit to your apartment. We think the killers have a source inside the Paris Police. They probably know what we know, and are not so sure Becky didn't tell you more than you've admitted to." Steed looked again at Levin, who indicated he should continue. "We've had a chance to look over the contents of your computer and we have been monitoring your phone calls since — "

"You assholes bugged my phones? What the hell?" I was angry.

"Calm down, Mr. Finch," Levin interjected. "We've found nothing to indicate your involvement."

"But — "

"Please. Let me finish," Steed said. "I assigned Agent Brookins to follow you, and one of the first things he noted was that he was not the only one tailing you. Apparently Becky's killers also found you a person of interest. Do you recognize this man?" He slid a glossy photo across the table. It had been taken with a telephoto lens and showed the nondescript face of a fair-complected dark-haired man in his thirties.

I studied the photo. "I've never seen him before."

"He's been tailing you ever since two days after Becky's death. The last we saw of him he was following you into the Jardin de Tuileres last Friday night. He called someone on his cell phone just before his friends on the motorbike appeared and tried to kill you."

I sat in stunned silence. Steed continued, "We theorize the killers believe you and Becky had been in communication. They don't know what she told you, but just to be safe want to see you dead, too. No loose ends." He paused. "We don't think they're going to give up until you've been silenced. Permanently."

Clair spoke. "But that doesn't give you reason to hold back information from the local police. If you know some of the people involved, why haven't you had them arrested?"

Levin answered, "Ms. Tate, I understand your concerns, but remember this. There is no statute of limitations either in this country or in ours for the prosecution of a murder. I assure you the killers will eventually come to justice."

"Eventually!" Clair slammed her fist on the table. "Just what is that supposed to mean?"

Levin thought for a moment and replied, "Look at it this way. Murder is not the only crime that has been committed, and should we not find a way to protect Mr. Finch here," he looked at me, "this sad affair may eventually involve multiple murders. No, Ms. Tate, this is a problem that cannot have a partial solution. I know you want your sister's killers brought to justice. So do we." He turned to me. "Mr. Finch, I know you'd like some assurance that you can live your life without fear of being murdered by some stranger on the street. We want that, too. And recall, also, this whole episode began with what appears to be an attempt to smuggle stolen art."

Levin thought for a moment and continued, "Perhaps the best analogy is that of the blind men and the elephant. Each of us sees the situation from his or her own perspective. Maybe in this case, it's our job as representatives of the justice and diplomatic arms of your government to see the big picture and act accordingly. Think about it, don't we all agree on certain things? Becky's killers must be caught and punished. Nate Finch shouldn't have to spend the rest of his life in Paris afraid of every shadow. Those responsible for trafficking in stolen art must be apprehended and punished. The paintings in question must be returned to their rightful owners." He looked first to Clair and then to me as if expecting an answer. Neither of us spoke.

Levin continued, "Sure, our priorities may be different, but there has got to be a solution that will meet all of our goals. We think we've come up with it, but we'll need your help."

"Mr. Levin," I said, "you've not exactly explained why this whole matter can't be handled by the French authorities. While the crimes may have peripherally involved the U.S., this is basically a local issue. The police here are highly competent."

"Oh, I agree completely, Mr. Finch," Levin interrupted, "but that's why I'm here as a representative of the State Department. There are other — shall we say, political? — considerations." Clair snorted and murmured something under her breath.

Looking at me, he continued, "You live here in France, and no doubt have an acute sense of the history of Franco-American relations. It's been a turbulent one to say the least. The French supported the American colonial side during the Revolutionary War, only to turn around and support the Confederacy during the Civil War. A couple of decades later they gave us the Statue of Liberty as a sign of friendship with the government they'd opposed. In World War II, Vichy French troops fought and killed American soldiers in North Africa but were cheering us as liberators when we marched in to Paris less than two years later. The formation of NATO helped prevent the Soviets from overrunning more of Europe, but de Gaulle did his best to destroy it by ejecting our forces from France in the sixties. I could go on.

"The latest rift, of course, is the U.S.'s policy in the Middle East. France has done its best to thwart us at every turn. From our perspective, we see much of this obstructionism as simple opposition to America's new role as the world's sole remaining superpower. The French have an inflated vision of their—"

"Mr. Levin." Clair spoke, obviously annoyed. "Just what does all this crap have to do with my sister's murder?"

"I'm sorry," Levin apologized. "I'm a diplomat by trade and I tend to couch my explanations in terms of the big picture. The bottom line is that if the word gets out the American government is interested in this case — not only as a murder of one of its citizens, but also as a case of international smuggling, what little cooperation we get now will evaporate.

The French will handle things based on their own priorities. "We have good reason to believe that while someone may be arrested and prosecuted for Becky's death, the smuggling issue will be swept under the table. And even if it's not, even if the paintings in question are recovered, we fear the French government is likely to confiscate them for one of their national collections rather than see them returned to their rightful owners. We are confident we can achieve everyone's goals by handling this part of the case ourselves. Therefore, at this point all we've told the French is that our sole interest is in seeing the killers of one of our citizens is caught and punished."

"Come on!" I said. "You don't for a minute really believe that, do you? The truth is that you — the State Department — is looking for an excuse to upstage and embarrass the French by turning a local murder into an international conspiracy and then crowing to the world how it took American law enforcement skills and resources to solve the case. That's bullshit, and I'm not going to have anything to do with it." I stood up to leave. "I'll see you guys later. I'm going back to my apartment to find and rip out your phone taps."

Levin stared at me speechless. He was not accustomed to my evident lack of respect. Steed picked up the photo he'd shown me a few minutes earlier. "Well, good luck, Nate. Check on this guy while you're out. Our men tell us that at this moment he's sitting in a metallic silver Peugeot 607 parked about fifty meters from your building. You need the tag number?"

CHAPTER
Seventeen

I PONDERED MY OPTIONS. They were very limited. I sat back down at the table. "Okay. If this were a game of poker, you'd be holding all the chips." I turned to Clair. "I want you to know I hold no disrespect for your sister's memory; I just find myself getting sucked into..." I stopped. Better keep my mouth shut.

Steed spoke. "This is first and foremost a criminal investigation. While State has input," he glanced at Levin, "our goal is justice. In this case that means the arrest of your sister's killers, Ms. Tate, your safety and freedom, Mr. Finch, and the U.S. government's apprehension of those behind this whole operation. Are we on the same page now?" Clair nodded reluctantly. I stared back at Steed.

"Let's continue then," he said. "Lora, can you get the lights?" He motioned to Brookins who typed a few strokes on his laptop. A photo of a strikingly handsome, well-dressed man flashed on the screen. He looked to be about forty, with blond hair and blue eyes and wearing a sharply

cut charcoal suit over a pinstripe shirt and a solid maroon
tie. "Nate, Clair — If we're going to work together I hope
we can be on a first-name basis — either of you recognize
this photo?" We shook our heads. "Let me show you some
others." He rapidly clicked through a dozen or more shots
of the same man, some by himself, others with groups.
Several were apparently taken at a ski resort in the Bavar-
ian Alps, judging from the background. The last shot was
a blow-up of the photo page of a German passport. "Let
me introduce Hans Ulbricht." For some reason I glanced
at Clair. She stiffened at the sound of the name. I looked
around the room. No one else seemed to notice.

Brookins flicked off the projector and Kazinsky turned
up the lights. Steed continued, "Hans Dieter Ulbricht, born
September 2, 1962 at what is now the Columbia-Presbyte-
rian Medical Center in New York City. His father, Helmut
Ulbricht, was nominally the cultural attaché for the German
Democratic Republic legation — the East Germans — from
1961 through 1974. In fact, he was the local representative
of the *Ministerium für Staatssicherheit* — better known as
the Stasi — and, as we found out later after the collapse of
the Soviet Union, the KGB's inside man in New York.

"The elder Ulbricht and his wife spoke flawless English and were quite a part of the social scene in those turbulent days of the late sixties. While they were attending
cocktail parties with Leonard Bernstein and other glitterati,
he was quietly encouraging and supporting every dissident
voice he could find, ranging from the Black Panthers to the
SDS. It was before my time, but I've seen his dossier. He
managed to pull it all off without once getting caught with
his hand in the cookie jar.

"His son Hans attended private school on the upper
East Side and was thirteen by the time they were called
back to Germany. In the late eighties, his parents saw the

handwriting on the wall and took a long 'vacation' to a dacha near Odessa on the Black Sea where they decided to take up permanent residence.

"After the fall of the Berlin Wall, Ulbricht senior was indicted by the German government for multiple crimes, but was still a free man when he died of old age about six years ago in Moscow. Hans meanwhile had finished his university education. Prior to his parents fleeing Germany, he had opened an import-export business whose remarkable success can only be explained by his access to — shall we say — 'sensitive information,' no doubt supplied by his father. By the time of the reunification of East and West Germany in 1990 he had became a major power broker at the tender age of twenty-nine. Quite a remarkable rise to power!

"So, for the last decade or so, and especially since his parents' death, Hans Ulbricht has continued to prosper. Nominally his fortune was made in international commodity trading — you know, Argentine wheat to Russia, Brazilian coffee to Germany and the like. As far as most people are aware, he's a wealthy and well-respected businessman living with his wife and three kids in an upscale Berlin neighborhood.

"We suspect he's been involved in illegal deals for years. These have involved mainly arms smuggling in Asia, the Middle East and Africa. He doesn't do it for the ideology, just the money. To give you an example, we've documented one shipment of AK-47's and ammo that originated in Viet Nam. Half it was off-loaded in the Gulf of Guinea onto a coastal freighter owned by a Liberian rebel group while the other half steamed into the main port of Buchanan bound for the Liberian government army. It's only been since the World Trade Center attacks that we've begun to focus on him as a possible source of terrorist arms and even terrorist funding. We think, but we've been unable to prove, that Ulbricht is a major facilitator in the funding of Islamic terrorist cells in Europe. We want to bring him down."

Steed paused and looked at Levin again seeking permission to continue. The Commissioner said, "Go ahead."

"The money wired to Tate Interiors was from an account controlled by one of Hans Dieter Ulbricht's companies in Berlin. Clair, we don't know if your sister dealt directly with Ulbricht or one of his surrogates, but we think he carries the ultimate responsibility for your sister's death."

"Then why don't you arrest him?" Clair demanded.

"Because we don't really have any first class evidence. And recall that this is France, not Fresno. The FBI has no power to arrest anyone here."

"Well then have the French police arrest him. Once you've got him in custody you could — "

"I wish it were that simple. To start with, he's a German citizen and subject to all rights of the European Union. With his wealth and the attorneys and politicians it can buy, he wouldn't spend fifteen minutes in custody. The case would get buried so deep that it would probably never even come to court. Even if we tried to get the French police to pick him up, we think he has his own people on the inside. Evidence could 'disappear.' Files could get 'lost.' We figure we'll only have one chance to get him and we want to make it count."

I asked, "And I assume Clair and I are a part of your master plan?"

"I'll answer that," Levin said. "In a word, yes. We need you. We think that if we can arrest Ulbricht in a jurisdiction subject to American law we can make a case that will stick with an American jury. Here in Europe, who knows?"

"Are you saying what I think you're saying, Mr. Levin, because if you are — "

"That's right, Nate, we want to arrest him on American soil and you two are at the heart of the plan."

CHAPTER
Eighteen

I LOOKED AT CLAIR. I couldn't exactly read her expression. It was either one of fear or hate, or maybe both. Levin sat quietly as if waiting for an answer.

"So what does this involve, Mr. Levin?" I asked.

"Several weeks of your time — a month at most."

"And I take it there is some danger involved?"

"Some, perhaps, but I'd say minimal. We'll be there with you."

"What exactly is it you want us to do?"

"We want you to make contact with Ulbricht and see if you can take over at the point the deal fell apart."

Clair, who'd been silently listening said, "Are you out of your damned bureaucratic minds?"

Steed answered, "No, not at all. Again, recall all we've just been over and consider the alternatives. We think we have a plan that will work." He paused. "You are under no obligation. We're not going to give up on bringing Becky's killers to justice. And Nate, we're not going to cut you loose at the mercy of whoever wants you dead. We think, though, if we handle everything right, and our plans work, we can close the book on this case permanently and take one of our enemies off the street for good."

The room was quiet. I could hear the hissing of the ventilation duct above and thought of the interrogation room at the Paris police building. I glanced at Clair. I did not want to be here. I looked at Levin and Steed and the other agents, their faces impassive, waiting for an answer. Only Dr. Berne toyed with his papers, nervously pulling at his earlobe.

Clair began, "So, If we — "

Steed interrupted her. "There is one thing, Clair." He paused, as if for effect. "You've got to come clean with us. Tell us what you know."

"Why do you...? What makes you think I...?" She hesitated, stammering a bit.

"It's our job. Nate, truth is, we believe you. Clair, we think you know more than you've been willing to admit." Steed waited for her reply.

Clair stared at the table for a moment, chewing her lip. She looked up, her eyes burning into Steed, "And you promise," she forced the word out, repeating it again, "promise, you'll find and punish Becky's killers?"

"As much as I can make that sort of promise, you have my word."

Clair looked at me. I raised my eyebrows and shrugged slightly. She looked at Levin, then Steed and the agents, locking eyes with each as if she wanted some assurance they each were personally committed to this quest. She looked back at me. I said quietly, "Okay."

She said, "Okay."

Levin said, "Good. Let's take a break. I'll have sand-wiches sent up and we'll start back after lunch." Everyone stood and began to wander out of the room.

I found the men's room down the hall. I felt vaguely nauseated and splashed water on my face. I stared at myself in the mirror. There were dark circles under my eyes. I must have lost some weight. The scar on my right cheek gleamed in an ugly shade of purple. Steed walked in and headed for the urinal. I tried to look like I was in control. Steed said, "Glad to have you on board, Nate."

"As if you've given me a choice," I replied sarcasti-cally. "Listen, Steed, I really don't know what you've got planned for us, but I hope you don't expect me to work with Clair Tate."

Steed glanced over his shoulder, shook himself dry, and headed for the sink. The urinal flushed automatically. "What do you know about Clair?"

"From what I've seen her repertoire includes exactly three acts: she can yell, she can slam her fist on the table and she can cry. She comes across as a goddamned airhead."

"What do you suppose she knows about you?"

I can take care of me, I thought. *It's her I'm worried about.* Instead I replied, "Very little."

Steed rinsed his hands methodically and reached for a towel. He dried them slowly and said, "There's a lot more to Clair than meets the eye."

"Thus far she's come across to me as some whiny little rich girl from Atlanta."

Steed inched closer, invading my space. "And what are you, Mr. Finch? Some farm boy from south Georgia who drags lonely American women on romantic April-in-Paris tours? Some guy whose wife gets pregnant by — "

I swung at him. He caught my right wrist with his left hand before it could connect. We stared at one another.

116

"Apologies offered, Nate. I was out of line." He released his grip. I dropped my fist.

"Okay, Steed."

We stood glaring at each other. Steed spoke. "She can hold her own, Nate. You'll see."

The restroom door opened and Brookins walked in. He immediately sensed a problem. "You fellows okay?"

"Sure," I said. "Agent Steed and I were just getting better acquainted."

Brookins glanced at Steed who smiled and said, "Nate and I were just on our way to see what the local Mickey D's has sent over for lunch."

Paris — gastronomic capital of the world — and the American Embassy sends out to McDonald's for lunch. I hoped this wasn't a hint of things to come.

~

I ATE A BIG MAC, one of the few American terms the French have allowed to take root, and *frites petites*. Clair dug through the pile until she found a Happy Meal, took a single bite from the hamburger and spent the next ten minutes posing and un-posing the plastic Chinese-made action figure that came stuffed in the sack. The others dug hungrily into their ketchup-covered fries while discussing the plot of some new Nicole Kidman movie that had not yet made it from Hollywood to Paris. It was as if we'd taken a break from a boring history lecture and were waiting for the next class to begin.

An olive-complected secretary with a big nose cleared the remains of lunch from the table. Levin said, "Ready to get started back?" No one indicated otherwise. "Okay, then, I'm going to turn this over to Agent Steed. Dr. Berne and I have to catch a flight back to Washington this evening, so we've got to head for the airport. He looked at Steed and the three other agents, "You fellows comfortable with the plan?" They indicated they were. "Then we're off." He turned toward Clair and me. "I know this has been difficult for both of you. On behalf of the U.S. government, I want to thank you for your help." Without waiting for our reply he hurried out the door, Dr. Berne shuffling along behind him.

Steed began, "Before we go any further, I think it's appropriate that you tell us everything you know, Clair. This is a team effort now, and our success is going to depend in part on our trusting each other."

Clair looked at me and said, "I think Becky knew from the beginning this was not an ordinary deal." She hesitated and said, "I didn't know — I really didn't — that she'd been having money troubles. You know the antique business was originally my mother's. She'd run things by herself after my father..." She hesitated again. *What was it with her father,* I thought?

"Anyway," she continued, "my mother was diagnosed with multiple sclerosis about six years ago. She went downhill rapidly. She's been in a nursing home for nearly four years now. My sister took over the business just because there was no one else to run it. I thought initially she was doing very well. I knew things were expensive with my mother's medical bills and all, but I never really asked about the money. Becky handled all that. I just assumed everything was fine.

"About two years ago Becky got involved with Nate." She looked at me. "She took it really hard when they broke up. I don't think she'd had half a dozen dates until about a year ago when she met someone. She wouldn't even tell me his name at first, but she was all giddy and finally acting like the Becky I used to know. For the first time in a long while she seemed really happy. She said he was German and had businesses all over the world. I know they spent a week at his villa near Ibiza, and I know they'd meet every time she was here. I think he even came to Atlanta several times to see her. She was secretive about it — maybe she was afraid of getting hurt again.

"Not long after that, Becky told me she'd lucked into some incredible find. Antique dealers are like that — they're always looking for that Rembrandt at a yard sale. She started to tell me about it. I remember her mentioning something about World War II and some 'Slosh' collection. I guess she meant Schloss. Anyway, she was all up in the air and said if she could just work this one deal out 'things would be fine.' I really didn't know what she meant at the time. She said — "

"Clair, pardon me for interrupting," Agent Kelly said, "but did she tell you how she came across this find?"

"Yes, that's just what I was about to say. She said her new friend had put her in touch with a dealer in Paris who had a couple of paintings on consignment but didn't really know their true worth. He had a business associate in Atlanta who was willing to pay top dollar for them if he could get them through American customs quietly. Becky said she'd get a finder's fee — a commission — of a million dollars if she could pull it off."

"Clair," Kelly said, "did Becky ever tell you her friend's — the German's — name?"

"Yes." Clair's shoulders drooped slightly. "She said his name was Hans. Hans Ulbricht."

CHAPTER
Nineteen

AT THE MENTION of Ulbricht's name Kelly, Brookins and Kazinsky began scribbling on their note pads. Steed stared at the ceiling and pursed his lips. Without looking at Clair he said, "You mentioned a million dollars. According to what we can reconstruct she only received five hundred thousand. Was there to be a second payment?"

"Of course. I thought you would have figured that out. She never told me the exact amount, but she said she was to get half of her commission up front and get the other half when the paintings were delivered."

"Did she say for whom they were being purchased?"

"No, in fact I don't really think she would have told me all she did if we hadn't gone out one night to celebrate her birthday. She was turning thirty so we had champagne. We were always so close. I could tell she had something she wanted to talk about and..." Clair stopped in mid-sentence. A tear rolled out of her left eye. She dabbled at it with a

McDonald's napkin. "I'm sorry. I just realized she won't be having any more birthdays."

Kazinsky spoke. "I know this is rough on you, Clair, but we need your help."

"That's all I know, really."

"You never met Ulbricht, then, and he never met you, correct?" Brookins asked.

"That's right."

"Do you think he would believe you if you called him and told him Becky had kept you informed about the whole deal from the beginning? That you need the money and want to go through with the original plan?"

"It's possible, sure."

"Wait a second," I said. "You're missing a few things. Something happened at the last minute to give Becky cold feet about the deal. She must have discovered something that threatened their plans enough to want her dead. Even though they're not sure what she told me, it looks like they're trying to silence me just in case. What's to stop them from trying to eliminate *both* Clair and me if we make contact and try to go through with the original plan?"

"Perhaps nothing," Steed replied, "but look at it this way: whatever it was that caused Becky concern probably happened on the day before she was killed when we theorize that she went to inspect the merchandise. She's been in Paris dozens of times since you two broke up, but she never called you. Why would she call just before a meeting that ended in her death? And if either you or Clair actually thought there was a problem, why would you want to get in touch with Ulbricht to go through with the original plan? We figure the bad guys aren't sure what you know, Nate, and want you out of the way just in case. On the other hand if you say you never talked with Becky before she died, that will just confirm what they've learned from the Paris police."

"So how do you explain my involvement? Why do Clair and I contact them together?"

"Easy. They were watching your apartment and no doubt found out that Clair was looking for you. She mentioned the money and talked you into helping in exchange for a cut of the profits."

"But that's not what — "

"They don't know that." Steed seemed satisfied at the soundness of his reasoning.

"Well, then," Clair asked, "How do you explain Nate's rescue from the guys on the motorcycle? Aren't they going to get suspicious about that?'

"Why should they? Paris is a big city. Lots of strange things happen at night in deserted parks. Hookers carry guns for protection. Maybe she wanted to rob you herself? Who cares? The police know nothing of the incident so it won't appear in any official report. We're certain that Ulbricht and friends have no idea the Embassy's interest goes any further than concern for one of its citizens who met an untimely death in the city. They have no idea we're watching them."

I spoke, "All right, assuming what you say is correct, we can't just call the guy up on the phone and say, 'Hey! I want to help you smuggle some stolen art to the States, and by the way we think you killed Becky Tate.' Where do we even start?"

Kazinsky produced a large white envelope from her briefcase. "Here," she said, and slid it across the table to Clair.

Clair stared at it. "What is it?"

"Open it up."

Clair peered in the envelope. "Oh, my god! Where did you find this? Becky never let it out of her sight!" She pulled a thick green leather-bound diary and address book out of the envelope. "The police gave me an inventory of her things, but this was missing from the list. How did you get this?"

"I took it from her hotel room," Kazinsky said. "After Becky gave me the slip at the Musée d'Orsay, I figured it would be a good time to search her room. I grabbed this and had intended to photocopy it and return it. After we found out she'd been killed I didn't want to have to explain to the police how it ended up in our possession. As far as they know it doesn't exist."

"Becky kept everything in this book. It was her diary, her business ledger, her address book. I remember she always said she'd just die if she ever..." Clair stopped, realizing what she'd said.

Not giving her time to react, Kazinsky continued, "We've gone over it in detail. Some of it's a bit sketchy, but the notes were clear enough to let us know she was owed another half million on the delivery of the goods. And Clair," she looked at her intently, "I want to read you something out of her diary." Clair slid the book back across the table to Kazinsky who flipped through the leaves until she found the right page. "The note written the day after her birthday says, '*Clair and I drank champagne at the Ritz-Carlton last night. Talked too much. 30 and lonely but maybe not for long if Hans is serious. Didn't tell Clair yet, but think we'll announce the engagement in April.*' I think Ulbricht had asked her to marry him."

For a time, no one said anything. Clair spoke first. "Okay. I've done enough crying. Let's get the bastards that killed Becky."

CHAPTER
Twenty

WE SPENT THE REMAINDER of the afternoon going over a way to approach Ulbricht. I called my office to check in with Michelle. She again assumed my absence meant I'd spent the weekend with some mystery woman. I told her a project had come up, and I might need to be in the field more than usual over the next few weeks. I assured her I'd stay in touch or she could reach me most of the time by phone. Michelle sounded suspicious, but in a pleasant way. "Nate, you've got to break away. Let Colette go. It's good you're seeing someone else, but you don't have to hide it from us. We're your family here. We care about you." She used the phrase "*Nous t'aimons*," which could also mean "We love you."

"Yeah, yeah," I replied in English and hung up.

Steed and Kelly hatched the plan. Steed did most of the talking; Kelly had little to say. The three parts seemed simple enough. First, I was to call Ulbricht and say I was calling on behalf of Clair. I'd say I'd heard Becky had been killed but didn't know much more than that. Her sister, Clair, had come to Paris to take care of the paperwork and see that Becky's remains were shipped home. She knew Becky had been involved in some sort of deal with Ulbricht, and that she was owed an additional half million dollars if Becky completed her end of the bargain. Clair had told me she'd be taking over Tate Interiors and she really needed the money. Since she didn't speak French, she'd asked if I'd help her out. I was to say I'd agreed to do so, but was suspicious of the legality of things and wanted a cut of the action.

Second, we'd need to arrange a face-to-face meeting somewhere in Europe. "Confidence building," to use Steed's words. We'd find out all we could about the delivery details, the origin of the paintings and the like. "Both of you need to be pretty good actors," Steed said. We assured him we could do it.

Finally, as the representatives of Tate Interiors, we'd have to arrange for the paintings to be delivered to a U.S. port. This was the sticky part. "We presume Becky would want to include the paintings with a larger shipment of antiques so as to not draw individual attention to them," Steed said. "For all we know, she may have already made arrangements. Your job is to demand Ulbricht take personal delivery, presumably in Atlanta. A charge of international smuggling with an arrest on American soil will give us all we need to keep him behind bars while we build a case for murder."

Steed promised we'd be constantly shadowed and in relatively little danger. "After all," he said, "you don't know what Becky knew, so why should you be a threat? Ulbricht wants to smuggle art; you're going to help him."

By five o'clock we'd run though our strategy in detail half a dozen times, going over various scenarios and contingencies. The agents made it clear all of our expenses would be paid. We'd put things in operation the next morning. Clair would come to my apartment and we'd call Ulbricht from there. The phones were bugged anyway, Kelly reminded me.

We left by separate unmarked vehicles from the Embassy parking garage. Kazinsky drove Clair to her hotel while Kelly dropped me off around the corner from my flat. In the fading light I could see the metallic silver Peugeot parked down the street as I approached from the opposite direction. I thought I recognized the man behind the wheel as the one in Steed's photo. I could see him talking on a cell phone as I ducked into my building entrance and bounded up the stairs.

The phone was ringing as I opened the door. I picked up the receiver. The line clicked dead. Was someone at the American Embassy was listening?

Without turning on the lights I opened the doors to the balcony and peered down at the street. The Peugeot was gone.

∞

CLAIR RANG MY BELL shortly before ten the next day. Paris was its usual busy self on a Tuesday morning. The traffic on the rue des Capucines was gridlocked by some accident blocks away. She'd left her taxi in the middle of the snarl and walked the last half-kilometer to my flat. "Has our friend in the Peugeot reappeared?" I asked. He wasn't there earlier when I'd looked.

"No, but I'm not sure I'd recognize him anyway." She crossed to the balcony doors and stepped out in the morning sunlight. "Look down there. See that guy sitting on the bench? Or the one in the doorway over there? Or that old woman at the bus stop? Any of them, Nate. Any of them could be watching, waiting." She took a deep breath and exhaled slowly. "We have *got* to get this over with."

Kazinsky had returned Becky's diary-*cum*-address book to Clair. We'd decided the day before to first try contacting Ulbricht through his office in Berlin. I found his name and dialed the number next to "Berlin Office" written in Becky's flowing script. Clair listened on the extension. An efficient-sounding female voice answered on the second ring, "Sinon Imports, *Guten Tag*."

I spoke in English. "Hello, my name is Nathan Finch and I'm trying to reach Mr. Hans Ulbricht. I'm calling for Miss Clair Tate."

The reply came in flawless English. "How may I be of assistance?"

"*Herr* Ulbricht had some business dealings with Miss Rebecca Tate, Clair's sister. I'd like to speak with him in reference to that."

"I'm so sorry, Mr. Finch, but *Herr* Ulbricht is out of the country on business at the moment. If it can wait, I'll give him your message when he returns. If it's an urgent matter I should be able to reach him within the next few hours."

"I would consider it urgent," I answered.

"If you'll give me your number then, I'll ask him to call you as soon as possible. Can I be of further service?"

"No, thank you. We'll wait for his call." I gave her my number.

❧

WE DIDN'T HAVE TO WAIT LONG. Kelly called just after I hung up to confirm they'd recorded everything and would be on standby when or if Ulbricht called. Half an hour later, he did.

The voice on the other end of the line said, "This is Hans Ulbricht. I'm returning Nathan Finch's phone call." His English was perfect, with an American accent.

"This is Nate Finch. *Herr* Ulbricht, I'm calling for — "

"Mr. Finch, of course! I feel like I know you already. Becky spoke so highly of you. It's all been so sad. I had thought about calling you but — "

"Then you know about Becky, then?"

"My god, yes! We were — " He stopped suddenly. "I take it you know what happened."

"I've heard, yes."

"Did I understand my secretary to say you were calling on behalf of Becky's sister, Clair?"

"That's right."

"Then we should meet and talk. It's strange how the fates spin their cloth. I was informed that Clair is still here in Paris." By whom, I wondered.

"Yes, she's here with me now."

"Well, actually, I'm in the city myself. I flew in this morning from Spain. Are you available this afternoon?"

I looked at Clair who was gripping the extension with such force that her knuckles were white. She nodded. "We can be," I said.

"Good. Would four o'clock be convenient?"

"I don't see why not."

"Then please meet me at Chez Papetier. It's a small restaurant in the Third Arrondissement near the Place des Vosges."

"I know the area well."

"Excellent. The *maître de maison*'s name is Raoul. He'll be expecting you. It shouldn't be crowded that time of day, so we can share some remembrances of our dear Becky."

"See you at four." I hung up.

Within thirty seconds the phone rang. It was Kelly. "Well that was quick and easy. He knows your name. Becky must have mentioned it."

"Apparently." I wasn't comfortable with the direction things were taking.

"Don't worry. We'll have our people there to back you up. I can't see Ulbricht trying something in a public place." I thought of the Eiffel Tower but held my tongue.

CLAIR LEFT TO MEET with the police again. They still refused to release Becky's remains, but the Embassy had promised they'd see it was done by the end of the day. I wondered if they'd been using that as an additional wedge to win her cooperation. I had mixed feelings about working with Clair. I didn't know her at all and had no idea how she'd react if things didn't go exactly as planned. And what would happen if things went really bad? What if she were wounded, or worse? Would I be somehow responsible? I wondered what might have happened if I'd been home to answer Becky's phone call that afternoon.

THE TAXI DROPPED US OFF promptly at four on a small street near the Musée Carnavalet. Chez Papetier filled a narrow building that must have at one time been a stationer's shop. The street-side window and muted sconces provided the only light for a dark oak interior crowded with a dozen tables covered with white linen. The *maître de*, who I presumed to be Raoul, stood guard at the door. In the dim light I could see that two of the tables were occupied, one of them by Kelly and Kazinsky acting the part of love-struck tourists on holiday in Paris.

I gave my name to Raoul and told him we were meeting someone at four. "Ah, Monsieur Finch, of course. Monsieur Ulbricht is expecting you. Please follow me." He proceeded toward the back of the restaurant. I noticed he didn't pick up menus from the stack next to his desk.

We threaded our way past the tables in the front, by a small bar and seating area, through a second narrow dining room and down a hall toward the kitchen and restrooms. To my surprise, we pushed through a swinging door into a narrow kitchen and approached a second door in the rear. Without hesitating, Raoul opened the door to reveal an alley. An S-series Mercedes with darkly tinted windows sat idling immediately in front of us. He opened the rear door and said, "Thank you for your visit to Chez Papetier. Monsieur Ulbricht will receive you at his home."

For an instant, I panicked. Should we get in the car or not? There was no way Kelly and Kazinsky could follow us. We'd lose our protection. Clair gave me a 'What do we do?' look. I turned to the *maître de* and said, "Thank you, Raoul. I trust we'll be back soon." I climbed in behind Clair and he slammed the door.

I could see the rear of the driver's head as we sped out of the ally. I asked, "Where are we meeting *Herr* Ulbricht?"

He turned and smiled, "At his flat, sir, on the Île St.Louis. My name is Henri, sir, if I can be of any assistance." I recognized him instantly. He was the driver of the Peugeot — The man in the photo.

CHAPTER
Twenty-One

THE CITY OF PARIS TRACES its origins to the murky pre-history of the third century BC when the Parisii tribe settled on an island in the Seine known as Lutetia. For more than a thousand years it remained a fortified island-city ruled, first by the Romans and then by a series of tribal kings and warlords. By the late Middle Ages, Paris had become a major trading and cultural center with growth spilling over to both sides of the river. Lutetia, now known as the Île de la Cité, remained the geographic and spiritual heart of Paris.

In the seventeenth century two smaller islands just upstream were joined and developed as a site for the homes of wealthy nobility. Renamed as the Île St. Louis, the island is now the quintessential Paris of tree lined boulevards with magnificent stone architecture, and home in the past to such luminaries as Voltaire, Cézanne and Chagall. An address on the Île St. Louis came with the unspoken assumption of power and wealth.

Henri was silent as he expertly maneuvered the big Mercedes through the Place de la Bastille and onto the island via the Pont Marie. We turned to the north, skirting along the Seine and finally entered the cobblestone courtyard of an eighteenth century building overlooking the Pont St. Louis and the gardens of Notre Dame. Clair and I had not spoken. We were trying to look calm.

We parked near an arched stone opening that concealed a modern elevator. Henri opened Clair's door and indicated we should follow him. I noticed a discreet video camera that swiveled to keep us in its vision as we walked across the courtyard. He inserted a key in a brass plate and turned it. The elevator door silently slid open. "This is a private elevator to *Herr* Ulbricht's apartment. Simply press the button and it will take you to the uppermost floor." There was only one button. Clair pressed it and the door hissed shut.

I looked around the elevator. It was big enough for a half-dozen people. The floor was green marble and the walls were of burnished walnut with brass trim. A small rosette oddly placed in one corner near the ceiling probably concealed another camera. The elevator moved slowly upward with none of the grinding and creaking of my lift on the rue des Capucines. This was an entirely different world: one of unlimited resources.

Clair started to speak, but I silently mouthed "camera" and pitched my eyes toward the rosette. She nodded and, hesitating for a second, reached out and squeezed my hand.

The door opened into an elegant foyer. Despite the building's age, it was clear it had been completely renovated with no costs spared. The floor held an intricate design of inlaid parquet using woods of various colors to create a pattern of geometric fancy. The furniture was mainly late Empire, the walls covered with antique tapestries and ornate mirrors. A primly dressed maid whose dark skin belied a third world heritage awaited our arrival. She spoke in Spanish-accented English, "Herr Ulbricht will see you in the parlor."

The apartment was huge, occupying the entire upper floor of the building. The maid led us down a wide hall past a dining room with a crystal chandelier and a smaller more intimate library with book-filled shelves lining the walls from floor to ceiling. Clair spoke to the maid, "*¿Tu acento es de Paraguay, no?*"

The woman gave her a surprised look, "*Si, Señora. ¿Conoce mi país?*"

"*Si. Estuve allá hace dos años pasado. En Asunción.*"

I could tell the maid wanted to ask more, but felt it improper. As for me, I realized I knew nothing whatsoever about Clair. For a fleeting instant I wanted to scream, "Stop," put everything on hold and try to figure out what was going on. At that moment, however, we were ushered into the parlor.

It was a large west-facing room with a series of glass-paned doors opening onto a balcony overlooking the Île de la Cité. The walls above the wainscoting were mirrored in the style of Versailles, giving a false sense of an infinite horizon in their reflection. The furniture was Louis XIV, with a carved marble fireplace occupying one wall. An ornate Aubusson carpet covered the floor.

I didn't see Ulbricht at first. He was sitting in a wing chair facing the balcony and appeared to be intently studying pieces on a chessboard. When he realized we'd arrived he stood up and walked toward us. I had imagined what he'd look like, this monster responsible for Becky's death and untold other crimes. I was wrong. He was handsome, with a relaxed air and a genuine smile. He acknowledged our presence, first extending his hand to me and then turning to Clair and saying, "Oh, my dear Clair, I am so very, very sorry about Becky." He gave her a small hug with a perfunctory European air-kiss. I could see her stiffen under his touch.

Ulbricht motioned for us to sit on a yellow, silk down-filled sofa. He sat down in an armchair facing us and directed the maid, who name was Maria, to bring us tea. "I think I owe you both an apology and an explanation," he said. He spoke perfect English with an accent that would be expected from an educated New Yorker. "This has become such a complex situation that I almost don't know where to begin." He paused and looked out toward the balcony. The Eiffel Tower gleamed in the afternoon sunlight. "Let me start by saying I was not trying to deceive you in requesting that you meet me at Chez Papetier. I don't know if you are aware of it, but you are being followed. By whom, I do not know. I suspect the police. I also must tell you that the reason I know that, Nate, is that I, too, have had you followed since shortly after Becky's death."

Clair had been staring intently. She had a hardened look on her face as her eyes burned into Ulbricht. She interrupted him, saying, "How well did you know my sister, Mr. Ulbricht?"

He gave her a somewhat surprised look. "Very well, I should hope. We planned to be married."

"But I understand you have a wife and three children in Berlin," Clair shot back.

Ulbricht looked both genuinely surprised and hurt. Either he was being sincere or was a very good actor. "So Becky never discussed our relationship?"

"No." Clair cut him off again. "I — we — know you were involved in a business deal of some sort with her. We came here to discuss that." She seemed to have conveniently forgotten the entry in Becky's diary.

Ulbricht glanced at the floor and then at Clair and me. "Then I do owe you much, much more than a simple apology and a quick explanation." He hesitated. "I think perhaps I should begin at the beginning.

"First of all, before I say anything else, I want you to know I was in love with Becky. To answer your question more directly Clair, yes, I am at this moment married, which probably accounts for why Becky never said anything to you. My wife and I have been separated for nearly two years now. Were I a man with lesser assets, we would have been divorced long ago, but the lawyers have strung out the process for months and months. We've finally hammered out an agreement that should provide for my children and make my wife a very wealthy woman. This unpleasant process should be finished in the near future."

Ulbricht paused as Maria arrived with a silver tray holding a small English tea service. She poured three cups and offered sugar and cream while she served them. Setting a plate of *petit fours* on a small table between us, she silently left the room.

Ulbricht resumed his explanation. "I first met your sister nearly a year ago in Atlanta. As you may know, I'm in the import-export business and as a result spend many days each month traveling. I have a good friend — a distant cousin actually — who is a German expatriate living in Atlanta. He is quite wealthy and has a large home he purchased in the Buckhead section of the city few years ago. Last spring, I think it was in late May, I was in Atlanta on business. My cousin gave a small dinner party in my honor. He'd bought several fine antique pieces from Becky so it was natural she'd be invited as one of the guests. She and I met and discovered we had a lot in common. We became good friends, which with time led to something more."

Ulbricht paused and took a sip of tea. I noticed Clair had not touched hers. She continued to stare at him with a hard look. He continued, "My work takes me to the States at least once a month, and of course Becky was here in Europe several times a year. Since my separation I've kept an apartment near my office in Berlin, as well as this apartment here in Paris, a house in Spain and a small flat in Hong Kong. You recall Becky spent last Christmas in China?"

Clair replied icily, "She was on a buying trip to explore the possibility of importing Chinese antiques."

"Yes, but she was with me most of the time. I asked her to consider marrying me once my divorce was final. She refused."

"But you said you planned to get married…"

"Yes, let me explain. Becky is — I'm sorry — was… It's hard to talk about her in the past tense." He paused and restarted, "Becky was concerned about appearances, and I couldn't help but agree with her. After what happened to your father, she was so sensitive about anything at all that might hint of scandal, and quite honestly she was right. No matter what the truth might be, she didn't want it said she was seeing a married man. When you're in love, you sometimes don't care about what people say, but I had to respect her wishes. That's why we were so secretive about our relationship. We agreed we'd remain as close friends and would discuss marriage when my divorce was final. Ironically, I got a call just today. Everything should be wrapped up within the next two weeks. I'd… I'd…" Ulbricht looked like he was going to cry. "I'd planned to give her a ring."

At that moment I couldn't help thinking Ulbricht was either telling the truth or was one of the best actors I'd ever seen. I made a mental note to ask Clair about her father. I recalled Becky told me he'd died when she was in her late teens, but I didn't know the circumstances.

"What do you know about Becky's death?" Clair asked, her tone a bit less harsh this time.

"I probably know what you know, and more," Ulbricht said. "My one goal now, my obsession, is to find her killers and see them punished." He thought for a minute and then asked, "Can I be perfectly honest with you? Can I trust you not to repeat what I want to tell you?"

"Yes," I said, answering for both of us.

"I don't trust the Paris Police." He looked out at the Eiffel Tower and continued, "I am not satisfied with the explanation they've offered."

"Have you been in touch with them?" I asked.

"Of course, I called immediately when I heard about Becky's death. I spoke to a Lieutenant Andrade, but he was not very helpful. Said it was a police matter and that is was 'under investigation,' and so forth. I've been fortunate in life and I suppose one of the advantages in being wealthy is the ability to use one's resources in ways that might not be possible for the average man. I have — and again, I'll ask you to keep this in your confidence — a source inside the Prefecture of Police. I've had access to Becky's case file — or at least I did until it was transferred to the Criminal Investigation Division. That alone makes me suspicious. I saw they had interviewed you, Nate, and on my own I decided to have you followed. I really didn't know whether or not you were telling the truth."

"Mr. Ulbricht," I asked, "when was — "

"Please, call me Hans."

"Okay, Hans, when was the last time you saw Becky before her death?"

"On the day before she died. I have an acquaintance here in the antique business who occasionally alerts me to outstanding pieces as they come on the market. He'd called me about midday to tell me about a wonderful Louis XIII chest that was available from the estate of an elderly woman who lived near the Bois de Boulogne.

"I called Becky on her cell phone. She was in a taxi at the time so she simply told the driver to take her to the woman's house. I recall she was in a bit of a hurry — said she had an appointment later in the day, but I don't remember her telling me whom she was meeting. I was in a rush to catch a flight to St. Petersburg to meet with a customer, so she met me at the house briefly to look over the piece. She said it was a very good nineteenth century reproduction but not especially valuable.

"I was due to be back in Paris on Sunday and we'd made plans for dinner here at the flat. I called her cell phone Saturday afternoon but she didn't answer. My assistant heard the news and called me late Saturday night. I couldn't get a flight back here until Sunday afternoon, at which time I contacted Andrade. I suppose you'd say that after talking with him I was angry. Angry at what happened. Angry that he wouldn't tell me everything. Angry most of all that they seemed to have no real suspects. I had this crazy idea I'd start my own investigation." His voice dropped off with the last sentence. He seemed to be truly hurting over Becky's death.

I was beginning to think he was telling the truth.

CHAPTER
Twenty-Two

I LOOKED AT CLAIR. I could see she was beginning to have mixed feelings about Ulbricht. I asked, "Do you have any idea about who might have wanted Becky dead, and why?"

"No, not really, but I've got to think it may have had something to do with her meeting on that Friday after I left for St. Petersburg. She didn't call me as far as I know, but she may have tried and couldn't get through. Russia is one of the few remaining places in Europe where the phone system is unreliable. You know, though, she always kept an appointment book, a diary sort of thing she'd use to make notes."

"I have it," Clair said.

Ulbricht sat up in his chair. "Where did you get it? The police report said they found nothing on her body except for Nate's phone number."

"It was in her personal effects at the hotel," Clair lied. "That's how I got your phone number. I guess the police overlooked it or didn't think it important. There's nothing in it about an appointment on that day. You don't have any idea about where she might have gone?"

"Not really. Several days earlier she'd mentioned talking with a Syrian living here in Paris who wanted to sell some ninth century Islamic ceramics. She seemed interested, but was concerned they might have been looted from an Iraqi museum during the second Gulf War. She didn't mention it again so I presumed nothing came of it."

"So why did you have me followed?" I asked.

"Because other than her killers, you were the last person Becky talked to — or perhaps tried to talk to."

"So you don't believe I'm telling the truth?"

"I do now."

"Did you know someone tried to kill me last week?"

Ulbricht, who had slumped back down in his chair, sat up and said, "My god, no! Where? What happened?" I told him about the Jardin de Tuileries, but said my assailants had been scared off when a couple of hookers emerged out of the darkness as potential witnesses.

"Do you think it was a robbery attempt? Crime is getting so bad here in Paris, especially since the EU opened the borders to so many immigrants from southern Europe. You know one of the antique dealers Becky bought from was killed in an armed robbery several months ago."

"Are you talking about Lavalle?"

Ulbricht looked puzzled. "How did you know his name?" Then, "Oh, yes, Becky told you about our little business deal."

Clair seemed to have recovered her sense of purpose. She said, "Nothing will bring my sister back, Mr. Ulbricht, but if we don't do something to keep her business solvent we're going to lose that, too. And without Tate Interiors, we can't afford to pay for my mother's medical bills. That's why we're here today. We want to pick up where she left off."

Ulbricht took a deep breath and looked out the window. "I don't know… I don't know if that's the right thing to do." He got up and walked over to the window. "When Becky died, a part of me died with her. I'd offered to just give her the money."

"Hans," I said, trying to get him back on course, "Clair told me you asked Becky to bring a couple of Old Masters into the US. Since I live here in Paris, she's asked me to help out. I'm willing to do that — to help Clair and because Becky and I were close at one time. From what I understand though, this is not a simple transaction that involves exporting fine art — it's more than that. You want to tell us about it? I've said I'd help, but — no disrespect to Becky's memory — if it's going to be risky I expect to be compensated for my time."

Ulbricht looked at me a moment, trying to size me up. I wanted to give the impression I was here for the money, not for the memory of Becky. Finally he said, "Okay, let me go over everything with you. It was something I was trying to do to help Becky. Of course I'll honor the same agreement for her sister. Again, can I have your word that this will be held in confidence?"

"You do," Clair replied.

"My business," he began, "is a simple one, and it's been very good to me. What I do is act as a middleman. I identify needs and I identify sources. I then try to match them up and take a commission for doing so. I send Brazilian tractors to the Ukraine, Canadian fir to Japan, American soybeans to Siberia and so on. I rarely, if ever, see the commodities I trade, and I always charge as much as the traffic will bear. Basically someone tells me what they want, and for a price I will see they get it. After a few years in this business you develop many contacts, some of whom become good friends. Sometimes I'm offered opportunities that would not be available were it not for my personal relationships with the potential buyers or sellers."

Ulbricht stopped to pour himself another cup of tea and continued, "Nearly a year and a half ago, I received a call from an acquaintance here in Paris, a fellow named Renko. His grandfather was a Russian Jew who fled to France in 1918 after the Bolshevik revolution and who become quite wealthy in the manufacturing business.

"Renko and I had done several very profitable business deals together. He wanted me to help him sell a couple of paintings from his grandfather's estate. My first reaction was to suggest he contact Christie's or some other well-known auction house. He said there was a slight problem with the provenance of the works and that a private sale might be more appropriate. He pointed out that I know a number of wealthy individuals throughout the world who might be interested and more importantly, he was willing to pay me a commission of twenty percent of whatever I could get for the paintings. He guessed they'd bring in excess of fifteen million dollars at a private sale. It would be less than the works would bring at auction, but the sale would be off the record and out of view from tax collectors and the like."

"Before you go any further, you used the word 'provenance.' Tell me what that means," Clair asked.

"Of course. Most real property — land, vehicles, buildings, etc. — has what is called a title, a certificate of ownership. In the art world there is not a comparable document, especially since some paintings may be hundreds of years old. Strictly speaking 'provenance' means 'origin,' but when applied to paintings or other works of art it means a record of ownership that can establish that the holder — or

142

in this case the seller — of the work has acquired and possesses it legally.

"Most paintings of significant value have a well documented history and their sale or purchase presents few legal risks. On the other hand every year there are hundreds of works stolen from museums or private homes, or sometimes looted in wars and insurrections. When — or if — these works come up for public sale they are subject to confiscation by governments or any number of international agencies throughout the world. The particular works in question were not stolen, but there is some question as to the rightful owner. I'll explain that in a moment. Is that clear?"

"I believe so," Clair said, and Ulbricht continued.

"Well, I will be the first to admit that while I know something about art, I am no expert. I hired a consultant whom I knew would be discreet and paid him well to evaluate the paintings. He met me here afterwards at this apartment in a state of shock. He said he believed that both works had been stolen by the Nazis during World War II and had not been seen in more than sixty years. It was assumed they'd been destroyed in the bombing of Germany at the end of the war, or stolen by the occupying Soviet forces. I think he used the phrase "hot potatoes" to describe them and said he wanted to have nothing to do with their sale. He advised me to call the authorities. I gave him a thousand Euros extra to buy his silence and dismissed him.

"I am not particularly afraid of the international authorities, but this was something I didn't think would be worth the risk, no matter how generous the rewards. At that point I met with my friend to explain this to him, and he gave me a very interesting tale of how his grandfather acquired the paintings.

"As you may know, my countrymen under Hitler's regime occupied France in 1940. They stole untold num-

bers of art treasures from every possible source. One of
the most famous private collections belonged to the family
Schloss. They had hidden it in the south of France before
the start of the war, and it was not discovered by the Germans until 1943. I don't recall exactly, but there were in
excess of three hundred works. It took a massive effort to
move and hide them.

"Renko's grandfather attended the same synagogue
as did the Schloss sons and was apparently responsible for
helping get the works out of Paris. He was under no suspicion so he was the one who paid the expenses and bribes
necessary pull the whole thing off. In gratitude the family
gave him two paintings, one by Brughel and the other by
Hals. Renko has a letter from 1940 expressing the Schloss
family's gratitude and specifically referring to the gift of
the paintings by name and description."

"Shouldn't that be sufficient proof of ownership?" I
asked.

"One would think, but recall that my friend's grandfather was a Russian Jew himself, and a condemned man
should the Nazis arrest him. He chose to store his newly
acquired paintings with the others in the collection. The letter he kept with other family papers. When the Nazis found
where the Schloss collection was hidden it didn't matter to
them who owned them. They were cataloged and for the
most part sent off to Germany.

"Now, I have no idea how the paintings ended back up
here in Paris. The speculation is that the grandfather still had
some Russian connections and that the works were looted
by the Soviets and somehow returned to Paris. Maybe they
never left — it's impossible to say. All anyone knows is that
they hung quietly in the library of the old man's house from
the late 1940's until his son's death last year. That's when
his grandson, Renko, inherited them, discovered the letter

detailing the gift among some old family documents and contacted me to try to sell them."

"All that really doesn't make sense," Clair said. "If he has documentation that he owns them, what more does he need?"

"Ah, there's the rub! Both the French government and the surviving members of the Schloss family have listed them as missing and stolen. Even if the government didn't grab them for 'safekeeping' right out, the case would stay tied up in court for years and have a very uncertain outcome. Recall these works are worth millions. Renko is a bit of a spendthrift and needs the cash. Now. The family and courts could argue that the 'gift' was made under duress, or that the letter was a clever forgery. No, for him, quick and quiet disposal is the best option."

"So what did you do?" I asked.

"I saw a chance to make several million dollars and I started looking for a buyer."

CHAPTER
Twenty-Three

I TURNED TOWARDS CLAIR. I couldn't read her thoughts, and wasn't really sure I wanted to. She seemed to be turning things over in her mind, absorbing what Ulbricht had said, formulating questions. Eventually she spoke. "So tell us what happened next. How did Becky get involved?"

"Let me take up where I left off," Ulbricht said. "Trying to act as the middleman for the sale of slightly suspect art is not exactly what I do best, but to be honest, I saw it as having the potential for turning a quick profit. And, too, connecting a seller with a buyer is not really that different from what I do in the regular course of my business. I put out a few discrete inquiries, always indirectly and being careful to keep at least one layer of deniability between myself and the proposed sale. Briefly put, I got some interest but no takers.

"After about six months I had about given up on any involvement with selling the paintings. Renko was putting some pressure on me, and I actually encouraged him to explore some alternatives. About that time I was in Atlanta on business and had lunch with my cousin. I trust him, so when he asked what I had been up to, I mentioned the paintings. He's made quite a bit of money and is always looking for some way to hide it. He's got a ranch in Montana and a pecan farming operation in south Georgia. It hadn't occurred to me he might be interested, but he said he wanted to look into it. I had no real objection; in fact I'd rather have him as a buyer than someone I didn't know. Over the next few months he flew to Paris twice to look at the works, even going so far as to hire two independent experts to authenticate them.

"Once he made up his mind, he was hooked, but he didn't want to pay what Renko wanted. They went back and forth and finally by last fall agreed on a price of fifteen million dollars, with ten percent down and the rest on delivery. At that point, I was proud of myself for making a quick profit and was making arrangements to have the works flown by private jet to Atlanta. You can't imagine what happened next." He stopped and looked up as Maria appeared at the door.

"*Herr* Ulbricht, you have a phone call. They say that it's urgent."

"Forgive me," he said and followed Maria down the corridor.

I looked at Clair. "What do you think?"

"I believe that 'rethink' is going to be a better term. I just don't know. I'm confused. Everything seems to match what we know, but —" She stopped suddenly. We could hear Ulbricht approaching down the hall.

"I apologize. People think such silly things are important. It was a minor issue that should be handled by one of my assistants in Berlin." He sat down. "Where was I?"

"You said you were making arrangements to have the painting delivered to Atlanta," Clair reminded him.

"Oh, right. I was just in the process of setting up delivery to the U.S. when there was a scandal involving a work by Caravaggio held by a private collector in Los Angeles. He'd made no real effort to hide the fact that he owned it; in fact, he had loaned to a major exhibition at the Los Angeles County Museum of Art. Unfortunately for him, there was an online catalogue featuring some of the works, including the Caravaggio. Turns out it had last been 'officially' seen in Prague in 1940. The collector had owned it since the fifties, but was rather vague about how he acquired it. The case is still tied up in court, and it looks like the painting is going to be returned to the Czech Republic without any compensation to the fellow in LA that claimed ownership.

"All this set my cousin off. He wanted out of the deal, but he was already in for a million and a half which Renko refused to return, not to mention the fact I was looking at losing my three million commission. I was determined to make things work — that's what I do."

Clair stared at Ulbricht intently, weighing his words. I thought I could sense doubt on her face, but I wasn't sure. He continued, "Meanwhile, Becky and I had started seeing each other regularly. I never tried to hide anything from her, and told her about the problems I was having with the paintings. It was her suggestion that my cousin should buy the paintings through a dealer, or better, a series of dealers. He'd have a valid bill of sale, and if the issue of ownership ever came up he could fall back on the letter of ownership from Renko. I thought it sounded like a great idea.

"Clair, it was also about that time I discovered your sister was in trouble financially. She tried to hide if from me, but there were little things, I remember being at her condominium in Atlanta and seeing a letter from the bank

148

she'd accidentally left out on her desk. There were the phone calls from collection agencies that she didn't return. That kind of thing. I begged her to let me help her, but she was proud. She refused. About four or five months ago, things were so bad that the bank was threatening to foreclose on the business. She was desperate.

"I had taken Becky's suggestion and was in the process of working out the details to have the painting sold through a dealer. I had recruited Lavalle. I'd bought a few things from him in the past and he's always been willing to look the other way for a few euros. It occurred to me that Becky — Tate Interiors, actually — could act as a middleman. On paper, Lavalle would represent Renko; she'd pay Lavalle and sell to my cousin. I would arrange for her to make a million dollars — half on finalizing the agreement and half on delivery of the paintings.

"It was obviously all contrived to let her make a huge profit, but honestly, it was her last hope. And it allowed her not to say that she'd taken the money as a gift — she'd had to work for it. Of course most of the money would not go through her account, only just enough to cover commissions and give the semblance of a legitimate transaction. That way, if asked by the various tax and revenue authorities here or in the US, she'd have something legitimate to show. It was all very neat."

"Just whose share, Hans," Clair asked, "did Becky's 'commission' come out of?" I noticed she called him "Hans."

"Mine of course."

"Why?"

"We were in love. Why not?"

CHAPTER
Twenty-Four

"HANS," I SAID, trying to sound sincere, "It sounds like you really cared about Becky."

"Yes, but I'm almost embarrassed to tell you all this. I'm a wealthy man, Nate. I'd give my entire fortune if it would bring her back."

No one said anything for a moment. I could hear the sound of a boat horn in the distance and the tolling of church bells. I spoke, "Where do we go from here?"

"Are you serious about wanting to go through with the original plans?"

"We don't have any choice, Hans," Clair replied. "I haven't looked at the books, but if things are as bad as everyone says, we need the money."

Ulbricht hesitated, pursing his lips. He seemed to be turning things over in his mind. "There are some uncertainties, you know. When it was just Becky, I was prepared to defend her should anyone question the transaction. Now, I'm not."

"We're willing to take that risk," Clair interjected.

He looked directly at her, studying her for a moment. Turning to me, he said, "And you, Nate, said something about wanting compensation, also?"

"I think I'm sticking my neck out to make you a profit."

"True." He studied me this time for a brief moment and said, "How much?"

I hadn't expected him to be that direct. The truthful answer was that I hadn't expected things to get this far. I should have said that I really hadn't thought about it. Instead I said, "Fifty thousand dollars."

"A small sum for a fifteen million dollar transaction. You'd never make it in the world of international trade."

"Yes, but from what you've said, this seems to be a done deal. I'm assuming we can have everything done in a matter of weeks."

Ulbricht looked out across the city, apparently thinking about my demand. He replied simply, "All right. I will agree to that."

"It shouldn't come out of the money that was originally going to Becky."

"Of course." He turned to Clair. "Is this arrangement acceptable to you?" She nodded assent.

"Then it's agreed." He stood up and offered his hand, first to me and then to Clair.

"Where are the paintings now?" I asked.

"In a warehouse near Rouen, waiting to be picked up. The plan was to ship them as part of a load of furniture and other antiques that Becky had purchased. She had already made arrangements."

"When are they scheduled to ship?"

"If I give the go-ahead, they'll be picked up tomorrow and taken to Le Havre. Today is the twentieth," he said, glancing at the date on the dial of his watch. "I believe that the container vessel is scheduled to depart on the twenty-fifth. Assuming there are no problems, it should arrive at the port of Savannah eight or nine days later."

"What do we need to do?" Clair asked. "I'm sorry to sound stupid, but I never really worked in the business. I don't know how things are done."

"I think it would be best if you checked the container once it clears customs, and then meet it when it arrives at your warehouse in Atlanta."

"Do we need to make arrangements to have it picked up?"

"Oh, no. That's all arranged in advance. Becky always liked to meet her shipments at the port, just to be sure they arrived safely and to pay any customs duties and the like. Once you do the paperwork, a truck will load the container and deliver it to your address."

"What about you?" I asked. "Are you going to meet us in Atlanta?" I hadn't forgotten that the supposed purpose of this whole charade was to lure Ulbricht to the U.S.

"I hardly think that's necessary. All you need do is simply deliver the goods to your warehouse and someone will arrange to pick them up."

"I think it would be best if we deal directly with you. You haven't even told us your cousin's name. We have no idea how to contact him, no idea where to deliver the paintings. And, too, it would be best if we had a certified check — no, two certified checks — in hand before we release the goods."

"You sound as if you don't trust me, Nate." Ulbricht looked wryly amused.

"Why should we?"

"You're right. I'll be there in Atlanta when the container arrives."

I GAVE ULBRICHT my phone numbers. He said he'd call me the following day with the shipping details. Henri dropped us off in front of a crowded student bar near the Sorbonne. Clair and I needed to sort things out. We could easily blend into the crowd, and I figured it would be the last place Steed and his agents would look for us.

A scruffy-looking band seemed to be doing a retro-reinterpretation of greatest hits of the Sex Pistols, butchering the lyrics into an unintelligible wail of French-accented English. They finished up "Friggin' In The Riggin'" and launched into a sick rendition of "Belsen Was A Gas." I managed to find a small table under a stairwell in the back of the bar where we had a bit of privacy and shelter from the noise.

We hadn't spoken since we'd left Ulbricht's apartment. "What do you think?" I asked.

"I don't know," Clair replied. "I don't know how I feel. I got on that elevator prepared to hate the man, and I got off of it thinking he meant it when he said he was in love with Becky. I mean, everything he told us matched exactly with what they said at the Embassy, but it all had a totally different spin on it. Sure, he may be involved in some shady dealings, but that doesn't make him a murderer. I guess the thing that struck me most was what he said happened on the day before Becky was killed. Steed and the others know she talked to Ulbricht, and just assumed she spent the afternoon with him. But they weren't there! They're just guessing about what happened. He says she had an appointment with someone else later that day. He said that he wasn't even in the country when she was killed! Why do they think he's the murderer?"

153

"I don't know the answer either, Clair, but I don't trust him. There's something about this that's too easy, too slick. Take me, for example. If his story is to be believed, before this afternoon the only thing he knew about me was that I might be a suspect in his future wife's death. I stroll in, ask for a ridiculous sum for doing nothing but being there and he readily agrees. No argument, no negotiation."

"Yes, but see the other side of it. He said he was in love with Becky. Surely they had a relationship, he couldn't have known the details of her life otherwise. Just assume for a moment he is doing this for her — for her memory." I could see tears in her eyes. She looked out across the crowded bar. The band had launched into the French version of "*L'Anarchie Pour Le UK*":

> *Moi, je suis l'anarchiste*
> *Moi, je suis l'anarchiste*
> *Je ne sais pas ce que je*
> *Veux mais je l'aurai*

The crowd cheered.

"Nate, translate the lyrics for me, will you?" she asked. "God, I need to learn to speak French!"

"I think it's an old Sex Pistols piece. The words go something like, 'Me, I'm the anarchist. Me, I'm the anarchist. I don't know what I want but I'm going to have it.' Kinda silly."

"You know, that's a pretty good description of where we're heading at the moment. We don't know what we want, but we're going to get it." She picked up a napkin and dabbed at her eyes. "Can you order me a drink? Something strong?"

"Clair, I will, but we need to talk. I really don't know anything about you, either."

"Then order two drinks."

CHAPTER
Twenty-Five

WE EXCHANGED SMALL TALK while we finished our drinks. I think in some sense of the word neither of us wanted to talk about the situation. We were not volunteers. Without coercion leavened with a large dose of fear, I'd be sitting in my flat reading a book. The FBI had dragged Clair into the mess by playing on her sorrow and need for retribution. She reminded me we should check in with Kelly and Kazinsky. They were probably frantic when they discovered we'd abandoned them at Chez Papetier. I punched a number into my cell phone. Kelly answered on the first ring. When he heard my voice he nearly screamed, "Where the hell are you?! Are you all right? We waited a few minutes and then walked toward the back of the restaurant. You must have slipped —"

"Hey!" I said. "Things are fine. We met with Ulbricht at his apartment and everything is on track."

"Where are you? We need to debrief you."

"We're okay. There's no emergency. I'll give you a call in the morning."

"You can't —" Kelly started. I hung up on him.

My next call was to Maurice Baltard, the owner of a small restaurant just off the Quai St. Michel. Colette had introduced us on my first visit to Paris when we were still students. It seemed lifetimes ago. Over the years, and especially since the divorce, he'd become a good friend. His establishment — appropriately named Maurice — was a discreet little hole-in-the-wall place best known for its individual dining rooms, each seating only two customers. It was a favorite haunt for prominent men and their mistresses, and others whose need for privacy was coupled with an appreciation of excellent cuisine. "Ah, Nate, you're bringing a woman! It's been so long. Colette was beautiful, but *c'est la vie*. You need a quiet table. I take it she's married, no?"

"Just a friend. An American. We need to talk and we want to avoid prying eyes."

"As you say, then." He clearly didn't believe me. "I'll alert my chef to give you our finest; we need to celebrate your renewed interest in the opposite sex."

We hailed a taxi and threaded our way through the intricate maze of the Latin Quarter's one-way streets before arriving at Maurice's poorly lit entrance a few minutes later. Maurice himself met us at the door. "Nate! So good to see you again." Turning to Clair he said in accented English, "Nate has been a dear friend for years. He's a good man. Be gentle with him." I saw Clair smile and then laugh for the first time since we'd met.

He showed us to a small dining room whose walls were hung with tapestries. An oval table faced the door with seating on a worn leather banquette. Wall sconces and a flickering candle on the table provided muted light. Maurice looked at Clair and said, "This is an occasion that calls for a special evening, Mademoiselle. My American friend has been too long without the company of a beautiful woman. So, tonight *l'addition* is my pleasure. I took the liberty of ordering for you. The waiter will bring you champagne while you wait. *Bon appétit!*" He disappeared through the curtained entrance before I could protest.

We had finished most of a bottle of a vintage *curvée* from a small estate near Reims before the first courses arrived. *Fruit de mer* from Normandy, then a green salad with *bleu d'Auvergne* and olives accompanied by a perfectly chilled viognier. I was beginning to get a little intoxicated by the time the *pigeonneau en croûte* was served as the main course. I sensed the same was true for Clair. The waiter poured us generous glasses of a 1992 St. Emilion and told us to ring the bell if we needed anything else.

We had talked, and even laughed, but had said nothing of substance. I began, "Clair, I don't really know how to say this, but I don't really know you. If we're going to be working together, I want to change that." I paused, my brain a bit foggy with wine. "Up until today — tonight even — I had seen just one side of you. But now I'm curious. There are little things. Your father and what happened to him. I want to know what that's all about. You don't speak French but you spoke to the maid at Ulbricht's in perfect Spanish. I don't even know what you do for a living. I don't understand —" I stopped in mid-sentence, fearing I'd said too much.

The smile disappeared off Clair's face. She looked at me for a moment, probably deciding how much of her life she wanted to share with me. "I guess I do owe you that. My sister was in love with you, and had it not been for that you wouldn't be here. But, you know, tonight — right here and now in this very moment — I had pushed all that to the back of my mind. It's been really hard…" Her voice trailed off.

"I know. And nothing I can say will change that."

Hesitant, she said, "Where shall I start?"

"Anywhere you want to."

"Okay, then. I guess I'll start at the beginning." She thought a moment and said, "I had a happy childhood. My father was a prominent attorney and my mother came from a wealthy Atlanta family. She was a Sinclair, if you know the name. My grandfather — her father — was a real estate attorney and had the foresight to buy up hundreds of acres north of town in the 1930's. By the time he died, it was worth millions. My mother named me for Katharine Hepburn — Katharine Sinclair Tate. She said she always wanted a little girl named Katharine, but she never realized I'd end up being called 'Kate.' 'Kate Tate' was just a bit too cute! When I was in the first grade I started calling myself 'Clair,' short for 'Sinclair,' and the name stuck.

"My father, on the other hand, grew up dirt poor in the mountain foothills up north of Gainesville. His parents were sharecroppers. They didn't even want him to go to college, but he left home after high school, worked for a couple of years in Atlanta to make money and then moved to Athens near the university. He worked his way through college and the law school there. Despite all his hardships, he was Phi Beta Kappa and was president of the Law Review.

"After law school he got a job as a clerk with my grandfather's law firm. I guess you can never really be objective about your parents, but I always heard he was one of the best litigators in the city. He met my mother at the firm's Christmas party, they dated and — over the objection of my grandmother who thought her daughter should marry a man with a better social background — got married a year later.

"First Becky came along, and then me. We were truly happy as a family, I think. We had a big house on Putnam Drive, memberships in the best country clubs, you name it. And then it happened." She stopped suddenly as if she didn't want to go on.

I waited a moment and then asked, "What happened?"

Clair poured her wine glass full, took a long drink and said, "My father's past caught up with him."

"I was fifteen, Becky was seventeen. By then we — our family — were at the top of the social heap. My father had worked his way up to become a managing partner of the firm, my mother was a director on the board of the High Museum, and the 'Tate girls' were the ones that every boy's mother wanted her son to marry one day." She stopped, choked with emotion.

"What happened?" I asked again.

Clair put down her wine glass and looked at me in the dim light. I could see tears in her eyes sparkling in the reflection of the candle light. "Nate, did you ever hear of the bombing of the St. Galilee African Methodist Episcopal Church? It happened back in 1968, about the time of the race riots?"

"Of course, who hadn't?" It has been one of the most egregious race crimes ever committed in the South. The dynamite bombing of a black church that killed five children and their Sunday school teacher, a seventy-eight-year-old grandmother. The investigation grew cold and for years the killers went unpunished. The case had broken open just as I started college with the deathbed confession of one of the bombers who named his fellow plotters and provided enough evidence for an air-tight legal case. I wasn't sure I saw the connection between the St. Galilee bombing and

Clair's family. "Did your father defend one of the suspects?" I asked.

Clair gave a sardonic smile. "I wish." She paused. "Nate, my father was Leander Tate. Do you remember now?"

CHAPTER
Twenty-Six

SUDDENLY EVERYTHING FELL INTO PLACE. Leander Tate, icon of Atlanta society and participant in the infamous St. Galilee AME Church bombing. Convicted on multiple counts of murder and conspiracy and sentenced to a dozen or more consecutive life terms in prison, having avoided the death penalty only because of his long and more recent history of community service.

"I never realized," I stammered. "I… I never made the connection."

"You'd have no reason to," Clair replied.

"Becky never mentioned…"

"She wouldn't have. We never talked about it. It was like a big black cloud floating over us while we tried to pretend that it was a bright and sunny day."

"I knew your father was dead. He died in prison, then?"

"No, Nate, he didn't die. He was murdered, by a black prison gang. They caught him alone in one of the storerooms, tortured him by breaking nearly every bone in his body, and then to be sure, they slit his throat and carved 'Honky Baby Killer' on his chest with a knife."

I didn't know what to say. Finally I mumbled, "I'm sorry."

"Oh, if you only knew the truth! It wasn't what the press coverage said at all. He didn't plan the bombing. He didn't condone it. He wasn't a part of it." I could see anger in her expression. "It happened when Daddy moved to Atlanta just after high school. He was an uneducated country boy in a big city. A fellow, an older guy he'd known in north Georgia, helped him get a job in a factory making radiator parts. He invited Daddy to some meetings. They weren't Klan meetings, but they were just as bad. A bunch of redneck idiots who saw the civil rights movement as a threat to their jobs.

Daddy told me later that he was ashamed to be there, but he was young and naïve. He was present the night they talked about 'bombing some nigger church.' He said he didn't want to have anything to do with it and left — he never went to another meeting. And then a couple of weeks later it happened. He didn't know what to do. He *thought* he knew who was behind the killings, but he was eighteen and scared and living alone in a strange town. He kept his mouth shut. Years later when one of the actual bombers confessed, he said Daddy was there for the planning sessions; that he knew all about it."

"Couldn't he have just told the truth?"

"He did. He said he had been a member of the group at one time, but had dropped out. There were others that confirmed that, but in the end it was his word against that of a dead man who identified him as a plotter. The prosecutors said the fact that he didn't come forward to help the police right after bombing indicated his guilt. Plus he made an easy target. Here he was, a prominent white attorney married into one of Atlanta's best families and accused of horrendous race crimes. The prosecutor was black, and both the grand jury that indicted him and the jury that convicted him were mostly black. He didn't have a chance."

"I'm so sorry," I said again, repeating myself. "Did you appeal?"

"Of course, all the way up to the Supreme Court. My mother spent everything she'd inherited to try to free him. We had to drop out of private school. We sold our house and moved to a tiny little place in Decatur. Our friends abandoned us. It was so hurtful, especially for my mother."

Clair stared at the candle for a moment and said, "Do you have any idea what it's like to have someone you adore and idolize called a murderer? I don't want to remember my Daddy as a broken man, taken in chains from the courtroom never to see his children alone again. I want to remember him as that sweet person who tucked me in bed and read me *Goodnight Moon* and who smelled of lime aftershave and whose beard scratched me when he kissed me good night." She broke down, sobbing. I said, "I'm so sorry" a third time and was quiet.

"Anyway," Clair resumed, sniffling and wiping her eyes, "we tried to pull together as a family and carry on. My mother started Tate Interiors so she could have something to live on. Becky won a scholarship to Emory, and for me — well, I just wanted to get as far away from Atlanta as I could. As soon as I graduated from high school I moved to Athens for college and majored in International Business with a minor in Spanish. I even considered changing my name. When I finished college, I got a job with the international division of Coca-Cola and was assigned to Asunción, Paraguay. I swore I'd never come home."

"That's a long way off," I said, trying to distract her.

"True. But it was a voluntary exile. I was getting used to it, actually. I almost married a guy named Fernando. I think his family owned about half the country. About that time the company wanted to transfer me to La Paz, Bolivia. They said it was a promotion," she laughed, dabbing again at her eyes, "but I wasn't so sure. Fernando wanted me to quit and stay home and have babies. He'd already picked out a wedding date."

"So what did you do?"

"I quit my job, broke up with Fernando and moved back to the States. By that time my mother had gotten sick and Becky was trying to run Tate Interiors by herself. I just couldn't stay away, but I still didn't want to be back in Atlanta. I got an apartment in Athens and a job as a sales rep selling medical supplies." She hesitated. "Pretty dull, I know, but it pays well and leaves enough every month to help out with my mother's medical bills. Over the last couple of years Becky and I had become closer. That's how I knew about you. Still, she kept things from me — she never told me about the money problems. I guess she was embarrassed."

I said nothing, waiting for her to continue speaking. "You know, I was thinking about a month ago that things were not really so bad after all. My job was going well, and I was reasonably happy. Sure, I'd lost my father and my mother was dying, but I still had my sister who for some strange reason seemed happier..." She paused. "Now, she's dead and when it comes right down to it, I guess I'm the only one left." She was quiet for a moment, her thoughts drifting far away.

"Nate," she said reaching out to place her hand over mine, "I just want to get through all this, and when it's over I want to settle down to a pleasant life of anonymity in some nameless suburb in middle America. I want to get married and have babies and drive a minivan and yell at my kid's soccer games and forget that my life prior to that point ever happened. I want to grow old and be a grandmother and go to bingo in the church basement on Wednesday nights. And when I die I want my tombstone to say 'She Lived Happily Ever After.'"

Again Clair stared at the candle in silence, finally saying, "I don't like to lean on people. I don't want to be a burden. I don't like to ask for help, but I think this time is different. When I look at Ulbricht I don't know if I am seeing the man who was in love with my closest relative or the man who had her killed. It's going to be hard. If I need you, Nate, will you be there? Please?"

"I will."

"Thanks," she said, and kissed me on the cheek.

CHAPTER
Twenty-Seven

WE STROLLED THE TEN BLOCKS to Clair's hotel in silence. We both needed to walk off the effects of the wine. The warm afternoon had given way to a cool evening. Neither of us had dressed for the chill. Clair linked her arm in mine, huddling next to me for warmth and occasionally giving a little shudder against the cold.

Perhaps it was her company, perhaps it was the alcohol, but for the first time in a long while I enjoyed being with someone, despite the emotional nature of our conversation. We said good night in the lobby. I gave her a hug and my cell phone, telling her I'd call in the morning once I'd spoken to Kelly or Ulbricht.

I emerged from the hotel intending to ask the doorman to call a cab, but one pulled up just as I reached the sidewalk. I recognized the driver as the same one who'd taken me to the safe house in Chaville after the motorcycle incident. Steed rolled down the passenger window and motioned for me to get in the back. "You stupid ass," he started, "you could have gotten both of you killed. Just why the hell did you — "

"Bag it, Steed!" I regretted not having hit him in the restroom at the Embassy. "You wanted us to meet with Ulbricht. We met with Ulbricht. You wanted us to arrange to get both him and the paintings to the U.S. We did that. Right now, I'm about half drunk and more in a mood to fight than talk. We can finish what we almost started at the Embassy, or you can take me home and we'll discuss it tomorrow when I'll be less likely to want to do you physical harm. The choice is yours."

They dropped me off at my flat. I said I'd call the next morning.

∞

I WOKE UP WITH A HANGOVER and a half-hearted self-promise to never consume more than two glasses of wine at any one sitting ever again. I had a low-grade throbbing headache behind my right eye and a tongue that felt like I'd been eating green persimmons. The bedside clock read 9:46. I was just stepping out of the shower when the phone rang. It was Kelly. "How's it going this morning, Nate?" Without waiting for me to reply he said, "Steed wanted me to call. Said he's sorry if he was hard on you last night. He was wondering if we could get together with you and Clair this morning to go over what you learned yesterday?"

"Probably," I said, "but make it this afternoon. I was out late last night and didn't sleep well."

"So I heard."

"Yeah, well…"

"Steed doesn't think you two need to be seen at the Embassy. We'll send our taxi around to take you back to Chaville if that's okay."

167

I was not in a mood to go anywhere, especially if it involved sitting in the back of a moving taxi. "How about meeting me at the Madeleine Tours office at three? We have a conference room that's quiet. I'll tell the staff that we're working on a group package for some embassy dependents."

"Sounds fine. I'll call you back if Steed has any objections. Meanwhile, get some sleep." He hung up.

I called Clair. She answered on the sixth ring with a sleepy, "Hello," and then, "God, Nate, what did we drink last night?"

"Well, we started with a drink at the bar and then had something on the order of three bottles of wine at Maurice's. Feeling a bit peaky?"

"I wish I could say I felt that good. I don't think I remember a lot of what I said. I didn't make a fool of myself did I?"

"No, of course not. We talked a little about your family."

"I must have been drunk, then. I am so ashamed of all that. I... I never tell anyone."

"Forget it. I had a good time. You're great company."

"Thanks, but I'm really hung over."

"Me, too. Look, the reason I'm calling is that Steed and Kelly want to meet with us. I told them three o'clock at my office. Can you make it?"

She said she could. I gave her the address and told her to take a taxi. I called Michelle to alert her I had a meeting at three and to keep the conference room open. I then took two Alka-Seltzers and three Tylenol tablets and crawled back in bed.

I had barely gotten to sleep when the phone rang again. The clock read 11:02 AM. It was Ulbricht this time. "Good morning, Nate. I trust you and Clair made it home safely."

"We did, thanks," I said, trying to sound as if I'd been up for hours.

"Here's what I've done. I've arranged to have the paintings packed as part of a shipment of other pieces that Becky had purchased before her..." he hesitated, "death."

"I own a majority interest in a small trucking firm here in France that she'd been using to pick up and deliver her purchases to the warehouse in Rouen. They're crated and packed there in a container and transported to the port in Le Havre where they'll be loaded on a ship that's scheduled to leave on this coming Sunday. I had to call in a favor or two to get it on board on such short notice."

My head still ached and I was still half asleep. "Okay. Container, you said —"

"Right. A standard forty-foot intramodal shipping container. The same thing she usually uses."

"Okay," I said again, still not thinking well.

"Are you all right?" Ulbricht asked. "You sound like you just woke up."

I lied, "A little stomach flu this morning, but I'm fine." I tried to sound normal. "What about the paperwork? Don't we need the name of the ship or the bill of lading number or something?"

Ulbricht chuckled. "Of course. The ship is the Menelaus — it's a Greek-flagged container ship. I've got all those details for you. Shall I send them around, or would you like to pick them up?"

I needed to buy some time. "Hans, to be truthful, Clair and I were out late. I drank more than usual, and at the moment I'm nursing my hangover. Could I call you in the morning?"

This time he laughed. "I thought so!" He gave me his cell phone number and hung up. I set the alarm for two and buried my head in the pillow.

⬥

I ARRIVED AT THE OFFICE at two forty-five. I was feeling better and trying not to look like I'd just crawled out of bed. Françoise was manning the reception desk and greeted me with a cheery, if gently sarcastic, "Good morning, Mr. Finch. Your clients arrived early and are waiting for you in the conference room."

I walked down the corridor to find Steed and Kelly sitting at the table thumbing though some travel brochures. They both stood up when I entered. "Did you bring Clair with you?" Steed asked.

"No," I said, glancing at my watch. "I spoke with her earlier and she said she'd be here at three. I'll tell the receptionist to show her back when she arrives." I stepped out in the corridor where I could see Françoise sitting behind her desk. I started to call her name when I saw her look up and gasp. She put her hand over her mouth and said in French, "*Mon Dieu!* I thought…"

I reached the desk in time to see her staring mutely at Clair as if she'd seen a ghost.

"Francoise, this is Clair Tate. You remember Becky."

"Sacred Mother of Jesus, I thought she… she was…" Fortunately she was speaking in French. Clair smiled, unknowing.

"They do look alike," I said in French to Françoise, and then switching to English introduced Clair.

"I'm pleased to meet you," Françoise said in English, still clearly shaken.

CHAPTER
Twenty-Eight

WE GOT DOWN TO BUSINESS immediately. Steed gave me the unspoken impression that, given his choice, he'd rather not deal with me at all. I really couldn't blame him; we hadn't exactly become the best of friends. Clair and I went over the preceding day's events in detail. The agents took copious notes. When we'd finished Kelly said, "That's it?" as if he'd expected something sinister to happen.

It was Clair who took the lead. "What did you expect? You'd painted us a picture of Ulbricht that resembled the devil incarnate, and he turns out to be a nice guy. You know, to hear him tell the story he simply seems to be an aggressive international businessman who on one hand sees a chance to make a quick profit, and on the other was in love with my sister. What proof can you offer that he was somehow responsible for Becky's death? He had a reasonable explanation for almost every point you made to implicate him."

"I really have to agree," I said. "How are you so sure you're not barking up the wrong tree? And one more thing, if Ulbricht is such a bad fellow, how is it that he visits the US several times a year on business? Why haven't you arrested him?"

Steed hesitated a moment and answered, "We — the FBI and other agencies — have access to some additional confidential information. I'm not allowed to share that with you at the moment."

"Then why are we here?" Clair asked, clearly angry. "Are we trying to apprehend my sister's killer, or are you using us as part of some bigger secret plan? If you are, then I'm out of here. I'm going to the Paris police."

"Hold on, Clair," Steed said. "I promise you everything we told you is true. We still believe Ulbricht was behind Becky's death, but whether he was physically there at the Eiffel Tower remains to be seen. That is still our number one priority. We could probably arrest him when he's in the States, or even find enough evidence to have him arrested here in Europe. The problem is building a case that his lawyers can't talk or buy his way out of, and doing so in a jurisdiction that will give us leverage with sentencing. In the bigger picture, he's not the only fish we'd like to catch."

"Look," Steed continued, "we need to go over the information you've given us thus far and formulate a plan about how to approach things once we have Ulbricht on U.S. soil. We need to check out the freighter and its schedule and get our stateside team ready to move on a moment's notice. Arresting him will just be the start. We're going to need to put together enough hard facts to convince an American judge that Ulbricht is a flight risk and needs to be held without bond — you get the idea? Nate, you need to pick up the shipping data."

"And I need to get home," Clair said. "I'm picking up Becky's ashes tomorrow and have a flight back to Atlanta on Friday afternoon."

"Then we need to meet again — briefly at least — on Friday morning. But we've got to have the shipping information."

"I'll pick it up," Clair said. Everyone looked at her with surprise. "I'm having dinner with Hans this evening."

⁓

"ARE YOU A FOOL OR WHAT?" I nearly screamed at Clair. We were in a taxi on the way back to her hotel. "Forty-eight hours ago you'd have gleefully strangled Ulbricht with your bare hands, and now you're having dinner with him?"

"Nate, he sent flowers to my hotel. Roses. And the kindest note. He said he wanted to see me, to talk about Becky. I couldn't say no."

"I think I should be there," I said.

"Why? I can take care of myself."

"But you — "

"To answer your question Nate, no, I'm not a fool. I'll call you at your place in the morning. I've still got your cell phone." The taxi had stopped in front of Clair's hotel. She leaned over, pecked me on the check and got out. She walked through the front door without looking back.

I sat in the taxi, staring at the hotel entrance. The driver turned around, waiting for me to decide where to go next. "Monsieur?" he said.

"Let's ride around for a while. Take me to the Bois de Vincennes. Just drive around the park. I need to think."

The driver shrugged. "As you say, Monsieur. A *coup de cœur,* no?" A blow to the heart.

"Perhaps," I said, unthinking. I really didn't know how I felt.

≈

MY PHONE RANG at eight the next morning. "Hi," Clair said.

"How'd your evening go?" I tried to sound normal.

"Fine. I think I learned a lot."

"Did you get the shipping info?"

"Yeah. I called Kelly when I got in last night. He drove over and picked it up."

"You out late?"

"Midnight. Henri drove me back to the hotel."

"So, what are your plans?"

"I've got to pick up Becky's ashes this morning and sign a few last papers at the police station. I should be finished by early in the afternoon. Then I guess I don't have anything to do until we meet with Steed and Kelly tomorrow morning. My flight leaves Orly at three so I need to leave for the airport by noon. What are your plans?"

"Nothing really. I need to show my face at the office and sign a few checks. Not anything of importance."

"Well," she said a bit hesitantly, "if you're not busy there's one thing I want to do. I could use some company."

"Sure, what's that?"

"I want to go to the Eiffel Tower. I want to be there at five. I just want to… to… well, I don't know what I want to do, but I just want to be there."

"Okay."

"Closure, you know? Or something like that."

"Okay."

"Pick me up at four? At the hotel?"

"I'll be there." I felt strange. Not a bad feeling, but strange.

∾

AT FOUR-THIRTY we were standing in line for the lifts at the Eiffel Tower. It was Thursday afternoon and the small queue moved rapidly. Clair had said little since we left her hotel. I hadn't mentioned her dinner with Ulbricht, and she hadn't brought it up. I bought two tickets for the third level observation platform.

We rode in silence to the second level and waited briefly for the lift to take us to the top. The elevator doors opened onto a magnificent vista of Paris. Clair walked over to the railing and gazed out across the city, slowly turning to take in every inch of the view, her eyes dreamy and far away. The wind tugged at her long hair as the sun ducked in and out behind wispy clouds, casting alternate shades of shadow and light on her face. After a moment she said, "It's so beautiful here. I'm fine now. Nothing will bring Becky back, but I'm here where her life ended, and in a sense I want to take up where she left off."

"How so?" I asked. I had no idea what she meant.

"Ulbricht," she said, her eyes filling with tears.

"Clair, you're not thinking."

"Yes, I am. After last night, I am."

"But you can't just..."

She looked at me with burning eyes. "I can, Nate and I will."

"He was your sister's lover. You can't be serious."

"Yes, and I realize now that he was also my sister's killer. I'm going to see him burn in hell, Nate."

CHAPTER
Twenty-Nine

WE ATE AT THE JULES VERNE restaurant on the second level of the Tower. I hadn't planned for dinner. In fact I hadn't really been sure I wanted to see Clair at all. Her back and forth changes in attitude about Ulbricht left me puzzled. There was no way I was going to let her leave Paris without trying to understand what happened the night before to provoke what appeared to be a grim determination for retribution. Reservations at the Jules Verne were nearly impossible on short notice and we weren't really dressed for the occasion. Fortunately I knew the *maître de* well, and a subtlety offered twenty-euro note seated us at a table with a view of the Seine and the setting sun on the western horizon.

We talked about nothing important while I ordered for both of us. The waiter brought two glasses of Dubonnet blanc as an *apéritif.* I nursed my drink and asked, "What happened last night?" trying not to appear too eager.

"In truth, nothing," Clair replied. "We had a pleasant dinner. He's a delightful host. He even had Maria make a wonderful *sopa paraguaya* for the occasion. It's a fantastic dish and no one other than a native Paraguayan knows how to do it just right. Nate, he speaks Spanish, not well, but adequately. He knows about art, about literature, about music, about antiques. He's handsome and rich and — assuming what he said about getting a divorce is correct — soon to be available. I guess you'd say in short that he's everything a girl might want in a man."

"Did he put the moves on you?" I was hesitant to ask and uncertain how to politely phrase it, but felt I had to know.

Clair smiled, a bit grimly, "He probably would have if I'd let him. Fortunately for me all the wine we drank at Maurice's the night before was still in my system so I stopped after two glasses." I thought to myself that we both must have made the same resolution. "No, he really was a perfect gentleman. I think he's too smart for that."

She took a sip of her Dubonnet and continued, "It's what *didn't* happen, Nate. That's what brought it all together. Try to look at it this way — if you examine all the little the little pieces of the puzzle you see nothing but all the little pieces of the puzzle. Think about it! Everyone has their own agenda. The FBI and whatever other agencies they're working with want Ulbricht for their own reasons. They say terrorist financing, but who knows? They talk a good line, but Becky's death to them is more of a convenient excuse than a quest to bring her killers to justice. I'm here because I'm her only surviving relative, and you're here because of some whim of fate backed by the coercion of the U.S. government. Can't you see? Both of us have become playing pieces in someone else's game."

"I don't understand what you're trying to say, Clair."

"I'm not sure that I do either when it comes right down to it. It's more of a feeling that all this is too easy, that everything falls into place without effort. Back off a minute and consider it. Why is Ulbricht so readily agreeable to this complicated arrangement to get a couple of paintings with suspicious provenance — see, I remembered the word — into the States. He can charter a jet for less than he's paying you."

"He said he was doing it for Becky and in turn *you* because you're Becky's sister," I said, playing the devil's advocate.

"True, he said that, but the woman he alleges he loved has been dead for less than two weeks and he's wining and dining her sister. Nate, right now I'm emotionally vulnerable, but I'm no virgin. At times I've allowed myself to be seduced, and at times I've been the seductress. I know his game. It would have been so easy to wake up in his bed this morning to look out across the rooftops of Paris and think I just might be falling in love. Remember what Levin said about the blind men and the elephant? That's you and me. We're seeing only part of the picture. We're walking in on the third act of a five-part play and trying to decide for ourselves what's happened before and what's to come."

"But who sees everything? Who's pulling the strings? Who's the man behind the curtain?"

"I don't know, and I don't know where to find the answer. If I had to pick someone *not* to trust it would be Ulbricht. It's a feeling, Nate, nothing more. Call it a sixth sense, a woman's intuition, call it Becky speaking from beyond the grave. I *know* somehow that he's responsible for her death." The waiter brought the first course. We dined in uneasy silence, each wrapped in our own thoughts.

After dinner we walked across the Pont d'Iéna to the Tracadéro. Strolling arm-in-arm beside the fountains, we climbed the stairs to the terrace of the Palais de Chaillot. Before us the Eiffel Tower thrust toward the sky, its massive iron filigree illuminated by the yellow glow of sodium vapor lamps. "Paris is so beautiful," Clair said.

"It's a city, nothing more," I replied and recalled to myself that this was exactly the spot where Hitler had posed for a photograph on his one visit to Paris in July 1940.

WE MET AT THE MADELEINE TOURS office at eight on Friday morning. Steed and Kelly were there ten minutes early as usual. Clair arrived by taxi promptly at eight. She'd checked out of the hotel and planned to leave directly for the airport. I helped her bring her bags in. I noticed she was cradling a small wooden box with brightly polished brass hinges. She followed my eyes and nodded. "It is what you think it is. I couldn't just pack it in my luggage. She was my only sister." For a fleeting instant she looked like she wanted to cry.

We met again in the conference room. Steed was at his formal best. "All right, here's where we stand. We've checked on the freighter. The *Menelaus* is a relatively small container ship owned by Dutch corporation but under lease to the Greek shipping line Polis Seaquest. The keel was laid in 1998 and it went into full service about six and a half years ago. It's three hundred ninety feet long, displaces forty four hundred tons and has a capacity of three hundred thirty-two standard twenty-foot containers, or half that many forty-foot ones. For the last two years it's been in steady service on the northern European-U.S. east coast route, mainly carrying small specialty cargo — wine, some textiles, auto parts and the like. Polis Seaquest is a well-respected company. We haven't as yet been able to track down the true owners of the Dutch corporation, which is owned by a holding company in the Caymans, which in turn seems to be controlled by a company based in the Republic of Nauru."

"Where is Nauru?" Clair asked. I'd had the same thought but didn't want to appear ignorant by asking.

"It's a small little island about a third the size of Manhattan located roughly twelve hundred miles from anywhere in the middle of the Pacific. It has a population of about thirteen thousand with probably half that many private banks. It's a tax haven, basically, the latest version of what Switzerland used to be. The fact that the line of ownership of the vessel goes through Nauru doesn't mean much. Just another international businessman trying to avoid taxes, likely. We'll keep working on it, though." Clair shot me a sheepish look.

"Anyway, the Menelaus is scheduled to dock for a few hours first at Brunswick, Georgia, then at the Port of Savannah for two days, then on to Charleston and points north. The company has reserved berth space in Savannah for late Monday afternoon, May third. They'll begin unloading as soon as she ties up and should have it completed in less than twelve hours. We checked with our people in the States and they're pretty sure the best thing to do is to inspect the container as it's offloaded in Savannah. We'll confirm that the paintings are on board and then make the arrest in Atlanta once Ulbricht takes physical possession. The lawyers tell us that will give us the best case. Once he's in custody we'll start putting the pressure on him."

"Mr. Steed," I said, "I still don't see where you've got a shred of evidence to connect Ulbricht to Becky's death. Neither Clair nor I give a damn about whatever smuggling laws he's broken. It was Becky's murder that got us here and that's the sole reason we're in this little game of yours."

"We know that," Kelly answered. "We think once we have him in custody though we can start to work on his organization with a few arrests in Europe, Asia and the Middle East. Someone will crack, which will lead to someone else cracking, and so on up the line. We'll get him."

We discussed the plan. Clair said she had to get back to work if for no other reason than to arrange for a personal leave until this whole thing was over. Kelly promised that would be the day after Ulbricht's arrest. Steed and the FBI's Paris bureau would coordinate the European end of operations. Kelly and Brookins would be in charge in the U.S.

"We're going to keep a low profile in the States until we make the arrest," Kelly continued. "We'll track Ulbricht's whereabouts, but you'll be on your own for the most part. We will want you both present in Savannah when we open the container for a 'customs inspection.' Technically the goods belong to Tate Interiors and it's a chain-of-custody issue. You'll just confirm that the shipment made it through customs. We'll reseal it until you open it again in Atlanta in Ulbricht's presence. Should be a piece of cake."

"Sounds great from your perspective no doubt," Clair observed, "but it occurred to me no one has said what happens to the money, the half million dollars that Ulbricht is supposed to turn over when he picks up the paintings. That and Nate's check, too."

Steed glanced at Kelly and smiled wryly. "We didn't forget. We've already run it past the lawyers. It will be the government's position that you earned those funds in the normal course of a business transaction." He paused. "Of course, you'll owe taxes and there may be some additional import duties."

The agents left shortly after ten. Clair had more than an hour to kill before she had to leave for the airport. "How about a late breakfast or an early lunch?" I suggested. "I know a *pâtisserie* about three blocks from here that serves great coffee from the Ivory Coast."

Clair smiled. "Sure! I won't see you for a while and for some reason, I've sort of gotten used to your company." She carefully laid Becky's remains on my desk and we walked out into the warm late April morning.

We drank strong dark coffee and feasted on cream-filled croissants. "I guess you're flying through Atlanta when you come over? Are you going to connect to a Savannah flight or do you have other plans?"

"Since our illustrious FBI has promised to pick up our expenses, I thought I might fly in a couple of days early and pick up a rental car. I haven't seen my parents in more than a year."

"Suppose I could catch a ride with you to Savannah?"

"I was planning to spend the night on the farm. Maybe a couple of nights."

"I could shovel hay or feed the hogs or something to pay my way if you'd let me come."

"Well, for a start you 'toss' hay and 'slop' the hogs, but I don't think you need to do either. We raise — I'm sorry — *my family* raises onions."

"You have a whole farm full of onions?"

"Tons and tons. I'll feed you an onion sandwich: a big thick slice of onion between two slices of light bread slathered with mayonnaise."

"It's a long way from the *foie gras* at the Jules Verne last night but I'll try it."

"You're on then. See you in Atlanta."

Part II:

Atlanta

"They consider only their own ideas of ingenuity; and, in searching for anything hidden, advert only to the modes in which they would have hidden it. They are right in this much—that their own ingenuity is a faithful representative of that of the mass; but when the cunning of the individual felon is diverse in character from their own, the felon foils them, of course."

-Chevalier Auguste Dupin, referring to the
police search for a stolen letter
From **The Purloined Letter**
By Edgar Allen Poe (1845)

CHAPTER
Thirty

Atlanta
April 30, 2004

ATLANTA IS HOT IN APRIL. It's one of those facts you know, but tend to forget until you're overwhelmed by a blast of warm, sticky air as you step off the plane onto the jetway. Paris, despite all its springtime balminess, is still more than a thousand miles to the north in latitude, roughly the same as Nova Scotia or Thunder Bay, Ontario. By the time I'd cleared immigration and customs, I'd stripped off my jacket and sweater and stuffed them into my carry-on bag.

The Air France flight was due in Atlanta at one fifty in the afternoon but we'd had minimal headwind and had arrived twenty minutes early. I arrived in the baggage claim area shortly after two. I saw Clair before she saw me. She was pacing back and forth, nervously glancing between the carousel that was now spewing out bags from the Paris

184

flight and the passageway that led to the flight concourses. I waved and she smiled, half tripping as she rushed to give me a hug. "How was your flight?" she asked. I felt strangely comfortable with her.

"Great," I said, not bothering to mention I had made the same trip a hundred or more times. "Are you ready for all this?" I asked.

"I think so. Kelly called yesterday. They've confirmed Ulbricht is booked on a Lufthansa flight from Berlin next Thursday, the sixth. He should arrive in Atlanta about noon. The ship is on time and due into Brunswick late Sunday afternoon, then on to Savannah on Monday. He says we'll need to be there late Monday afternoon — I've got the details written down. And there's lots more. I've been going over the books at Tate Interiors, trying to sort out the business." she stopped suddenly. "I don't want to bore you with all this right now. I'll give you a ride to your hotel, and we can talk later."

"Looks like we're on track." I tried to sound confident. In a worst case scenario I figured I'd be wasting a few days of my time, but the upside was I'd be making an easy fifty grand and would have a chance to pay a long overdue visit to my family. I had also set up a business meeting with Colette, something I was not especially looking forward to. And then there was Clair — I wasn't sure how I felt about that.

I planned to spend a couple of hours Friday afternoon at Madeleine Tour's Atlanta office, stay overnight at the Grand Hyatt Buckhead, then pick up a rental car and head for the farm with Clair. We'd spend a couple of nights at my parents' house, drive to the Port of Savannah on Monday afternoon, then back to Atlanta either that night or the next day to await delivery of the paintings. I was holding an open return ticket and planned to leave for Paris as soon as Ulbricht handed me the check.

Clair retrieved her car from short-term parking and was waiting when I walked out of the baggage claim area. She drove a clunky-looking minivan. "Company car," she explained. "I spend most of my time going from one doctor's office to the next selling medical supplies — you know, bandages, gloves, small instruments and that sort of thing. Stuff that you could buy cheaper at Wal-Mart if you really wanted to. But I'm convenient and friendly, and I smile a lot."

"It pays the bills," I observed. Clair didn't have much to say as we drove into the city. She seemed vaguely upset about something.

It was always a bit strange to come back to Atlanta. I'd lived there for years but unlike Paris, the city was constantly changing, and not necessarily for the better. Neighborhoods once filled with modest houses and hundred-year-old oaks had been swept away and replaced by mass-produced high-rise apartments. Stately homes once magnificent on large wooded lots now huddled together with herds of "infill housing," over-built McMansions for the upwardly mobile who were willing to pay outrageous prices to live in the right part of town.

Years of corrupt and inept city administrations had left the streets poorly maintained and the expressways in perpetual gridlock. Those who could afford it lived in gated developments to the north of town while the central city decayed with inelegant shabbiness, like a malignant tumor whose rapid growth had starved its core of nutrients.

I enjoyed staying at the Grand Hyatt. It was a well-run hotel, even by European standards, and within walking distance of our office on Piedmont Road. And, for me at least, it was cheap. Madeleine Tours used the Park Hyatt

Paris-Vendôme exclusively for our upscale clients so the room for my usual stay of a night or two was complimentary. Clair dropped me off at the valet entrance, handing me a card with her cell phone number.

Dinner?" she asked. "I owe you from Paris."

I said I'd call when I'd finished meeting with Colette. I went to my room, took a quick shower, called the office to say I'd be there at four-thirty, and lay down for a half-hour nap.

PROMPTLY AT FOUR-THIRTY I pulled open the door of the Madeleine Tour's Atlanta office and strode in casually. I had been here a dozen or more times since the divorce, but I dreaded every visit. The ten-minute walk from the hotel was inevitably accompanied by sweating palms and a vague, unfocused anxiety. It usually disappeared once Colette and I got underway with our meeting, but it was that first look, that view of the woman I once loved and desired and trusted with my innermost secrets, that swept over me like a tidal wave, destroying my confidence, wrecking my resolve and drowning me in a sea of undeserved guilt. The staff greeted me warmly. I don't think they took sides in the divorce; after all, the status quo and their livelihood depended in part on how well Colette and I got along.

Brandi, our twenty-something tattooed and pierced receptionist grinned and said, "She's waiting for you in the conference room." Then in a whisper, "She's in a good mood, so relax."

I tried to. I found Colette going over a stack of printouts she'd unfolded across the long table. "Hi. How's it going?" I tried to sound nonchalant.

"Fine, Nate," she smiled, speaking in English. "I'm glad you could come." She walked over and gave me a little hug. "That was so tragic about your friend Becky. I guess I was out of line the other night. I'm sorry." She reached out and squeezed my hand. Colette rarely apologized for anything. She hadn't touched me since the divorce. "We're doing well," she continued, holding up a sheet of figures. "Between our group bookings and FIT's, I'll wager that our dollar volume will be up close to ten percent this year."

We spent the next hour and a half going over figures, fine-tuning itineraries, and discussing the staff. Colette usually preferred to speak French to me, but I noticed she spoke in English this time except when we were discussing personnel matters. Something was up. We were just finishing as Brandi stuck her head in to let us know she was leaving and would be locking the door on the way out. Colette folded up her printouts and stuffed them in a large file folder. "So, how have things been?" I asked.

Colette looked at me a bit strangely, somewhat startled. "Er... fine. You should know; we just went over those figures." She opened the folder and appeared to be studying a page of numbers, avoiding my gaze.

"No, I mean with you. Carl junior okay?"

"Of course. Why do you ask?" She seemed defensive.

"Colette, I'm just asking, okay? We haven't talked in a while."

She seemed relieved. "He's fine, thanks."

"And Carl senior, I take it he's well, also?"

"Of course! Why shouldn't he be? We're fine. I told you already." I sensed I had hit a nerve and decided to press the point.

"I don't know. I just had a feeling that you were, well, a little upset about something. The business is fine so I thought perhaps it was a problem at home."

She was suddenly angry and spat back at me in French, "What happens in my marriage is none of your business. Everything is just fine. I am perfectly happy." She broke down sobbing and laid her head on the table.

I stood there for a moment listening to the sounds of her gasps and then, perhaps foolishly, I walked over and placed my hand on her shoulder. "You want to talk about it?"

"Oh, Nate, I've been such a fool. Carl's been working so hard lately. He's been on call a lot — going out late at night on emergencies. Sometimes he'd have to spend the night at the hospital. I believed him, Nate! I gave him everything he wanted… and now, now…" She broke down sobbing again. I stood over her quietly, my hand on her shoulder, not speaking.

"Why did I ever do this? Why did I ever get involved?" she moaned softly, her head buried on her arms folded on the table. "I've always loved you, Nate."

I felt a cold chill rush over me. "You want to tell me about it?"

"He's having an affair, Nate. With a nurse who works in the OR. He's got a wife and a precious little son at home and I find out that he's been spending those on-call nights with that whore."

"Colette," I said, lifting my hand from her shoulder. She raised her head and peered at me through tear-reddened eyes. "Now you know how it feels."

CHAPTER
Thirty-One

I STROLLED BACK TO THE HOTEL slowly, turning over Colette's words in my mind. Ever since the divorce, I'd told myself I was still in love with her and would take her back in a minute. Meanwhile, another more rational voice inside my head screamed that she'd betrayed me in the worst way, and her obvious suffering was only so richly deserved. Either way, the situation was one of her own making, and she'd have to sort things out by herself. I shoved it all into the back of my thoughts and called Clair on my cell phone. She said she had a lot to go over with me and suggested we find a quiet place to eat and talk. McKinnon's Louisianne was another short walk from the hotel. I told her I'd meet her there at eight.

I guess I'm a creature of habit; I usually manage to eat at McKinnon's at least once when I'm in town. Compared to the great cities of Europe, Atlanta is just an infant, scarcely even a hundred and fifty years old. Its explosive growth has given rise to hundreds of restaurants all vying for the expense account-fueled buying power of conventioneers exploring the *de facto* capital of the New South. Like dogs raising their hind legs to mark territory, each chef struggles to create some signature dish to celebrate his or her own culinary superiority, but with a "Southern flair." This has given rise to such bizarre chimeras as "pecan and molasses encrusted sushi grade *ahi* tuna served on a bed of turnips greens sautéed with smoked country free-range ham." McKinnon's, on the other hand, is quiet and serves consistently good simple Louisiana dishes.

Clair's minivan was parked in front of the restaurant when I arrived a few minutes after eight. I found her in the bar, sipping a glass of Evian and still appearing somewhat disturbed about something. We took a quiet table in the back dining room. She ordered the jambalaya. The waiter said the crawfish were fresh, so I had etoufée. I picked a Chilean Merlot and asked him to bring the bottle while we waited for the first course. We exchanged a few pleasantries. I could see she wanted to tell me something but didn't know how to start. She said she'd gotten a leave of absence worked out with her job and she'd been staying at Becky's condo. Becky's friends wanted to schedule a memorial service later in the month. I knew she planned to spend the week going over the books at Tate Interiors, but she said nothing about what she'd found. Finally I asked, "How is the business doing?"

"Not great, but I think we can survive. I spent a long day with the accountant. Becky was on schedule with all of her notes at the bank, and sales have been up substantially in the last four or five months. The half million she got from Ulbricht turned things around. She has several really dedicated employees — one of them is an interior designer — and they've kept things going over the last few weeks."

"So things are looking better then?"

"Definitely so, according to the accountant."

I sensed there was still something bothering her. I tried, "You said you a lot to go over with me. Sounds like you've got everything under control."

"No, Nate. That's just it. I don't. I want to tell you about it, but at the same time I don't even want to talk about it. You think you know somebody, especially your sister. We grew up in the same house, we went to the same schools, we even dated the same boys. I knew that what happened to our father changed her; it changed me and sent me running off to Paraguay. I guess I knew she was bitter about it all, but I never realized how deep her hatred had become."

"Hatred of what?

"Of the system and the people she blamed for Daddy's death. She felt — I guess I should say we all did — that my father was wrongly accused, or at least didn't deserve the punishment he got. Nate, they turned him into the poster child for every racial injustice that has ever taken place in this state and then threw him in with a prison population that's half black. It was a death sentence." She paused, taking a sip of wine. "I was looking through Becky's computer. She had been keeping a diary. No, that's not the word. It's more that she had been venting her frustrations by writing long essays to herself. I can't imagine she ever, *ever* intended for anyone to read them. They're really vile, Nate. Racist in the worst sense of the word. It's almost like something that would have been written by those men that bombed the church and killed those little girls."

I didn't know what to say. "Clair, she never said anything like that to me. I know I was with her only a few months."

"But did she tell you *anything* about what happened to my father, or why?"

"No."

192

"And it's not likely she would have said anything to anyone else. It's one of those dark family secrets you never talk about. What I can't understand, though, is why this seems to have come up just lately. Time is the greatest healer, but most of what I read was written over the last few months."

"Do you suppose your mother's illness together with all the problems at the business had reawakened some dormant feelings?"

"I don't know, and I'll never have the chance to ask her. Her rantings — that's really the only word — are almost scary."

"How so?"

"She keeps talking about revenge, about the need for retribution, about punishment for whomever she holds responsible for my father's death."

"Who is that?"

"The blacks, Nate. All of them."

I was stunned. "That's so unlike the Becky I knew."

"That wasn't my sister. I don't want to remember her like that," Clair said, looking distressed.

"What did you do?"

"I erased the files. Every last one of them."

CLAIR SEEMED RELIEVED to have gotten it off her chest. The rest of the evening went smoothly. She said she was considering quitting her job and trying to run Tate Interiors on her own. "I don't know anything about the business, but I've talked with the staff and they're willing to help me learn. I think I'd enjoy it. I don't think I'd feel right about doing anything until Becky's killers are caught and punished. If we can just make it through next week."

"By this time next week we should have everything wrapped up," I said.

"You know, it just occurred to me that the sixth, next Thursday, is the anniversary of my father's death. I guess I should go out to the cemetery."

"Need some company? I probably won't fly back to Paris until Friday."

"That would be great." She paused. "We've been so busy talking about me that I forgot to ask. How did your meeting with your ex-wife go?"

"Fine, I guess. We try to meet in person at least once a month. Either here or in Paris. Business is good."

Clair studied me for a moment and said, "You still love her, don't you?"

I hadn't expected the question. "No, of course not," I replied quickly. Then, "That's not right. The answer is I don't really know how I feel. You know what happened. I thought I knew her and then... well. I guess you really don't ever know a person, or what they're capable of, no matter how close you are to them."

Clair swirled her glass, watching the rivulets of thick wine run down the sides. "That's just what I was thinking when I read the files on Becky's computer."

CHAPTER
Thirty-Two

AVIS DELIVERED MY RENTAL CAR to the hotel the next morning. I had ordered a medium sized vehicle but ended up with a Chevrolet Tahoe. They said it was all they had left on the lot thanks to a national conference of software engineers who'd snapped up all the low-end vehicles. I picked up Clair at Becky's condo. She was waiting on the front steps as I pulled up. Thankfully, I didn't have to go inside. Too many memories.

We headed east for more than an hour on I-20, then south cross-country on Highway 15 for another hour and a half. The city and its endless stretches of cookie-cutter malls and subdivisions named for English villages gave way to small towns separated by long stretches of pine forest. Just south of the crossroads town of Adrian, we turned left on a county-maintained paved road that led to the Finch farm, and beyond to Soperton. "It's strange how much south Georgia reminds me of Paraguay," Clair observed. "It's got the same red dirt, the same little settlements."

We passed through a dark forest of mature pine trees and then burst into the sunlight. Gently rolling open fields dotted with regular rows of green shoots disappeared into the distance on both sides of the road. Small brightly painted signs read, "Finch Farms, Inc. Home of Finch's Finest® Vidalia Onions." Clair rolled down the window to catch the breeze, her long dark hair whipping in irregular strands as she peered back and forth. Warm air carrying the smell of fertile earth flooded the car. "So this is where you grew up," she observed.

"Part of me never left," I said.

My parents' house came into view as we topped the next hill. I had told them I was bringing someone home with me. My mother seemed quietly excited about the prospect. After the divorce she urged me to "move on," and always wanted to know if I'd "started going out" whenever we talked. I'd told her Clair was just a friend and that we had some business in Savannah, nothing more. I'd never told them about Becky.

My father met us on the front porch. He greeted me with a hug and turned his attention to Clair. I introduced them and he said, "Your mama's out in the kitchen feeding the hands. We were just finishing dinner and fixing to go back out and get started again. I 'pologize Miss Clair, but this is our busy time of year — we're harvestin'." Turning to me he said, "Nate, your brothers are out on the farm or over at the packing house. They said they'd see you tonight. Want to meet your lady friend here." He winked. "Y'all come on in and get some food before it's all gone."

We found my mother in the kitchen presiding over a long table full of home cooked dishes that were filled and refilled as the field hands wandered in and out for their mid-day meal. She smiled broadly when she saw Clair, and had given her a huge hug before I'd had a chance to introduce her. "I want you to feel right at home here. We're not quite as fancy as y'all are in Atlanta, so you just relax and enjoy yourself. The men are going to be out in the fields so I'd planned for you to spend a little time with me and my son's wives, unless you and Nate had something else planned."

Clair glanced at me. I shook my head, "Be careful, she'll have you cooking for the farm hands."

"I can handle it," Clair said, smiling.

WE HAD A GREAT WEEKEND. I ended up helping at the packing house on Saturday afternoon while my mother and sisters-in-law took Clair off on a round of visits to several neighboring farms. I think they were showing her off. On Sunday morning, with the four brothers and their families together for the first time in years, we all went to services at the Poplar Springs Christian Church. The preacher spoke on sin and forgiveness. After dinner everyone disappeared back to their homes. Clair said she thought she'd take a nap. My father suggested we go and look at some new harvesting equipment one of my brothers had just purchased. We climbed in his worn pickup and headed out across a dusty field road. I knew it was an excuse. He wanted to talk.

"You know, Nate," he began, "your mama and I are nearly seventy-five years old and still working just about as hard as we did the day you were born. We've not gotten rich, but we've had a good life, raising four fine boys, having a bunch of healthy grandchildren. We tried to raise you with the simple creed that if you work hard and do the right thing the Lord will reward you. For us that's been true. But I worry about you. I know what happened with Colette was bad — it made you feel worthless, inadequate — like you'd done something to cause it when you knew deep down you hadn't." He stopped the truck and switched off the ignition.

He turned toward me in the seat leaning back against the door and continued, "You're well past thirty now, and I can't give you anything but my thoughts and advice. You haven't been to see your family in a long time, and when we have seen ya or talked on the phone you seem sad, bitter even, like life keeps slapping you in the face. Oh, you probably think things are fine, I mean you've got a good business, you're making plenty of money, you live in an excitin' foreign city that most folks just dream about, and so on. But I don't see you as happy, Nate. And I think you're not happy because you feel like you can't trust anyone anymore."

"I don't —" I tried to get a word in.

"Let me finish and then you can talk." He said this, waiting for me to object. I nodded. "You know we go to church and all that, but I'm not an especially religious person. I'm not gonna sit here and talk to you about faith and belief in things you can't see. I do like to read though, and I was thinkin' about you the other night when I was reading a story by Nathaniel Hawthorne — it was called 'Young Goodman Brown.' Ever heard of it?"

I said I hadn't.

"Well, it's about a fellow name of Goodman Brown who's said to be a fine man. He seems to have a good job, a nice home and most of all, a good wife. The story takes place somewhere up North right after the pilgrims came and back when they all believed in witches and witchcraft. 'Parently there was a lot of rumors of that sort of thing in the community, but this Brown fella, he's glad he's got him a good, honest, loving wife.

"So one night he wakes up and his wife's not in the bed with him. He calls out to her and she's not to be found. To make a long story short, he heads out all alone hunting for her, and pretty soon he comes up on a group of witches dancing all naked around a bonfire in the woods and celebrating some sort of unholy goings-on. He gets real upset, runs back to his house and eventually falls asleep. When he wakes up the next morning his loving wife is right there in the bed with him like nothing ever happened, and come to think of it, he's not sure if it did happen or if he just dreamed it. From that day forward he was a changed man, Nate. Even though nothing in his world changed, and even though as far as everyone knew he had the most perfect wife, he never trusted her again. He couldn't open himself up to her love, so he grew old and miserable and in the end died a lonely death."

My father paused, waiting for me to speak. I said, "So what does that have to do with me?"

"Son, it's a question of faith and trust. You can never really know someone deep down, but unless they give you a concrete reason to think otherwise, you oughta trust them if that's what the situation calls for. Now, I know you're still holding on to Colette."

"It's not that way."

"Let me finish. And you'd probably welcome her back like nothing had ever happened. But, Nate, she's done danced with the witches. If you were together, you'd never be able to trust her again. Let me give you an old man's advice. Find you someone new — someone you can love and trust." He stopped, looking me directly in the eye and waiting for me to respond.

I'd said scarcely a dozen words since we'd left the house. "I think you know me all too well. It's just a lot easier said than done."

"Nothing good in this world's easy, son. I ain't gonna be here forever to remind you of that, so take it to heart." I nodded. "Good, then. Let's go see that new harvester."

∞

AN HOUR LATER WE ARRIVED back at the house. From a distance I could see Clair pacing back and forth on the porch. She rushed up as we drove into the yard.

"Kelly called," she said. "We need to talk. There's a new development."

"A problem?"

"He's not sure. It may be."

CHAPTER
Thirty-Three

"WHAT'S UP?" I asked.

Clair grabbed me by the hand and pulled me over to the swing under the oak tree in the back yard, far out of earshot of my father. "I don't really know. It may not be anything at all, but Kelly called from Savannah about half an hour ago. He and Brookins are back in the U.S. and say they're working with Customs to get the container off-loaded and inspected as soon as the Menelaus ties up in port. Said he's been trying to contact us for a couple of days — the cell phones don't work very well out here — and finally tracked us down by calling your parents' number. They want to go over things in more detail with us later, but thought we should know the FBI has discovered that Ulbricht's driver, Henri, is not who he says he is."

"I'm not sure what you mean. He never told us who he was in the first place."

Clair gave me a frustrated look. "No, that's not what I'm saying! You remember they showed us the surveillance photos taken of him in Paris when he was tailing you, right?"

"Right."

"Well, they didn't know who he was at the time and according to what Kelly said, didn't think it was important to find out. Nate, he's in the U.S. He came over on a flight to Washington on Wednesday of this past week. He's using a French passport with the name," she paused and reached in her jeans to extract a scrap of paper, "Henri Jean Broussard. He made it through immigration without any problems, but later they found out he's a Serbian whose real name is Henri Mavik. Kelly says he's under indictment for murder and various war crimes committed in Bosnia about ten years ago. They want to meet with us at the FBI's Savannah office tomorrow at three and will give us the whole story then."

"Washington, DC, is a long way from Soperton, Georgia. Why's Kelly so concerned?"

"I don't really know. The FBI tried to pick up his trail, but he's disappeared. They've put out bulletins to all the airlines, car rental companies and the like, but nothing's come in yet. Mavik or Broussard or whatever his name is has a ticket for a return flight from Washington to Paris next Sunday, the ninth. They intend to arrest him when he shows up at the airport."

"Clair, it's hard for me to see what this has to do with us. Maybe the guy's just taking a vacation."

"I don't know. Kelly seemed worried, though, and thought we should know. He told us to look out for him."

"Yeah, maybe, but I think a French-speaking Serbian war criminal is going to stand out like a sore thumb in south Georgia. I don't think we'll need to post a guard."

Clair laughed. "I know it sounds crazy, but it's not any weirder than anything else that's happened." She leaned her head back and looked up at the branches of the massive oak tree that spread out above us like a giant umbrella. "I know it's changing the subject, but I want to thank you for bringing me here. With Becky's death and all that's been going on I needed to get away. I love your family. They have a great life here — simple, hardworking, uncomplicated. Did you ever consider coming back and living here? You'd do well."

"Sometimes I wonder why I ever left."

"I'm glad you did, though," Clair said.

"Why's that?"

"We never would have met if you hadn't." She laid her head on my shoulder. I saw my father peek out the kitchen window. He smiled briefly and disappeared from view.

THE FBI'S SAVANNAH FIELD OFFICE was on the fourth floor of a red brick and concrete box of a building on East Bryan Street a couple of blocks from the riverfront. Iron bars covered the windows on the lower two floors. To describe it as an eyesore festering in an otherwise charming historic area would have been an understatement. The front door opened into a foyer no larger than a large closet equipped with an intercom and a crudely worded notice that visitors should announce their presence to be allowed in. Kelly and Brookins were waiting for us when we arrived at three. We met in a standard government-issue conference room that could have been next door to the one in the Paris embassy.

"I'm glad you made it here safely," Kelly began. "Clair, Nate, I was sorry to have to have to disturb you yesterday, but I thought you should be aware of what's going on. We don't have any evidence that Mavik's connected to this current investigation, but we wanted to keep you informed."

"If you thought it was important enough to call us, you must have your suspicions," I replied. "I presume that you're going to tell us the details?"

Steed looked at Brookins who said, "Might as well. Let me fill you in on what happened. By way of background, you're aware that several of the provisions of the Patriot Act and other legislation passed over the last couple of years requires we tighten immigration procedures at our borders.

"One of the things the government's working on but hasn't yet fully implemented is biometric data collection from all foreign visitors to the United States. Several systems have been set up as pilot programs at a dozen or more US international airports. We've been collecting a lot of data: photographs at some sites, fingerprints at others, sometimes both. The problem has been what to do with it. If Osama bin Ladin himself walked through in disguise we could get his prints, but if we don't have some way to check them on the spot the whole process would be useless.

"Right now the Immigration Service is testing the concept of comparing fingerprints collected at US airports to several international databases to see if there are any suspicious hits. If you have a traveler who, for example, is wanted for murder in Burma, it's not going to do much good to compare his prints to the FBI's central files.

"Anyway," Brookins continued, "at Washington-Dulles they're beta-testing a system that uses a combination of biometrics from facial photos and right index finger prints compared to Interpol's central files. The system's not perfect, but it works pretty well much of the time. Of the prints and photos tagged as suspicious, roughly seventy–five to eighty percent correctly identify the individual. Another twenty to twenty-five percent get kicked out for hand review. Of that group probably two-thirds are erroneous, or just plain wrong. Only a human expert can make the call.

"On Wednesday afternoon, April 28th, an Air France flight arrived from Paris carrying Henri Jean Broussard. He went through immigration routinely, but the ID system flagged his data, not as a bad guy, but for hand review. As I said, we get lots of false alerts. We just can't turn away up to a quarter of all foreign visitors, so pending a review by an expert, we allow local supervisors to make the call about what to do.

"In the case of Broussard, we got a hit through the Interpol database that matched his prints with those of a Serbian who'd been killed — assassinated actually — about eight years ago. The supervisor on duty thought it was pretty obviously a false positive, so Broussard got waved on through without any fanfare. He said he was in the U.S. on a vacation and he planned to be sightseeing in Washington for about ten days. He said he'd be staying at the Arlington Hilton — he even had a reservation — but they have no record that he ever checked in.

"Broussard went through immigration at about six in the evening, which was midnight at the Interpol offices in Brussels. The supervisor sent through a routine request for a hand-check of the prints and facial photos, but that was not completed until about an hour later, which was seven here. Since no one had flagged the request as urgent, it was the next morning, Friday, before we got back a positive ID. By that time his trail had gone cold, and I guess you'd say that's also the point where the shit hit the fan." Kelly winced at Brookins's terminology, evidently thinking such language was below the dignity of an FBI agent.

"Why so?" I asked.

"It seems that Henri Jean Broussard and Henri Mavik are one in the same. Back in the late sixties, a certain Captain Tarka Mavik was assigned as military attaché to the Yugoslavian Embassy in Paris. He was married, but kept a French mistress named Sara Broussard. They had an illegitimate son she named Henri Jean. Captain Mavik was a man on his way up, and in the early seventies went back to Belgrade and on to a series of promotions that eventually led to his being one of the top generals in the Yugoslav, and subsequently the Serbian, army.

"When Captain Mavik's son, Henri, turned fifteen he went to Belgrade to live with his father and took the name Henri Mavik. He joined the military at eighteen, and by the time of full-blown Balkan hostilities was a captain in the infantry. Apparently with his father's knowledge and encouragement, he led a bloody campaign of ethnic cleansing in Srebrenica, Bosnia. He was reputed to be responsible for the deaths of thousands of Muslims, including women and children. After NATO intervened both the father and son were recalled to Belgrade. They were indicted for war crimes by the Hague Tribunal and extradition proceedings were begun.

"Shortly thereafter in late 1999, Tarka Mavik was shot and killed by an unknown assailant one afternoon as he was leaving his office. The consensus is he was killed by his own people because he knew too much, possible at Milosevic's behest. His son Henri and two bodyguards were killed three weeks later when a remote control bomb destroyed their car. That, at least, was the official story. The son's body was too badly damaged to be identified, but at the inquest there were witnesses who swore they'd seen him get in the vehicle just before it exploded.

"What we think happened was that Henri Mavik saw the handwriting on the wall and knew he was a marked man. We presume he faked his own death, and then disappeared across a couple of borders to France where he resumed the identity he'd had before he left to live with his father. Henri Jean Broussard was in fact his given name, and he legitimately had a French passport confirming that fact. After the death of Henri Mavik in Belgrade, no one thought to look in France for Henri Broussard. We also presume he had no idea his fingerprints and photos still existed in an Interpol database."

Kelly spoke, "I suppose you're wondering how or if this all ties in with Ulbricht. We've been trying to figure that out. Certainly, Mavik's supposed death was something he couldn't have pulled off on his own. We're not sure, but we suspect Ulbricht financed it. It would have been a convenient arrangement for both of them. Mavik gets a job that will keep him out of the public eye and Ulbricht gets Mavik's utter loyalty, not to mention having someone who is capable of heartless violence if the situation calls for it."

"But is there *any* evidence whatsoever of a connection between the fact that Mavik is in Washington and Ulbricht is on his way to Atlanta to take delivery of the paintings?"

Brookins and Kelly looked at one another. Brookins spoke. "No, but like everything else that's going on, there are just too many coincidences." He paused, looking at his watch. "Unless things go really wrong, though, we'll have Ulbricht in custody in less than seventy-two hours, and will pick up Mavik in less than six days. We'll find out."

"It's all been too easy," Clair said. "Just all too easy."

CHAPTER
Thirty-Four

"THERE ARE A FEW OTHER LOOSE ENDS," Brookins continued, "but we feel confident we can start putting a case together once we have both Ulbricht and Mavik behind bars." He nodded his head toward an institutional-style clock on the wall. "The Menelaus should be tying up at the port in less than an hour. We don't want to take a chance of alerting anyone about our plans, so we're arranged for Customs to hold a routine 'random' inspection as soon as she's secured. They'll ask to check three containers, one of which will just happen to contain the paintings. We'll pull them out of line as they're offloaded and take them to the Customs warehouse out of sight of any prying eyes. Dr. Berne flew in this morning and will do the official authentication; we're going to need him as a witness if it comes to a bail bond hearing. Once we've documented everything, Customs will issue a routine release for the container. I take it you've made all the arrangements for delivery to Atlanta?"

"I checked into that last week," Clair said. "Everything's taken care of. I was told that I have to show up and pay any customs duties."

"I assure you there won't be any," Kelly interjected.

"Thanks," she said and continued, "Then I'll sign some paperwork and call the truck line. They've promised to have it delivered before noon the day after tomorrow."

"And the day after that, Ulbricht shows up — checks in hand. We grab him, and you two are home free with half a million in your pocket," Kelly continued her sentence.

Clair shot him a sharp look. "Money is not going to bring my sister back, Mr. Kelly."

"I'm sorry" he said, embarrassed. "I didn't mean to imply that." He paused, momentarily at a loss for words. "Clair, our goals are the same as yours. We want to see Ulbricht in prison as much as you do. Because of what we think his role was your sister's death, and also to take someone out of circulation that we consider at threat to world peace." "Just don't lose sight of why we're here," Clair said coldly.

Brookins glanced at the clock again. "It's almost four, so we'd better be heading for the port. We're picking up Dr. Berne at his hotel in half an hour. Can you two meet us at the Georgia Ports Authority Administration Building at about five thirty? I'll draw you a map."

"Sure," I said. "We're just parked around the corner. We'll do a little sightseeing for an hour or so."

❧

THE GREEN COOLNESS of Reynolds Square was half a block away. We sat on a park bench under the watchful bronze eyes of a statue of John Wesley. Horse-drawn carriages filled with tourists slowly clip-clopped their way past us over cobblestone streets. We hadn't spoken since leaving the FBI office.

"What do you think?" I asked.

"I don't know," Clair said. "I just want this whole thing to be over." She peered off in the distance down Abercorn Street toward Oglethorpe Square, lost in thought. After a moment she said, "Are we supposed to be worried about Mavik, or what?"

"Who knows? Let's just get through it, okay?"

She didn't reply for a long while, then, "Afterwards" she paused, "Will I see you again?"

I let her voice echo about in my head. "I don't know." I tried to put the right words together. "Clair, seems like we've been through a lot together, but…" I stopped, not knowing what to say.

"But what?"

"I don't think I'll ever be able to…" I stopped again.

She waited a moment and said sharply, "Able to what? Nate, am I going to have to finish all your sentences for you?"

I looked at her, surprised. "I think, when it comes to relationships, I'm damaged goods. Ever since the divorce I've had this idea that given enough time I'd be back to 'normal,' whatever that means. But it hasn't happened. One part of me keeps saying that in spite of everything I'm still in love with Colette. Another part of me says 'Forget her! Get on with your life.' And god knows I've tried! I'm great at romantic dinners and one-night stands, but then something —"

Clair stood up abruptly, looking at her watch. "We need to go," she said and began walking toward where we'd parked the Tahoe.

THE PORT OF SAVANNAH was located a few miles upriver from the historic district, occupying nearly two square miles of a former cotton plantation. Brookins was waiting for us in the lobby of The Ports Authority Administration Building just outside of the entrance. He handed us ID badges as we followed him to his government-issued Crown Victoria parked in the lot beside the building.

The sun darted in and out of the clouds in the western sky, illuminating plumes of dust raised by the busy flow of trucks through the port's nearby gates. "The Menelaus tied up about an hour ago," he said. "Customs announced a 'random' inspection and they're offloading the containers now. They should be at the warehouse by the time we get there."

We flashed our badges at the guard as we drove through the access gate and headed toward what looked like a small city composed of square, multicolored buildings. As we drew closer, we could see that the "buildings" were in fact stacks of containers arranged in neat boxes on a massive paved storage lot.

Transport trucks scurried about like so many ants, feeding giant forklifts that gingerly raised and lowered the heavy containers to build and rebuild the ever-changing landscape. "This place operates like this twenty-four hours a day, three hundred and sixty-five days a year," Brookins said. "At any given time there's something like thirty thousand containers sitting here either coming in or going out, and this is just the trucking terminal. "Over there," he gestured with his head, "is a rail link yard that can get a container from here to, say, Detroit in forty-eight hours. I guess you can imagine why we worry so much about security. Just trying to inspect a small percentage of what comes through here is a huge job."

"You mean the government doesn't inspect every container that's brought into the country?" Clair asked.

Brookins laughed. "No way! Commerce would grind to a halt if we even tried. No, the official line is that Customs inspects 'one hundred percent' of all suspicious containers. In fact, the reality is they do good to inspect about five percent of 'em. Most of those are chosen because of the country of origin, or because they'd had a tip or a previous problem with a particular shipping line or broker. And what passes for an 'inspection' frequently means running a container past a large x-ray machine, on a bigger scale but not too much different from the kind they use at security checkpoints in airports. Like that one over there." He pointed to container parked next to a warehouse. Large automated steel boxes moved in tandem slowly down its sides.

"It's frighteningly easy to smuggle about anything you want into the U.S. Most of those drug and contraband seizures that you hear the Customs Service crowing about are the result of hot tips, not random finds as they'd have you believe. The actual number of visual inspections done as compared to the number of containers coming through the ports is minimal."

"Scary," Clair observed.

"Sure, but Customs is like the IRS. They try to do enough 'random' inspections to give the bad guys something to think about." He pulled into a parking place next to long, windowless warehouse. A set of steps led up to a door labeled "U.S. Customs. Authorized Personnel Only." We waited in the car while Brookins went inside to see if they were ready for us.

"Really scary," Clair said again after he'd left.

CHAPTER
Thirty-Five

KELLY STUCK HIS HEAD out the door and motioned for us to come in. We passed through a small office area into a massive warehouse. A sloping concrete ramp on either end allowed a smooth flow of containers to be carried in on "jockey trucks" for inspection and then out into the swirling activity of the port and on to their final destinations. A forty-foot gray container labeled Norseland SeaLane in bright blue letters was being driven into an inspection area. "That's it," he said.

Brookins, Berne and three other men wearing Customs uniforms stood to one side in a small knot watching as the driver parked his rig. I noticed Dr. Berne was wearing the same shirt and stained tie he'd worn in Paris. Clair and I were introduced to the group by our first names only, with Kelly's explanation that "they are working with us." A Customs agent whose nametag read "Stinson" clipped the seal on the rear of the container and lifted the latch. We huddled behind him as he pulled open the panel-like doors to reveal a cargo of meticulously wrapped tables, chairs, chests and mirrors interspersed with sealed crates, all lashed down to prevent damage on the trans-Atlantic voyage. Stinson studied a bill of lading and said, "We should be looking for fairly small crates labeled," he squinted at the list, "'N-34-A' and 'N-34-B.' Let's get to work."

The three customs agents began unloading the items, checking each number off the list as they did so. Only a dozen pieces had been taken out when one of them said, "Got 'em" and pointed to two flat wooden boxes, each about three feet high by two feet wide and no more than six inches thick. The numbers N-34-A and N-34-B were clearly stenciled next to "Fragile!" in bold red letters. The first crate was handed off and placed on a worktable in a pool of bright white light from a metal halide lamp suspended overhead.

Berne excitedly paced back and forth, watching as the customs agents removed the long screws that held the panels of the first box in place. They slid off the top to reveal styrofoam pellets cushioning a flat object swathed in soft white plastic foam. Two men lifted it out and cautiously began to unwrap the cover.

It was not much to see at first: a painting of flowers in faded colors on what appeared to be a simple wooden board. There was no frame. A small, yellowed tag was affixed to the back with a thumbtack. Berne donned a pair of white cotton gloves and held it up with a sense of reverence, turning it back and forth under the light, marveling at the brushstrokes. "Amazing!" he said to no one in particular. I moved closer. I could see that the tag was stamped with an eagle and swastika above a long handwritten notation and series of numbers.

The second crate was opened with equal care. Although larger and with brighter details and colors, it too was unframed and painted on a wooden panel. There were some numbers scrawled on the back in what appeared to be white chalk, but the painting bore no tag or other label. Brookins broke the silence, "They're not painted on canvas?"

Berne gave him a look of disdain. "No. No, of course not! Most works of this era were executed on flat panels of aged oak, carefully dried and smoothed to an almost mirror-like finish. They were then primed with gesso, and —" Catching himself, he stopped suddenly and said, "No, they were usually painted on wood."

He held the larger painting as he had the first and studied the brushstrokes under the bright light. "Do you realize what we're seeing? These paintings are nearly four hundred years old and are as exquisite as the day the artist first touched his brush to the canvas, or in this case, the *wood*, Mr. Brookins." He held up the smaller of the two. "This one here, the Brueghel, is unusual in that the artist usually painted his floral works on sheets of copper. That fact alone makes it unique and quite priceless. But more than that, do you realize these works have been missing for over sixty years! Consider for a moment what the world lost."

"Dr. Berne," Kelly interrupted him. "I know you've got a lot of documentation to do and we need to keep things on schedule. Why don't we just get out of your way and let you do work?"

"Oh, yes. Right," Berne said, as if he'd been awakened from a daydream. We moved away while he unlatched a sturdy aluminum case and extracted a camera, a set of magnifying loupes that clipped to his glasses, and what appeared to be a battery powered ultraviolet light source. "It'll take me a good hour for both. Did you know that artists of this era compounded their own pigments?" When we didn't reply he opened a small notebook, scribbled an entry and began to examine the paintings.

Kelly and Brookins bought Cokes and crackers from a vending machine. We made idle conversation in the break room while Berne toiled away under the watchful eyes of the Customs agents. Forty-five minutes later Stinson stuck his head in and said, "I think you'd better get in here."

Berne was standing over the table illuminated by bright light in the otherwise dimly lit warehouse. The paintings were neatly laid out before him. He was staring at them through a hand-held magnifying glass while shaking his head in a barely perceptible motion and muttering to himself. "I can't believe it," I heard him saying as we walked up.

"Is there a problem, Dr. Berne?" Kelly asked.

"Uh, no. Well, yes. There is." A pause. "Or there isn't depending on how you want to see it." Another pause. "Or perhaps I should say that there could be a problem depending on your perspective."

"Would you just get to the point, please?"

"Sorry. Of course. It's just that I've never seen anything like these. They're... they... how shall I put it? Exquisite. But that's the word I used before. No, I'll have to say that they're unbelievably good. In fact they're the best I've ever seen."

"Dr. Berne, we realize all that." Kelly was clearly annoyed. "You yourself said that they're worth millions of dollars. If that's not enough, they're quite likely the cause of at least one, and possibly two, deaths. I don't pretend to know anything about art and its value, but works by Brueghel and Hals —"

"No, no. That's just it. They're not by Brueghel and Hals."

"What are you talking about?"

"I was saying that in all the twenty-five years of my academic career, I've never seen such good work." He put down his magnifying lens and looked straight at Kelly. "They're fakes, Mr. Kelly. The best I've ever seen, but still fakes."

CHAPTER
Thirty-Six

KELLY OPENED HIS MOUTH as if to speak and then shut it, not knowing what to say. The sound of a honking horn could be heard above the hum of the cranes in the distance. The persistent ringing of an unanswered telephone somewhere in the warehouse finally stopped.

"Are you telling us, Dr. Berne, that these paintings are not originals?" Kelly demanded, having found his voice.

"Oh, no, they're originals all right. Just not *the* originals. They're very, very well done forgeries; at least I *think* they are. They had me fooled at first. In fact, they're almost perfect."

"But how?" Kelly said.

"Let me finish. I was fully prepared to sign off on them as seventeenth century works by Hals and Brueghel, but knowing that I'd probably have to testify in court, I thought it would be good to have a couple of other routine tests that most experts would consider quite superfluous. There's a white pigment called titanium dioxide that wasn't even discovered until the 1820's and not available in a form suitable for artists' use until at least a hundred years later. I did a simple little test for it that should have been negative. It was positive. I couldn't believe it — I thought it had to be a mistake — so I did another test for lead carbonate. That's the substance that was used as the primary base for most white paints through the end of the nineteenth century. It was negative when it should have been positive." Berne picked up the floral painting, tilting it back and forth in the light. "I… I just don't know. I've never run into something like this. The quality of the work, it's... it's astounding."

"So you're saying that these are forgeries?" Kelly asked.

"Well, yes, or maybe no. I *can* say with certainty that they date from the twentieth century, but they came close to fooling me. This Brueghel here has a classification tag stamped with a swastika and dated 1943. It looks original but who knows? I've got to do some research as to when these works were actually added to the Schloss collection. There's always a possibility they were fakes from the outset.

Perhaps some clever forger created them for the sole purpose of selling them to a rich and unsuspecting art collector like Adolphe Schloss. Or that somewhere along the way someone snatched the real ones and replaced them with these copies. These paintings — real or fake — could be the very ones that were confiscated by the Nazis. It's even conceivable that the so-called originals never even existed and what the art world has been searching for all along are merely twentieth century copies. It's been known to happen before. I really need to get this to a laboratory where I can do more sophisticated testing. I'm going to need a scanning EM, infrared photography capability, stereoradiography."

"So we have no evidence these particular works were definitely part of the Schloss collection?" Kelly asked.

"Nope. In fact, they probably don't even qualify under the usual definition as being antiques. I'm sorry."

Brookins slammed his fist into his hand. Kelly bit his lip and murmured, "There goes our case," then more loudly, "I need to check with Washington."

Clair and I had watched the exchange with an increasing sense of disbelief. "Mr. Kelly," she said, "are you saying that now you don't have a case against Ulbricht?"

"No." He hesitated. "Well, I'm not sure. If we're going to arrest him, we've got to have a charge that will allow us to keep him behind bars and incommunicado while we make a coordinated series of arrests at half a dozen spots in Europe and the Middle East. We've got to rethink our strategy. I'll call Commissioner Levin."

One of the Customs officers stuck his head out of the office door and yelled, "Agent Kelly. Your office is on the phone. They say it's urgent."

"Hang on a sec, Clair. Let me take this call and I'll be right back." He half ran toward the office area.

I put my hand on Clair's back. "It'll work out."

She whirled around and glared at me. "Just where did you get that idea? And don't tell me you're sorry again. You've said it so many times in the last three weeks, you're beginning to sound like a broken record. It's not your damned fault! It's nobody's fault. Somewhere out there amongst the gods and goddesses who make the world spin around someone's laughing. One of them — maybe a whole gaggle of them for all I know — are rolling on the floor of heaven saying, 'Hey, let's see what else we can throw her way. Why don't we —'" She was suddenly quiet as Kelly reappeared at the office door. His face was grim as he motioned for Brookins to come over. They huddled for a moment, speaking rapidly in muted voices. Brookins listened intently, glancing in our direction every few moments. They seemed to reach some kind of agreement. Kelly nodded and reached for his cell phone. Brookins walked toward us, smiling mechanically. His body language said he was trying to look calm.

"Something's come up," he said. "We need to talk. Kelly's making a call. He'll meet us in the break room in just a minute." We followed Brookins back inside the office area and sat down, waiting for Kelly.

"I take it there's a problem," I said.

"Of course," Clair said. "One more little hang-up. One more little twist of the knife." She sounded bitter.

Kelly appeared at the door. He shut it and sat down. "Clair, Nate, I just got word that the Secretary of Homeland Security has raised the Alert Level from yellow to orange."

"Meaning?" Clair asked without waiting for him to explain.

"Meaning that there is a high and immediate risk of a terrorist attack inside the borders of the United States. Every available agent is being called back to duty. All non-essential investigations are temporarily being put on hold. Unfortunately, that includes this one. We're being sent to New Orleans. The official announcement hasn't been made yet but will be within the hour. Apparently they've picked up on some specific, credible and verifiable information that al Qaeda operatives already in the U.S. are planning an attack either in the city itself or on one of the chemical complexes to the north along the Mississippi River. They've got some good leads, but to follow them up is going to require massive manpower."

"So where does that leave us?" Clair asked, clearly angry.

"We're not stopping this investigation by any means, and I want you to understand and believe that. It's simply become a matter of priorities. We've got an entire city and millions of people at risk. I can promise you we'll be back on the case just as soon as we have the situation in south Louisiana under control."

"And in the meantime?"

"Well, I hate to admit it, but we'd probably have to scuttle our plans to arrest Ulbricht anyway. The charge of smuggling stolen art works just fell apart."

"What do you expect us to do, then?" I asked.

"Go through with the deal as planned. We'll have other opportunities. We'll get him. Look, it's better to build an airtight case and make an arrest that will stick than to risk having his lawyers spring him because we didn't do our homework. No, as long as he doesn't suspect that we're after him we're still in the game. Sooner or later he'll let his guard down."

"Bullshit!" Clair spit.

Kelly took a deep breath. "I know how you feel, but it's beyond our control at this point. Just trust us, will you? You have the FBI's promise — my promise — that we'll see this through to the end. I'll do whatever I can to help you."

"You know, Mr. Kelly," Clair said, "there is one thing you can do. You can answer a question. I think you owe it to me. There's something that's been gnawing at me for weeks. Something Steed said in Paris."

"What's that?"

"Do you remember the meeting we had at Nate's office the day after we first saw Ulbricht?"

"Yes, there were four of us there, you two plus Steed and me."

"Steed made some reference to 'additional confidential information' and said that 'I'm not allowed to share that with you.' Remember?"

"Vaguely, yes."

"I want to know what it was. Did it have something to do with Becky?"

Kelly hesitated and looked at Brookins who gave a small shrug. "Yes. Why do you ask?"

"Curiosity, mainly. A sense of closure. I can't really say. I just want to know."

"It probably doesn't matter now, anyway," Kelly said, looking again at Brookins who gave an almost imperceptible nod. "We believe it has little or nothing to do with her murder, or even with Ulbricht."

"Tell me," Clair demanded. "I want to know everything."

"Okay." Kelly took a deep breath. "Part of the mission of the FBI, together with other governmental agencies, is to keep a close watch on groups that have the potential for domestic terrorism. Take Timothy McVeigh and the Oklahoma City bombing. One of the arguments in the press was that if we'd been doing our jobs the whole tragedy might have been prevented. On the other side of the coin, you have civil libertarians screaming that we — the government — are constantly violating their First and Fourth Amendment rights. We have to walk a very thin line in what we do. So long as we don't restrict what is said, the courts have generally allowed us to monitor public speech, and various public forums such as internet chat rooms, web logs, et cetera.

"You recall that I said we were monitoring Becky's emails? One of the things we discovered was her active interest, if not her participation, in what I can only describe as racist groups. We don't have any idea how long it had been going on, or how she got involved. Her anger — and that's the only word to describe it — seems to have its origin in what happened to your father. She used an assumed name, of course, but we had no trouble tracing the origin back to her computer. There were a number of postings in which she expressed her desire for retribution — revenge even — against the people she blamed for your father's death."

"Who were?" I asked.

"The blacks. The city of Atlanta. The prison system. But I want to make it clear she didn't advocate open violence, we'd probably have paid her a visit if she did that. No, from what I saw she was hiding deep in her soul an abiding anger and an unsatisfied need to somehow punish those whom she believed had hurt her family." He turned to Clair. "Did you know she felt that way?"

"I had no idea, but it seems to confirm some suspicions I've had."

"Meaning?"

"It doesn't matter. She's dead and it's best forgotten."

"I want to ask, but I won't," Kelly said, glancing at his watch. "We really need to leave. We've got to get back into town, pick up our gear and get on a plane for New Orleans. Dr. Berne is going to have to find his own way back to his hotel." He paused, and then said, "Before we go though, I have a question for *you*, Clair. Something that's been rattling about in my mind."

"Looks like we're being upfront with one another for a change. Shoot."

"When we were debriefing you about your meeting with Ulbricht, you said he mentioned something about Becky talking with a Syrian wanting to sell some antique Islamic ceramics. Remember that?"

"Yes, but it didn't seem to have any bearing on anything else."

"True." Kelly stroked his jaw and looked at his watch again. "But you'd mentioned 'suspicions.' You don't think Becky held any hostility that would — how should I phrase this? — lead her to seek retribution against the American government or any particular target in the U.S.?"

"No, of course not! Why would you even ask?"

"Because we were monitoring Becky's phone calls, remember? This contact, this Syrian who allegedly wanted to sell her something. We know she met with him at least once."

"So?"

"He's an operative for the Syrian government. A go-between for the various radical Islamist movements they support. Like you said, it probably doesn't matter now but I just thought you might want to know."

CHAPTER
Thirty-Seven

BROOKINS AND KELLY DROPPED us off in the parking lot of the Administration Building. We hadn't exchanged a dozen words since leaving the Customs warehouse. I opened the door for Clair then climbed in and started the Tahoe. The clock on the panel read seven forty-nine. The sun was beginning to dip below the tree line in the western sky. "Where to?" I asked. "If we push it we can make it back to Atlanta by midnight."

"I don't want to go back to Atlanta, Nate."

"Want me to call my parents? We can be there in a little more than an hour."

"No."

"All right." I sat and waited for her response.

"It's been a bad day. A really bad day. I don't want to ride through the dark for four or five hours wondering what might happen. Wondering why Becky — "

"Okay, then." I stopped her. "It's not Paris and I don't have any pull with the maitre de's here, but I'll bet we can find a good restaurant and decent bottle of wine if we try."

"You're on." It was the first time I'd seen her smile all day.

∽

FIVE COURSES, THREE HOURS and two bottles of Sancerre later, we were the only patrons left in the dining room of the small restaurant on Broughton Street. Our waiter shifted back and forth on his heels while a low hum of voices and an occasional burst of laughter could be heard from the attached bar next door. We'd talked, not about Ulbricht, or the paintings, or the FBI or Becky, but about France and Paraguay, about the music we liked and the books we'd read, and about how we both were suspicious of men who wore white tennis shoes, especially with short little anklet socks. The waiter finally crept over to say, "Sir, the kitchen has been closed for an hour. Do you think perhaps I might find you a table in the bar area?"

We both looked at our watches and realized we'd lost track of the time. "Forgive me," I said. "We were enjoying ourselves so much, we didn't realize the time." I called for the check and left him a large tip.

We'd parked the car in one of the municipal parking lots nearby. I felt for the keys in my pocket. The night was warm and a full moon had climbed halfway up the eastern night sky. "I really don't think it would be a good idea for me to drive. Why don't we see if we can find some rooms for the night? And maybe take a walk on the riverfront?"

"In which order?" Clair smiled, slightly tipsy.

"I think a little walk in the fresh air might do us both some good."

227

Clair linked her arm in mine as we strolled in the direction of Bay Street and the riverfront parks. "The last time we did this was in Paris," she reminded me. "But it was so cold!"

"I remember," I said. "I was just getting to know you."

"Do you think you know me now?"

"Can you ever really know anyone? And even when you think you do, how can you be sure? People are like onions."

"Vidalia onions?" Clair laughed. "Crunchy and sweet, to hear your mother talk."

"No, not like that. They have layers. You peel one off and find another. And then another. You never know what's coming next."

We ran hand-in-hand across Bay Street and half-stumbled down the stone steps to the riverfront. The sound of a jazz band filtered out of one of the bars. Clair sat down on a bench.

"But what would happen, Nate, if you really could know someone completely? What would you have if you took that onion and peeled off layer after layer until there were no more?"

"I don't know. What?"

"You'd have nothing. You would have seen it all. There'd be nothing new to anticipate. No uncertainty, no mystery, no hope even." She looked up at the moon and brushed her hair out of her face. "You're right, I think. People *are* like onions, but to know them completely — to know everything about them — is to destroy them."

"But what about — "

"It's called trust, Nate. Or faith. Or the foolish conviction that no matter how bad things seem they have a way of working out for the best in the end."

A large container ship quietly loomed into view as it headed out to sea from the port area upriver. Pretending to watch its progress I said, "Once upon a time I thought I knew someone."

"People don't come with guarantees. Maybe you *did* know her at one time. Maybe she changed — or maybe it was you that changed." Clair peered at the ship, now only a couple of hundred yards away.

"So what is one supposed to do?"

"The same thing we all do at one time or another. Let our shields down. Become vulnerable. Risk failure but hope for success. It would take a change — especially for you."

"I sometimes wish I knew where to start."

"Let me give you a push." Clair turned and placing her hands softly on my cheeks, kissed me. I presume the captain of the container ship was watching us as he passed. He gave a long blast of the ship's horn.

I WAS AWAKENED by the sound of Clair speaking with someone. "I am *so* sorry, I overslept," she was saying. For a moment I couldn't remember where I was. I opened my eyes. Sunlight streaming through half-opened shutters cast a pattern of light and dark striations on the wall and ceiling. The deep sound of a ship's horn echoed off the river in the distance.

She paused, listening, then, "Okay, let me speak with him, please." Another pause, "Mr. Miller, this is Clair Tate. I'm calling for Tate Interiors. I apologize, but I was supposed to call you at eight this morning and let you know the container cleared customs without problems and it's ready for you to pick up. I won't make up any excuses; I just overslept."

I turned over in the bed, pushing a large feather pillow out of my face. I could see Clair sitting on the other side, her long dark hair cascading over her naked shoulders. I could barely hear a male voice replying to her on the phone. "No, that wasn't me. I'm sorry, I just woke up and I guess I'm not making myself clear. I'm Clair Tate from Tate Interiors in Atlanta. We just got a container in through the port here in Savannah that you're supposed to deliver to Atlanta."

A pause.

"That's right. Tate Interiors."

Another pause.

"No, I *didn't* call!" I could sense her annoyance. "That's what I'm saying. I forgot and overslept. My instructions were to call your office by eight this morning to confirm the container had cleared customs, so you could pick it up and take it to Atlanta."

The voice on the other end seemed to be explaining something. Clair looked back at me and silently mouthed, "Good morning," then frowned at the phone. "No, Mr. Miller, that can't be right. I was asleep." She listened for another moment and said, "No, I'm pretty sure no one from my office called, especially at six-thirty in the morning."

She looked back at me and smiled, shrugging her shoulders and pointing at the receiver.

"Well, okay. I'll wait for your call." She read him the number from the phone and hung up the receiver.

"What's up?" I asked.

"You're going to be in a minute," she laughed, and slid back between the sheets. "Just some little mix-up at the trucking company about getting the container picked up. They're going to get it straightened out and call me back. In the meantime..."

HALF AN HOUR LATER the phone rang. Without raising her head from my arm Clair reached out for the receiver. She listened for a moment, sat up suddenly in bed and said, "What?" The voice on the other end spoke rapidly. She glanced at the bedside clock and said, "We'll be there in half an hour."

CHAPTER
Thirty-Eight

IT TOOK US THIRTY-FOUR MINUTES to get dressed and drive from the inn on Bay Street to the Savannah terminal of Stetson Freight Lines. As we moved upriver, the city shed its tourist-perfect riverfront facade to reveal the gritty business end of town. The trucking yard was located in a run-down district near the port. A twelve-foot high chain link fence topped with barbed wire perfectly described the neighborhood. A surly looking guard at the gate waved us through when we gave him our names. Inside the fence a dozen-odd dark green tractor-trailers were being washed and serviced while several others seemed to be undergoing repairs in a large steel-framed shop.

We parked in front of a flat-roofed brick building and entered through a glass door marked "Office." Brown paneling that matched the color of the stained brown carpet sheathed the interior. Three drivers sat lounging in a small waiting area, smoking and drinking coffee from white styrofoam cups. A heavy-set, middle-aged man wearing a short-sleeved white shirt and a nervous expression was waiting for us. He extended his hand, "Ms. Tate, I'm Leonard Miller. I think we may have run into a little problem here, but I'm sure we can solve it." Clair introduced me. I could sense frustration in her voice.

We were shown into a small brown-paneled conference room. Miller offered coffee, we declined. He shut the door, sat down and began, "Ms. Tate, according to our records someone called this morning at six twenty-eight and said they were calling for Tate Interiors. They told us your container had cleared customs and we could pick it up routinely at the Garden City Terminal. Now, I went over this carefully with the girl who took the message. All she could tell me was that the caller was a man and he had all the right information — the correct container and bill of lading numbers, your address on Miami Circle in Atlanta, and so forth. Just a routine call, really. No reason to suspect anything."

"I can assure you that neither Nate nor I called," Clair replied.

"I know, and I believe you! Before I called you back I checked with your place in Atlanta, thinking maybe they'd called. They said they hadn't. Anyway," he continued, consulting a clipboard, "we dispatched a truck at six-fifty. The driver called at seven forty-two to say he was leaving the port gate and would be heading for I-16 and then on up to Atlanta. You called me about nine-thirty, and I then called you back shortly after ten. I'm not exactly sure what's going on, but I don't like it. I haven't been able to get the driver on his phone, but then there are some patches along the interstate that have poor coverage. Now, I want you to know we're responsible for your goods, and we're going to find out what's going on. I haven't called the police as yet."

233

"Mr. Miller," I interrupted him, "what are you implying? Do you think the container has been stolen?"

He glanced away quickly and then back at me. "Well, no. Not at this time anyway. It may be that we have a problem with the driver, though. His name's Pete Norris. He's fairly new, and well, heck, let me just show you something. You can see for yourself why I'm a little worried."

Miller led us down the corridor to a large open room. On one side, four employees were hunched over desks, simultaneously talking on cordless headsets and typing data into their computers. On the other, three large computer screens displayed maps of the southeastern United States. "This is our dispatch center." Miller explained. "The folks here at the desks are taking orders and pairing them with our drivers on the road.

"We operate mainly on the east coast, but we'll pick up or deliver cargo anywhere in the U.S. if we can make a profit on it. Now over here," he said, pointing at the maps on the screens, "is what we call our Tracking Center. All of our owned or leased trucks are equipped with GPS receivers and bi-directional satellite communication gear. At any given point in time, we can tell exactly where our trucks are, down to ten or twelve feet one way or the other. The system's been a real help with scheduling and also making sure our drivers don't get lost or otherwise go astray."

Clair frowned slightly and gave me a worried look. "Just get to the bottom line, Mr. Miller, will you? Has your truck gone missing?"

"Oh, no," he replied hastily, "Not at all. It just looks like our driver has decided to take a little detour. Let me show you." He sat down at a keyboard in front of a large flat panel monitor. "Now, with this system, we can tell exactly where a truck's been, how fast he's traveled, and how long he spends at every stop. I know it sounds kind of

'Big Brother', but it's probably saved us its cost ten times over." He tapped a few keys and a map of the Savannah area filled the screen. A few more strokes caused a blinking green dot to appear next to the Savannah River.

"Okay. Here we are at seven-thirty this morning. You see this green dot here? That's the truck that's hauling your container. Now, if I use the mouse to click on this button here, I can track what happens next." He clicked on an icon on the screen and the green dot began to move, leaving a broken red line behind it. A small digital clock at the upper left of the screen tracked the time. Miller continued, "Here you can see that the truck gets on I-16 headed toward Atlanta shortly after eight." He clicked on the icon as the green dot headed west. "Now, here's where something strange happens. About fifteen miles up the road, he pulls off at Exit 143 and heads toward the little town of Blitchton on Highway 80.

"The town's not much more than a wide spot in the road, so your first thought might be that maybe the driver had to go to the bathroom or something like that. Instead of stopping, though, he heads west on 80 and then turns off on a dirt road right here." He clicked on another icon and the map zoomed in to show the blinking green dot a short distance off a small road. The clock on the screen showed eight forty-six.

"And where is he now?" Clair asked.

"Right there, I'm afraid," Miller replied, clicking on a box labeled "Real-Time." The clock on the screen displayed the current time. "Looks like he's been parked there a couple of hours."

I could see that Clair was getting angry. "Mr. Miller, that truck — that container — is carrying antiques worth thousands of dollars."

"Don't worry, Ms. Tate. It's going to make it, I promise." Miller looked nervous.

"But you said you couldn't reach the driver on his phone. What's going on?"

"Well, it may be that he's in a dead zone, but I've talked with a few of the other drivers and I suspect something else is going on."

"Such as?"

"I'm embarrassed to say it, but I think this Norris fellow's got a girlfriend up there. He's only been with us a couple of months, but one of the other drivers said he's been having some marital problems and had started seeing a woman who lives between here and Statesboro. He's probably just taking a little detour to get him some, I mean, he's probably just visiting his friend."

"Mr. Miller." Clair was livid. "I want you to call the police. Now!"

"Ms. Tate, let's not do that right yet. I'm sure that — "

"Now!" She glared at him. "If you don't I will."

"Hold on, hold on!" Miller was sweating. "We don't really need to get the police involved. That generates a whole lot of paperwork and reports. I think we can handle this within the company. I promise you the fellow's gonna lose his job."

"Okay, then *I'm* calling," Clair said as she reached in her pocket for her cell phone.

"Wait a minute! I have an idea. Why don't I just ride up there and check on things myself? It's not much more than half an hour's drive from here if I take the interstate. I'll take a backup driver with me. That way if the situation is what I think it is, I'll fire the guy on the spot and have the other driver take over the delivery. Please let me handle it this way. I'd really appreciate it." He seemed to be begging.

Clair fingered her cell phone, thinking for a moment. "On one condition," she said.

"Name it."

"We're going with you."

Miller took a deep breath, considering his options. He clearly was not eager to have company. "All right. Let's get moving." He typed few letters on the keyboard and a nearby printer spit out an enlarged map showing the location of the blinking green dot. "I've got the map. We can take one of the company trucks."

Miller spoke briefly to a secretary and then to one of the men that had been lounging in the small lobby. "This is Mike," he said. "He's going to be our backup driver." We walked across the parking lot to a dark green extended cab Ford F-250 pickup bearing the cowboy hat logo of Stetson Freight Lines. Clair and I climbed in the back. Miller drove in silence while Mike fidgeted and kept reaching for his shirt pocket, wanting a cigarette but knowing better than to ask permission to smoke.

As we turned on the interstate ramp Clair whispered, "There're just too many things going on, Nate. I don't like it."

CHAPTER
Thirty-Nine

WE DROVE WEST in the bright morning sunlight for twenty minutes. Mike tried to make conversation but rapidly ran out of things to say. Miller made several attempts to assure us that Stetson rarely had any problems with their drivers, their safety record was one of the best in the industry, and so on until Clair finally told him politely to shut up. The sign for Exit 143 read "To Hwy.80." We left the interstate and drove north through pine plantations to the crossroads town of Blitchton. Miller's description had been accurate. The only viable enterprise appeared to be a large convenience store selling groceries and off-brand gasoline. An abandoned filling station had been reincarnated as Doodle's Café promising Blue Plate Specials and "Kuntry Kookin." Several boarded-up businesses with peeling paint were scattered haphazardly up and down the highway.

Miller consulted his map and turned west on Highway 80 toward Statesboro. "It looks like we should come up on a dirt road on our left about five miles down this way." Mike slapped at his shirt pocket and shifted back and forth. Clair and I said nothing. We drove past a long dead motel whose sign still offered "Clean Cheap Rooms." Small saplings poked up through the broken pavement of the parking lot. A small waving field of cattails grew in the abandoned swimming pool. Just beyond a burned out single-wide mobile home, we tuned south on a well-maintained dirt road.

"If he hasn't left, the truck should be somewhere up here on our right," Miller said. "It's going to be off the road — probably down a driveway or parked at someone's house. We'll be coming up on it in just a minute, so keep your eyes open." The road led through a forest of young planted pines marked by small tags every hundred yards or so, indicating the land was owned by International Paper.

Just beyond a sharp curve a graveled driveway led to a wide logging road that disappeared into the woods. Miller slowed the truck while Mike rolled down his window and peered out at the tracks. "There's been some heavy traffic through here," he said, pointing toward the road.

"Doesn't look like the driveway to a house," Miller observed, obviously worried. We turned in. A yellow gate barred the entrance. Mike got out to check it, inspecting the tracks in the moist earth.

"I'd say a big rig's been in and out of here this morning," he yelled. "I can see two sets of tracks." He reached the gate and unhooked the chain. There was no lock. He pushed it open and climbed back in the truck. We drove slowly into the woods.

"We've probably missed him. Odds are he was just meeting someone back in here. Probably some married woman. Drops her kids off with her mama and tells her she's going to the grocery but really plans to meet her boyfriend." Miller sounded somewhat relieved. "Happens all the time, but if they're going to screw around I wish like hell that they'd do it on their own." He stopped suddenly as we rounded a curve in the road. A large clearing lay before us. Parked in the middle was a dark green truck cab bearing the Stetson name and the cowboy hat logo. The trailer with the container was nowhere to be seen.

"What the hell?" Miller said simultaneously with Mike's "Shit!" Clair and I just stared.

Miller pulled the pickup to the edge of the road and switched off the ignition. The four of us walked cautiously into the clearing. Mike seemed interested in the pattern of tracks. Miller stared at the truck. He turned to Clair. "Ms. Tate, we *do* have a problem."

Mike said, "Come 'ere. Look at these tracks." He pointed at the ground. "I'd say he had another truck cab waiting here for him. Just pulled in, dropped the load from the company truck, hitched it up to his'un, and he's on his way. Stupid son of a bitch! He oughta know he ain't gonna get very far."

Miller climbed up on the running board of the Stetson truck and peered through the window. "Least he left the keys in it." He opened the door and climbed in, inspecting the seats and looking back into the sleeper compartment. "Now here's a crazy thing. The guy left his duffle. Guess he figures he won't need it."

Clair had said nothing. Turning to me she asked, "How much worse can it get, Nate? The paintings turn out to be fake, the FBI's put Becky's murder investigation on the back burner, the whole damned container — not to mention the paintings — has been stolen. What else could go wrong?"

"I don't know, but why do I think we're missing something?" I replied. "This driver — whoever he is — wouldn't have any idea of what the antiques in the container were worth, and even if he did, he couldn't just fence them at his local pawn shop. No, there's something bigger going on here. It's got to be an inside job. You don't suppose Ulbricht would have anything to do with this? Or maybe someone at the port?" Clair just shook her head.

Mike was leaning against the truck smoking a cigarette. Miller was speaking rapidly to someone on his cell phone. He clipped it back on his belt and yelled over to us, "I've called the sheriff. They say they can be here in about fifteen minutes. I'm going to walk back out to the road to make sure they don't miss the driveway. In the meantime they say that we need to stay away from the truck and the clearing. They want to look for footprints and take casts of the tire tracks. Okay?"

Mike walked to the edge of the clearing and leaned against a small pine. We came over and stood next to him. At one time the open area must have been a logging yard. The timber beyond had been cut and loaded here, and the land restocked. Now young planted pines aligned in straight rows disappeared toward the western horizon in the distance. "There's something wrong here," Mike observed. "Ain't nobody in his right mind gonna be so stupid as to steal a trailer like that. Miller wants to blame this fellow Norris, but something funny's going on."

"How do you mean?" I asked.

"Yeah, the guy may be having some problems with his old lady, and yeah, he might make a few grand selling a stolen trailer, but it don't make sense — ain't worth it. And, too, if I was him the first thing I'd do is smash that damned GPS tracking system." I noticed he'd been looking out across the pines. He was quiet for a moment, then said, "See them birds up there?" He gestured with his cigarette toward two large black birds flying tight circles over the pines. "Buzzards. One I'll give you. When there's two of 'em, I'm gonna worry. Come on. Let's check this out."

241

Stubbing out his smoke on the tree, he set out down a row of pines, gesturing for us to follow.

We had walked only a short distance when Mike pointed at the earth. "Fresh tracks. Let's move over one row so's we don't mess 'em up." A hundred yards further on we found the body of Pete Norris, the back of his skull blown away by a point-blank gunshot to his forehead.

CHAPTER
Forty

CLAIR PACED BACK AND FORTH as she had for the last half hour, watching as the techs from the GBI crime scene van measured, photographed, and dusted for fingerprints. Stopping for a moment, she leaned against the blue and white Georgia State Patrol cruiser and pronounced, "We've got to call the FBI."

"What are they going to do that's not going to make things worse?" I asked. "This case has turned into a truck hijacking and murder investigation. Anyway, they're probably going to get called in no matter what — those are Federal crimes. I worry more about telling Ulbricht. Since the paintings are fakes, the FBI doesn't have an excuse to arrest him. That means we've got to deal with him. What are we going to say to him when he shows up Thursday to pick them up and finds out they've been stolen? He's got to believe that they're real, and whomever he intends to sell them to must believe it, too. Otherwise the guy wouldn't be forking out fifteen million bucks. Explaining that the FBI has joined the hunt for the container is only going to spook him. And that's just our immediate problem."

"How so?"

"If the container gets recovered, it's probably going to be held as evidence. They'll be sure to make an inventory and appraisal of the contents, and that's going to lead to the 'discovery' of the stolen art works. They're good enough to have fooled several of Ulbricht's experts. Who's going to get the blame for trying to smuggle them into the States?"

Clair frowned, "Becky of course — or me."

"Right! And that means we'll have to call in experts to prove they're fakes. How do we explain to Ulbricht we knew all along that they were simply good copies? I can't see the FBI stepping up to take credit for a botched sting operation. I really don't see any good options."

"Nate, you know we've got to at least contact Kelly and Brookins — even if they don't do anything about it. We need to let them know what's happened. And we've got to try to reach Ulbricht. They said he was booked on a flight from Berlin the day after tomorrow. If we just explain to him what's happened he probably won't come. That will at least give us some breathing room. You know the Feds still want him, and he seems to be the only real link to solving Becky's murder. When this whole Orange Alert thing blows over we can meet with the FBI and work out another game plan."

"Yeah, but what if he thinks *we* arranged to have the truck hijacked? Consider this: what kind of man would hire Henri Mavik as his driver? He's got to know his background. And I'm still not sure he wasn't the one who tried to have me killed in Paris. Remember, he told us he'll do whatever it takes to make a deal work. We're talking about paintings he thinks are worth at least fifteen million at a private sale and twice that or more on the open market. As far as he knows, we're the only other people who know the true contents of that container. He'll read the police report and see that some man called in this morning and told them to pick up the load. Remember what Miller said, the caller had the right bill of lading number, the correct address in Atlanta. Who would know that besides you and me? Clair, I'm not an especially big believer in the goodness of mankind. A lot of people wouldn't hesitate to commit murder for fifteen million bucks. Your call to Miller at nine-thirty this morning could just as well have been to establish an alibi."

"You suppose the GBI and local sheriff are going to develop that line of thinking?"

"Who knows? You bring Brookins' and Ulbricht's phone numbers with you?"

"No, they're back at the hotel."

"Then we need to get back to Savannah. Fast!"

WE WERE QUESTIONED for an hour, first by the sheriff's investigator for Bryan County and then by an agent named Sonny Griffin from the Georgia Bureau of Investigation's Savannah Office. We gave them only the simple facts, avoiding all mention of the FBI, Ulbricht and the supposedly stolen art works. They were courteous and direct, giving no indication we were in any way suspected of having a part in the crime. Clair gave them her home and business numbers in Atlanta. I told them I could be contacted through the office of Madeleine Tours. A State Patrol officer named Durden gave us a ride back to the hotel in Savannah.

We reached Kelly without problems. He said he had just arrived in New Orleans and was assigned to "following up leads." He wouldn't say more. When we told him what had happened he simply said, "Damn!" and was speechless for so long that I actually thought we'd been disconnected. I explained to him our concerns and he promised he'd pass them on. "This terrorist issue is real, though, Nate," he explained. "I can't give you the details — they're confidential — but we're so sure we're right on this one that we've pulled in every available agent from across the U.S. We're talking about a whole American city here; we can't afford to have another 9/11."

"What can you do to help us?"

"Don't know at this point. That investigation has been put on hold for the moment. I'll pass it on. We want to keep the FBI's name out of it if at all possible. Too many questions to answer. I promise you this though; I'll make sure you two don't get in any trouble. Gotta go. Call me if they recover the trailer." He hung up.

"Any luck?" Clair asked.

"Not really. Their focus is on New Orleans at this point. He said he'd keep us out of trouble, whatever that means." I looked at Ulbricht's number. "Do you want to talk with him, or shall I?"

"I probably should. You only met with him that once. I think the bastard still harbors hopes of getting into my pants. We probably should start with his cell phone." Clair dialed the number on the bedside phone, using a credit card to pay for the call. I listened on the extension in the bathroom. After fifteen rings she hung up.

"Want to try the Berlin office next?" She glanced at her watch. "It's just past ten at night there. Suppose someone will be answering the phone?"

She punched in the numbers. An efficient sounding male voice answered on the second ring, "Sinon Imports."

"Hello, this is Clair Tate calling from the United States. I need to reach Hans Ulbricht. It's very urgent."

"Of course, Ms. Tate," he replied in flawless English. "*Herr* Ulbricht is currently traveling abroad, but I will attempt to contact him for you. Is there some message for him or do you wish to leave a telephone number?"

"I really need to speak with him. He's due here in the States later this week but there've been some developments — some problems."

"Well, I don't know his schedule, but I will certainly see if I cannot contact him and ask him to call you. It may take some time, though. I'm not exactly sure of his whereabouts at the moment."

"Just tell him I need to speak with him as soon as possible." Clair gave the operator her cell phone number and received an assurance he'd call her back if he could not reach Ulbricht within the next few hours.

We were just trying to decide exactly what to say when Clair's cell phone rang. She glanced at the number and flipped it open. "Hans?" A grimace. "Oh. Sorry." She listened for a moment and said, "I see. He can't be reached then?" A pause accompanied by a frown this time. "Okay, then. Thanks for trying, but if you do reach him, please ask him to call me. It's very important. Good-bye."

"That Ulbricht's office?"

"Yeah. They said he's unavailable by phone. The person that the operator talked with did say that she knew he had a business meeting scheduled for late Thursday afternoon in Atlanta with someone named Tate. Apparently he's planning on being there. Any ideas?"

The sick feeling suddenly returned to my stomach. "We better start coming up with excuses. Good ones."

CHAPTER
Forty-One

WE HADN'T PLANNED on spending a second night in Savannah. I'd imagined we'd drive back to Atlanta on Tuesday and await the container's arrival the next day. The inn, seeing we hadn't checked out, assumed we were staying and had booked us for another night. To say that Clair and I were both worried would have been an understatement. In the course of three weeks, we'd been intimately involved with two murders, one attempted murder — mine — and a truck hijacking. We had dealt with law enforcement officials from multiple jurisdictions on two continents who had, in the end, essentially abandoned us. That, in turn, left to us the unpleasant task of having to explain to the prime suspect in one of the murders how his multimillion-dollar shipment of contraband had disappeared from under our noses. The excitement and passion of the night before gave way to an uneasy sense of impending doom. We ate a light meal in the hotel restaurant and went to bed before ten, neither of us in the mood for anything more.

The ringing of my cell phone awoke me on Wednesday morning. It was Sonny Griffin, the Georgia Bureau of Investigation agent. "'Morning Mr. Finch. Sorry to bother you so early, but I wanted to bring you up to date on where we stand with the investigation.

"We retraced the route the driver took yesterday and had a little luck. A surveillance camera outside of a convenience store near the port shows a man climbing in the passenger side door while the truck was stopped at a traffic signal. The tape's not great and you can't really tell if the fellow forced his way in or if the driver was expecting him. We got one more break that confirms the first. I don't know if you noticed it, but there's a truck weigh station just before you turn off the interstate at Exit 143. Video cameras there picked up two men in the truck, but you can't see much more than that. At least we know Norris was not alone when he drove down that road.

"Right now it seems pretty obvious that this was a truck hijacking, the big question being whether it was a random act or one targeting this particular load. Obviously there was a lot of planning involved — whoever did it had a truck waiting at the clearing. We interviewed the victim's wife. Name's Sabrina Norris. They were having a few problems, short of cash, the usual thing. It may be that Norris was an active participant, but right now I'm leaning against it. Other than that, there's not much to tell. Still no sign of the trailer. I think we're dealing with professional hijackers."

"What do you think the chances are of recovering the trailer?" I asked.

Griffin took a deep breath and exhaled. "If you asked me to guess, I'd say between slim and nil. The way these guys operate, whatever was in that trailer has probably been repackaged and is halfway to Mexico by now. You've got insurance coverage, right?"

"Right," I said, while thinking that it was not going to do much to placate Ulbricht. "Can you fax us a copy of your initial report? We're going to have to explain to someone what happened to a shipment of antiques he was expecting."

"Sure," he said. I handed the phone to Clair who gave him her fax number in Atlanta.

We ate breakfast. Clair called Tate Interiors and spoke with Harriet, the interior designer. She was aware of all that had happened but had nothing new to report. She said that when she came in there was a message on the answering machine from someone named Hans Ulbricht. The message was he'd changed his flight and would be getting into Atlanta late Thursday afternoon. He'd plan on meeting Clair at Tate Interiors at six that evening and hoped that would be all right. "He didn't leave a number," Harriet said. "Do you need me to wait around and be here when he arrives?"

"Thanks, but no," Clair replied. "We're driving back this morning. I should be at the shop by three this afternoon. That shipment contained some paintings that Becky had agreed to import for him. I just hate to face the guy and tell him they've been stolen."

⁓

THE FIVE HOUR DRIVE to Atlanta seemed to last an eternity. We talked. Clair held my hand. We listed to the radio. She took a nap. We arrived at Becky's condo shortly before three. Clair unlocked the door while I got her bag out of the car. She asked me if I wanted to spend the night there. Before I could answer, my cell phone rang. It was Colette. "Nate, are you back in town?"

I said that I was.

"Good, I want you to come by the office. I need to go over these revised marketing plans with you."

"Colette, I've really got some other obligations right this —"

"It'll only take a minute." She hesitated. "Please, Nate. I need to talk with you." Colette never begged. Something had happened.

"Okay, sure. I'll be there in fifteen minutes."

Clair was standing in the doorway, waiting for my answer. I slipped the phone back in my pocket and said, "I need to go by the office for a few minutes."

"Sure, Nate. No problem. I remember what you said in Savannah about romantic dinners and one-night stands. I'll see you tomorrow. Try to be at the shop by five if you can break away from Colette." She slammed the door, leaving me standing on the stoop. I had intended to say that I wanted to stay.

❧

ATLANTA TRAFFIC MOVING with its usual sluggishness, it took me half an hour to drive the four miles to the Madeleine Tours office on Piedmont Road. I kept mentally kicking myself for not beating on the door and telling Clair she was wrong. I tried calling her cell phone. After six rings it went to voice mail. I left a message. I called the condo number and hung up after twenty rings. I was still brooding about my stupidity as I pulled open the office door to see Brandi's smiling face, this time under a hennaed red thatch she'd acquired since my visit the week before. "I thought you were into the Urban Goth look," I winked.

"Nate, that is *so* passé. Can you imagine me showing up at a club with *black* hair, *black* eye shadow, *black* nail polish and —"

"Uh, unless my memory is really off, that was you last week."

"See, that's what I'm saying. That was so last week." She broke into a broad grin. "Colette's waiting for you in the conference room. Be careful."

"What's up?" I asked. Brandi had a great feel for Colette's ups and downs.

Brandi glanced over her shoulder and lowered her voice. "I'm not sure. She's been really tight-lipped, but there's a problem somewhere. I don't have any proof, but I'd suspect that things at home are getting a little rocky."

"Thanks," I said and headed down the hall. Colette didn't initially hear me. She was sitting at the table, her back to the door, deep in thought as she stared at the wall. A thin folder lay in front of her on the table. I cleared my throat.

"Oh, Nate! Hi. You startled me. I was, uh, thinking." She spoke in English.

"Sure. Sorry, I wasn't trying to creep up on you." I sat down across the table. "You said you wanted to go over the marketing plans. I thought we'd covered that last week. Something come up?"

Colette got up and shut the door. She sat back down. "I... I lied."

"Okay." I waited for her to say more. When after a moment she hadn't, I said, "You must have wanted me here for some reason. Do you want to tell me why, or shall I just sit here and wait you out?"

She placed her hand over the folder. "It's this."

"Which is?"

"A letter. From Carl. He wrote me a *letter*. He said he couldn't face me. He... he..." She stopped, unable to finish.

"He what?"

Colette took three deep breaths as if she were about to dive into a pool for a long underwater swim. "He admits it. He admits everything. He's been seeing this nurse, this *woman*," she spit the word out, "since just after our baby was born. He says he still loves me, Nate, but then he says he thinks it's best if he moves out. He talks about a 'trial separation' or something like that... I don't know. You read it."

She pushed the folder over to me. I opened it. Inside was a two-page, typewritten letter that had been ripped in half and then taped back together. I wondered what sort of man would type a letter to his wife telling her that's he's leaving her. Maybe he just dictated it to his secretary. I glanced at it, closed the folder and slid it back across the table to Colette.

"I don't think it's any of my business, Colette."

"But, Nate," she pleaded, "you've got to help me. I don't have anyone else. Oh, I guess I have a few friends, but how can I face them with something like this? My family's all dead. You're the person who really knows me."

"Looking back on it, I'm not sure I ever really knew you at all. I don't want to sound harsh, but this is your problem, not mine."

Colette got up and walked around the table, sitting next to me. "You're right. I know that, but please believe me. I didn't mean to get involved with Carl. I didn't mean to get pregnant. It just happened. I didn't want to leave you, but what else could I do? I didn't want a divorce. I could have lied to you and told you that the baby was yours. I felt like I didn't have a choice. I had to do what I thought was best for my son." She reached out and took my hand. "I know I've made horrible mistakes, but now I don't know where to turn. Please forgive me. I still love you and I know you still love me. I need you, Nate. Please help me."

For more than two years I'd played this moment in my mind. Colette admitting she'd made a mistake. Admitting she still loved me. Saying she needed me. A thousand times I'd gone over my response. I'd tell her how much she'd hurt me. I'd tell her how hard it would be to forgive her. I'd tell her that despite everything I still loved her. I'd pretend to hesitate, and then say that I'd take her back. Instead I said, "Colette, I'm sorry. Things are not the same. I don't know whether or not I still love you, but I do know that I can't help you. You are just going to have to work this one out for yourself." For the second time in less than a week I walked out of the conference room leaving the woman that I once loved alone with her problems.

CHAPTER
Forty-Two

I SPENT ANOTHER NIGHT at the Hyatt, sleepless this time. Four calls to the condo went unanswered. Two more messages on Clair's cell phone got no response. When the call finally did come she got right to the point. "Before you start apologizing again, Nate, let me make one thing really clear. You've said 'I'm sorry' enough. Let's just forget that part and all that happened the other night and get on with what we've got to do. Ulbricht will be here in less than twelve hours. We've got to sit down and figure out exactly what we're going to tell him."

"Clair, I need to say one —"

"It's okay! You've said enough. I understand, and I don't really want to talk about it. How about this? Instead of you saying 'I'm sorry' for the umpteenth time, how about I say it for the both of us? I'm sorry for all that's happened. I'm sorry you got dragged into this mess, and I'm sorry for what happened in Savannah. That's it! Enough said. We won't mention it again, and hopefully by this time tomorrow I'll be out of your life and you'll be out of mine. Got it?"

"Got it." I didn't know what else I could say.

"Good, meet me for breakfast at the Waffle House down Piedmont. We need to get our stories straight."

∽

FORTY-FIVE MINUTES LATER I was finishing my grits and ham while Clair toyed with her waffle, not saying a lot. She'd dressed down for the day in a tee shirt and denim jeans, her hair braided in a loose bun at the base of her neck. "You're not eating much," I observed.

"I'm worried. Don't you think we need to call Kelly or Brookins again? Or the GBI guy, what's his name?"

"Griffin."

"Yeah, Griffin. Maybe there's been some news on the truck."

"We probably should." I looked at my watch. His office wouldn't be open for half an hour. "But more than that, we've got to decide exactly what to say to Ulbricht. I'm still afraid he's going to think we arranged the hijacking."

"Harriet said the fax of the police report came yesterday. That will help."

"Maybe, but it would be good to have some back-up. What if Griffin's there to tell him in person?"

Clair raked patterns in the syrup on her plate. "Not a bad idea. And he's a cop, too. At least we'll have protection if Ulbricht goes ballistic."

"I can't see it. He came across so low-key in Paris. But then I haven't spent much time around him. You had dinner with him. What do you think he'll do?"

"I don't know. And it's not what I think he'll do as much as it is what I think he's capable of doing. That night, he was too cool, too calm. There's a part of him I can't read. It's more of a feeling than something I can put into words. Sounds weird, I know, but that's why I'm sure he knows more about Becky's death than he's told us."

"Okay, let's do this: we'll go to your shop and call the FBI just to see if anything new has come up. Assuming things are smooth on their end, we'll see if we can't get Griffin to meet with Ulbricht. He can break the news. Tell him the container's been stolen and that the GBI is on the case, that kind of stuff. Once that's done, we're home free."

"Yeah. Home free." Clair stabbed the last bit of waffle with her fork and plopped it in her mouth.

THE COMBINATION SHOP, office and warehouse of Tate Interiors, LLC filled an impressive red brick building on Miami Circle just a few blocks south of the Waffle House. Originally developed as an area of small warehouse distribution centers, the street had slowly evolved into a collection of high-end art galleries, overpriced antique shops and other resources catering to the herds of interior designers who serviced Atlanta's *nouveau riche*. The last time I'd been here I was with Becky.

Clair parked her minivan in front of a display window dominated by an ornate mahogany George III breakfront filled with Staffordshire figurines. I parked next to her and followed her inside. To the left of the building, a wide driveway led to a loading dock and attached warehouse in the rear. I recalled Becky telling me that when her mother bought the building it was an appliance showroom. She'd gutted the structure, rebuilding it with elegant display areas from which she sold off her own family antiques to pay for the investment. By the time her illness forced Becky to take over the business, Tate Interiors had become one of the most respected names in Atlanta design.

Clair introduced me to Harriet, the manager and in-house interior designer. She said she'd heard my name from Becky, making it clear from the tone of her voice that she wanted nothing to do with me. While Clair was off attending to some urgent problem, I found an unoccupied desk and called Kelly on his cell phone. I brought him up to date on the hijacking and asked if he'd heard any more about Ulbricht's whereabouts. "As far as I know, he's still booked on a flight to Atlanta, but honestly, we've been up to our ass in alligators down here." He sounded a bit annoyed.

"I guess he'll just show up here at six, then. Any advice about how to handle things?"

"Just tell him the truth. My god, what do you think he's going to do?"

"I don't know. I can't help but worry that he might think we stole the paintings. As far as he knows, they're worth millions and we're about the only ones that could have known both that and how they were being transported to Atlanta."

"Nate, I don't mind your calling me, but don't you think you're being a little paranoid? Ulbricht knows you two could never pull off a truck hijacking. Like I said, just tell him the truth. Sure, he's going to be pissed, but it's not your fault. If he wanted you dead, he would have had you killed in Paris." I heard a horn blowing in the background. "I've to run. Call me if something important happens, otherwise I'll get back to you later."

No help from him, I thought. I tried the GBI office number on Griffin's card. He wasn't there but returned my call ten minutes later. "Nothing new to report on this end," Griffin said. "That container, or what remains of it, is probably sitting in some warehouse right now waiting to be cut up and sold for scrap."

"We may need a little help explaining things. Any possibility you'd be willing to meet with a client who owned some paintings that were in the shipment? Our excuses would sound a whole lot better if you were there to confirm the story."

"I wouldn't mind at all, but right this minute I'm down south of Waycross on the Florida line following up some leads for another case. I doubt if I could make it to Atlanta by this evening even if I could get away. Won't the police report I faxed up there the other day be enough? Hell! Tell you what — give the guy my phone number. Tell him to call me if he doesn't believe you." I thanked him and hung up.

Clair appeared at the door. "Any luck?"

"I'm batting zero for two. Kelly's got other things on his mind and Griffin's in south Georgia. Looks like it's going to be just me and you."

"It's got to work out. I — we — keep imagining all the things that might happen. We'll meet him. We'll explain the situation. He'll leave. Simple. Then we get on with our lives." She turned and headed back toward the display areas. I stared at the phone, trying to think whom else I could call. Clair reappeared at the door. "Simple," she said again and disappeared.

CHAPTER
Forty-Three

BY TEN-THIRTY I'D RUN OUT of ideas. Anyway, I reasoned, in twenty-four hours I should be on my way to the airport to catch the early flight back to Paris. It wasn't that I wanted to leave, I just didn't want to stick around any longer than necessary. Colette's marriage was imploding and I wanted to be as far away as possible when the end came. I might have found an excuse to stay for Clair, but I'd blown whatever chances we might have had.

I wandered around the shop, stopping every now and then to examine some knickknack or overpriced piece of porcelain. Clair was off somewhere in the warehouse. Harriet hovered in the background, eyeing me with the gaze of a classroom monitor. When it became evident she couldn't take it any more she said, "Mr. Finch, don't you have something to do? The person you're planning to meet is going to be here until six."

"I'm waiting on Clair. I thought she might want to join me for lunch."

"Why don't I ask her?" Five minutes later she returned to deliver the message that Clair was busy, along with the suggestion that I return about five-thirty.

Seven hours to kill. I drove back to the Hyatt and booked a seat on the next day's Air France flight to Paris. I spent an hour loitering among the bookshelves of the Barnes & Noble a few blocks down Peachtree. By two, I was on my third cup of coffee and nearly finished with a spy thriller by some allegedly best selling-author who should have kept his day job.

Then Colette called. I could tell she'd been crying. "I know you don't want me to bother you, but you've got to help me. I didn't want to call you. I wasn't going to, I promise." She broke down sobbing. I listened, not speaking. "Nate, he moved out last night. Carl left me. He's staying in a hotel."

"Colette, does this have anything to do with the business?"

"No, of course not. The business is fine. I've been such a fool. I never should have…" I held the phone away from my ear. I could barely catch snatches of words now: "…*always*…," "…*regret every day*…," "…*still love*…." I pressed the "End" button, holding it down until the power turned off. I stuffed the phone in my pocket and went back to my novel.

THE FIVE-THIRTY NEWS on the radio was just starting as I parked the Tahoe next to Clair's van. Cocktail hour had arrived. Miami Circle was mostly deserted now, the hot designers with their wannabes and hangers-on having migrated to nearby watering holes to begin the late afternoon ritual of martinis, gimlets and networking. Harriet walked out as I was walking in. She acknowledged me with a disdainful look and a chilly, "Good luck. Lock the door behind you when you go in."

Clair was half-slouched on an Eastlake fainting chair in the rear showroom, flipping through an old issue of Veranda. She'd changed into black slacks with an off-white sweater and a single strand of pearls. The look screamed understated elegance. She looked up and smiled when she saw me. "I owe you an apology. I shouldn't have run you off today like I did. I was," she hesitated, "hurt, for lack of a better word. I know you're going back soon…"

"Tomorrow."

"I don't want to end things like this. Let's say good-bye as friends. We've been through a lot over the last few weeks."

"I'd like that."

"Good." She gave me a hug. "Ready?"

"As ready as I'll ever be. Any word from Ulbricht?"

"Nothing."

"Your employees?"

"I sent them home. Want a drink? A glass of wine? A client sent over a bottle of a good Merlot I've been wanting to try."

"Sure," I said. I felt awkward. I wanted to tell her what was going on with Colette, but that might gouge open a healing wound.

Clair opened the bottle and poured two oversized glasses. I noticed she gulped hers down and then, embarrassed, said, "A little liquid courage, maybe?"

My watch read five-forty. Twenty minutes. Time enough to explain things. Time enough to make it clear that for the first time I realized I wasn't still in love with Colette.

A sharp knocking from the direction of the front show-room stabbed into my thoughts. Clair sprang up startled, knocking her glass over in the process. It shattered on the floor. "I'll see who it is," I said. "If that's Ulbricht, he's early."

Across the showroom I saw a figure silhouetted against the still bright day outside. Male, about the right height, wearing a sport coat and open-necked shirt. He saw me emerge from the back room and raised his hand to signal. I waved back. He turned around, peering down the street. I moved closer and could see the back of his head clearly now. Blond hair. He turned back around and smiled at me. Ulbricht.

I released the thumb latch on the door and let him in. He seemed glad to see me. "Nate, how are you? I know I'm a little early, but I didn't think you'd mind. Where's Clair?"

"In the back. She just knocked something over and broke it — an accident. She'll be right out."

Ulbricht walked over and picked up a finely painted Mandarin charger. He held it near a lamp to examine it more closely. "Eighteenth century. Too good to be export. This is a fantastic piece. I certainly hope it wasn't something as fine as this one."

"No. Just a wine glass."

"Well, let me say hello to her." Without waiting, he headed toward the rear showroom. I remembered that he'd been here before and surely knew the building well. I fol-lowed a few steps behind him. Clair was dabbing up the last drops of wine as we entered. She stood up awkwardly, crumbling the paper towel in her right hand.

"Clair, my dear! How are you?" He gave her a quick embrace.

"Fine, Hans. And you?"

"I'd be better if the world wasn't such an evil place. We all would." It seemed to me a strange thing for him to say.

"How was your trip?" I asked.

"Good, thanks. I'd planned on flying directly to Atlanta from Berlin, but something came up and I've been in New York for the last couple of days. I'm sorry I missed your call, but my assistant tells me you got my message."

"Yes," Clair said, hesitant. "Hans," she paused, searching for the right phrase. "We've had a little problem. I don't really know how to begin to explain…"

"It's terrible, isn't it? Of all the thousands of trucks that go through that port every day why do they have to pick ours to hijack? I'll tell you, America is becoming a dangerous place to do business."

"You know?" I said. "About the stolen truck and the murder?"

Ulbricht looked surprised. "Of course. My company is the freight agent on the European end. We received notification a couple of days ago. I had one of my people call your FBI, but I understand they're all tied up in some silly terror alert in New Orleans or somewhere like that."

"But you're not upset?" Clair asked. "You're not angry?" I couldn't tell if she was relieved or incredulous.

"Of course not. Why should I be? Or better, against whom should I direct my wrath? The trucking company? The shipping line? Or you, even? No, Clair, you seem to be forgetting that this is my work. I'm in the import-export business. Goods get lost every day. Trucks get hijacked. Ships sink. Planes crash. You don't relish it and you don't encourage it, but you expect it. You factor it in as a cost of doing business."

Clair eased herself down on the sofa. "So you knew about it. You knew the container was missing. You've known about it since right after it happened?"

"Yes."

She bit her lip, first looking at me and then at Ulbricht. I knew what was coming next. "If that's the case, then why are you here?"

CHAPTER
Forty-Four

"WHY AM I HERE?" Ulbricht looked amused. "Well, now, that's a good question. I suppose you'd say that I'm here because I told you I'd be here. No, actually I'm expecting a shipment that should be arriving at any moment. As I'm sure you'll understand shortly, my presence is quite necessary to ensure safe its delivery to its final destination."

He wasn't making sense. Not from my perspective, at least. Clair shot me a puzzled look. The low sound of a large motor rumbled through the showroom, followed by a hissing and short squeal of airbrakes. "And unless I'm wrong," Ulbricht continued, "it's right on time." We could hear the beep-beep of a large truck in reverse. It came from the direction of the access drive leading to the warehouse behind the showrooms.

Ulbricht knew the layout of the building. Without another word he walked rapidly down a hall past the workshop area and pushed open the door to the warehouse. He flipped on the overhead lights, then headed directly to the roll-up door that accessed the loading dock. The beep-beep had stopped with the hiss of airbrakes. The sound of an idling diesel engine echoed through the wall and across the huge space.

Ulbricht kicked off the pin locks on the bottom of the door and pressed the green button next to it labeled "Open." With a metallic creaking, the door crept up to reveal the rear of a tractor-trailer three feet away from the edge of the platform. Stepping outside, Ulbricht signaled to the driver to back up, holding his hands apart to indicate the distance to the edge of the dock. The beep-beep started again as the driver eased the huge vehicle toward the door, stopping again with a hiss of air when Ulbricht made a cutting motion with his outstretched palm.

For some reason it didn't hit me at first. Maybe I was focusing on the cab, a faded red Kenworth with "H & B Trucking, Macon, Georgia" stenciled on the door in neat white letters. The trailer with its container was big, about forty feet, grey with blue letters that spelled out Norseland SeaLane. It looked familiar. In fact, it looked very familiar. Clair must have had the same thoughts. I could read fear in her voice as she whispered, "That's not —" suddenly stopping as the truck door opened and the driver climbed out.

Ulbricht said, "Of course you remember my assistant, Henri?" He held a small pistol in his hand, pointing it at us.

WE SAT IN THE REAR showroom at either end of a Sheraton dining table topped with book-matched burl veneers. Our arms were lashed with plastic ties to the chair's arms, our legs the same way to the chair's legs. Henri sprawled on the Eastlake sofa, intently reading the same magazine that Clair had been flipping though an hour earlier. "You know,"

he said to me in French. "You Americans just have too much. Take, for example, this." He waved the copy of *Veranda*. "There's nothing in here but photos of possessions of the rich. You know what I think? It's all designed to make you want even more — as if you don't have enough already. To make you work even harder so you can have more money to spend on more things. I read on the plane flying over that the average American works forty-four hours a week? Did you know that? And that twenty-six percent of you don't even take a vacation? Now in France, it's different. By law we only work thirty-five hours a week. And we are required to take our nine weeks of vacation. And more, even with less work, our productivity is higher. It truly amazes me."

"What is he saying?" Clair interrupted.

"Just being a typical French asshole."

Henri walked over and slapped me. "My English is not perfect, but don't make the mistake of thinking I'm incapable of understanding you." Turning to Clair he continued in heavily accented English, "My regrets, Madame. Your friend here insulted me."

Ulbricht had been watching the entire exchange from the hallway leading to the warehouse. "Henri! Be a gentleman. This is not Bosnia, and these people are not enemy combatants. They most certainly didn't enlist for this operation." He spoke in English. Henri, looking chastised, sat back down and pretended to study the magazine.

Ulbricht stared at his watch and thought for a moment. He sat down on one of the side chairs between us. "I presume you realize by now that the trailer parked at your loading dock is the same one that was allegedly hijacked near the port?"

"What's your game, Ulbricht?" I said. I needed to figure out his plans. "We're in this with you. Why are you holding us here like this?"

"Oh, Nate, Clair, you are definitely in this with us, but not in the way you'd like to believe. You've been swept up in a rather elaborate smuggling operation, through no fault of your own, of course. You're about to become innocent victims, like the poor truck driver." A cold shiver washed over me. I needed an angle. Some way to gain his confidence.

Before I could say anything Clair blurted out, "The paintings are forgeries!" I wanted to kick her, to yell at her to stop, but she wouldn't shut up. "The FBI knows all about them. They've been on top of the whole operation all along, even before Becky was killed. They — "

"Clair, dearest, do you think I'm a total fool? I know all that, and more. I know that right now your alleged protectors Brookins and Kelly are in the swamps of Louisiana trying to track down a vicious cell of al Qaeda terrorists — who don't exist, by the way — bent on doing great harm to your country. No," he laughed, "this is a case of the tail wagging the dog. Unfortunately, the cavalry is not going to ride up at the last minute. The good guys are not going to win this one."

"You killed my sister, you bastard," Clair snarled. I wanted her to shut up.

"Well, not exactly. Henri, there, did the actual deed." Henri looked up from his magazine at the mention of his name, shrugged and went back to reading. "I was there, I'll admit, and it was not something I wanted to do. I cared about her very much. If the circumstances were different we actually might have been married. As it is, though, it looks like you and Nate have become the sacrificial lambs."

"What the hell are you talking about?" Anger seeped from my voice. "Sacrificial lambs?"

"Sacrificial lambs on the altar of commerce. You, my friends, have become unwitting participants in the largest business deal of my career. It's been a horribly complex project. And as occurs in any such endeavor, there were the usual series of complications. I made a mistake. A small strategic error. Becky hadn't figured it all out, but she might have if I'd let her live. And then suddenly you — you two — step up to take her place. I thought we were going to have to scuttle the whole thing, but then you appeared, *deus ex machina*, to set things back on track."

I repeated myself. "Ulbricht, what the hell are you talking about?"

He looked at his watch again and then said to Henri in French, "How long do you think it will take us to get there?"

"I've driven the route a dozen times. This time of day, twenty-two minutes minimum, thirty-four minutes maximum. Depends on the traffic and how we catch the lights."

"That gives us nearly an hour before we need to leave," Ulbricht said, looking at Clair. "Becky was a fine woman. Perhaps you deserve an explanation before you die."

CHAPTER
Forty-Five

"YOU KNOW," Ulbricht said, "This whole project, this deal, has been rather like a huge construction project. A girder here, a girder there, each by itself merely a shaped bit of steel. But you start to put them together, and soon you can detect a pattern, a form, a familiar shape. Now it's almost finished. One more little part to be aligned and bolted into place, then *voilà!* What began as a seemingly random series of small steps will come to fruition in a matter in hours in an event that may well change the history of the world."

Clair spit.

"Ah, Clair, you think I exaggerate. But let me tell you the story. I'm proud of it. Last spring, just before you Americans began your foolish excursion into Iraq, I had to be in Teheran on business. I've worked with the Iranians for years. Over the last decade or so I've handled a few sensitive transactions here and there without problems. They like that. I don't want to advertise the fact, but they've been

271

some of my best clients. They've come to trust me, I think. They know I'm expensive, but I get the job done.

"Anyway, I was about to leave town when a government official I know summoned me to his office. You wouldn't recognize his name, but suffice it to say that he's well placed and frequently handles the less public side of Iranian diplomacy."

"Like supporting terrorists," Clair hissed. I glared at her.

"Do be kind. Wasn't it my countryman von Clausewitz who said, 'War is the continuation of politics by other means?' Surely you must realize America has declared war on those who disagree with her? Your president labeled the sovereign nation of Iran part of the 'axis of evil,' just as he did with Iraq. Now your troops are in Baghdad. Who's to say Teheran is not next on his list? It's foolish to think that such a small county can defend herself against American mischief by conventional means. Why not acknowledge the fact that what you call terrorism is, like war, only the continuation of politics by other means?"

Clair glared at Ulbricht, then started to speak. He glanced at his watch and held up his hand. "Please let me continue. We've got a schedule to keep, and I think you'll be interested in what I have to say. Now, this Iranian gave me a challenge. He wanted to strike a major blow against America. But as a rational man, he realized that to do so directly would rain destruction on his country, much as happened with Afghanistan. And, too, as an intellectual he pointed out to me that great empires rarely collapse because of outside force. No, instead they weaken internally. Their resolve fades. Their national unity splinters. They turn inward and declare war on themselves as they struggle with their own identity. Look at the Romans, or the Ottoman

Empire. It's always the same. No, America shall meet her end not by force, but from internal decay.

"He knew about Timothy McVeigh and the Oklahoma City bombing. He'd seen how confused your country became to think there might be red-blooded, flag-waving Americans who would commit such an act. And he had come to the conclusion, he said, that if an external attack like the World Trade Center bombing could bring you together, an internal attack might just as easily tear you apart. It was a concept, not a plan. He wanted me to turn his idea into action.

"He chose me for several reasons. First, perhaps I understand you Americans. I spent the first years of my life here. I know your weak points, your hot buttons. Second, I'm not from the Middle East. I'm not the hook-nosed, bomb-hurling Semite portrayed in your newspapers. Third, I have connections. I have experience. I can get the job done. I'd be perfect, he said. I told him no, I said I wasn't interested. It would be too dangerous. And then he said, 'We are prepared to pay the sum of one hundred million dollars.'"

Clair gave a little gasp. I said, "Fuck you! You're no different than —" Before I could finish, Henri's hand grasped my throat, his fist raised to strike me.

"Henri, please," Ulbricht said calmly. "They have every right to be upset. We are not going to abuse them."

"As you wish," Henri replied in French. "I'm going out back to have a cigarette." He disappeared toward the warehouse.

"I apologize for Henri. He's rough around the edges, but totally loyal. Now, where was I? Oh, yes, I was talking about money. I don't know about you, but to me that's a fortune. With what I've got plus that, enough to quit. Get out of the game. Retire completely to some quiet villa on the Costa del Sol. So I said I'd think about it. I made no promises, mind you. I really thought that the scope of what he required was quite beyond even my capabilities. But I started looking about, thinking about it.

"Well, it so happened I had to be in St. Petersburg a few weeks later. Through various connections I was offered a chance to buy some black-market plutonium that had been recovered from decommissioned nuclear weapons. It'd been snatched from a shipment on its way to an underground storage facility east of the Urals. My first reaction to that, of course, was negative, especially since I couldn't for the life of me decide what I might do with it once I had it. Then I discovered a little morsel that changed my mind and gave me an idea.

"It was rather ingenious, the way they'd prepared the plutonium for shipment. They ground it into a powder, and suspended that in a thick fluid of some sort to separate the particles and keep them from interacting with one another. That mixture, in turn, was solidified and formed into large flexible sheets, somewhat like you'd find in a plastic bag, but thicker. So you had millions of radioactive dust specks dispersed in a flexible matrix. These sheets were then placed on top of lead foil and rolled up — sort of like your jelly roll pastry — to fit inside drums for storage. Very neat!

"The fellow that was trying to sell it to me pointed out it would be quite easy to unroll the sheets, place lead on *both* sides to block the radiation, and then incorporate them in the walls of, say, a truck. It was a brilliant idea! The perfect basis for your so-called 'dirty bomb.' One of the things Americans absolutely fear the most. So we cut a deal. Of course, I had Henri kill him later. I didn't want to have any loose ends."

Henri sauntered back in and flopped on the sofa, picking up a copy of *Southern Accents* this time. I couldn't read Clair's expression. Disgust or horror, or both.

Ulbricht continued, "I thought the next step might be to get the plutonium into the hands of some dissident group here in the States. One of those militia groups, or violent anti-abortion factions. But when I looked into that, I realized they were so heavily infiltrated by your anti-terrorist police that the chances of success were nil. I was quite discouraged and had decided to tell the Iranians I didn't think what they wanted was possible, no matter how much they offered to pay me.

"Then fate stepped in. I was here in Atlanta visiting my cousin. I met Becky. I was immediately taken with her. We started seeing one another, at first occasionally, then regularly. Things were not going well at home with my marriage. I realized one day I was falling in love with her.

"We'd known each other several months before she told me about your father, about the bombings. She was so bitter, so angry at the system. But she knew as well as I did that there was nothing she could do about it. Then it occurred to me, what if she wanted to do something about it? What if she were bent on revenge? What would she have done? I asked her about it — picked through her thoughts. Becky was normally a mild and gentle person, but one afternoon she said, 'I wish I could just blow them all up!' She was talking about the courts and the prisons and so on, but the idea was there, the concept. She could have become the perfect domestic terrorist. A female from a prominent family. No criminal record. No history of violent acts. A burning hatred for those who'd heaped ruin on her family. One day she snaps and decides to take action. The more I thought about it, the more realistic it sounded.

"While listening to Becky, I knew I'd found America's Achilles heel. What issue has greater potential to spread discord, to turn allies into enemies? Racial distrust, turned into racial hatred by a spectacular crime committed by so-called 'domestic terrorists.' Something that would wrench cries of outrage from blacks. That would bring back the race riots of the sixties. That would result in a wholesale roundup of militant groups on both sides and a curtailment of your beloved 'civil liberties.' The perfect distraction from America's adventurous foreign policy. I presented the idea to my contacts in Teheran. They loved it!

"So we struck a deal. Five million in cash for expenses. Unlimited technical assistance. Ten million dollars in a numbered account in Andorra as a down payment. Another ten million when the plutonium was safely in the U.S., and the remainder once the deed is done. I think it's safe to say that by this time tomorrow I shall be back in Berlin, sipping cognac and preparing to spend the rest of my life on extended holiday."

Clair strained against the ties that bound her arms. "Are you saying you were planning to set my sister up in some sort of terrorist act, some sort of bombing?" The veins in her neck pulsed with every beat of her heart.

"Oh, no. Initially she had nothing to do with it. But then things changed. As I said, there were complications. As it turned out, I needed to have her play a certain role. Without knowing it, she became the mastermind behind what will surely go down in history as an event even more memorable than the September Eleventh attacks in New York. After all, you surely must recall that today, May sixth, is the anniversary of your father's death.

"How could you?" Clair said, barely whispering.

"Clair, my dear! A hundred million dollars is a lot of money. I can just buy her replacement."

CHAPTER
Forty-Six

"I DON'T KNOW WHAT you've got in mind," I said, "but it can't work. You'll be caught. Your fingerprints are all over this operation. Clair was telling the truth. The FBI has been watching you all along."

Ulbricht laughed. "Don't you think I know that? The truck that's parked at the loading dock. You think it contains stolen works of art. Indeed it may, but it also contains a hundred kilograms of plutonium-239 and fifty kilograms of Semtex. Quite enough to contaminate hundreds of square kilometers around wherever I choose to detonate it. We're sitting here discussing my plans to explode a dirty bomb in the middle of an American city. Where is your vaunted FBI? They're off chasing wraiths in the swamps of Louisiana. Hasn't it occurred to you that your government wants to arrest me for the petty crime of smuggling stolen art when in fact they should be doing everything in their power to prevent the events that are about to take place? Did you ever for a moment consider the fact that I planned for things to work out this way?"

I didn't know what to say, so I was silent.

"No, I mentioned complications. We had some, and I had to change my plans, but I'll tell you about that in a moment. My original intent was simply to bring in a container full of plutonium and blow it up in a city or a sports arena or somewhere so as to produce maximum psychological impact. I was going to work out a way to blame it on some violent local group, the Ku Klux Klan or skinheads or the like. It's been done before. Look how your government shielded the true culprits by blaming Kennedy's assassination on Oswald. Please understand, Becky had given me the idea, but she was never part of the initial plan.

"I think I mentioned that I own a small trucking company in France. One of our sidelines is repairing and refurbishing shipping containers. My associates in Teheran were kind enough to send in a group of technicians with expertise in fabrication and the handling of radioactive materials. Thank god for the short French workweek. My employees all want to leave at noon on Friday. The Iranians had the entire weekend undisturbed to strip the interior out of a container, place lead-shielded plutonium between the outer and inner walls, fabricate plastic charges with detonators and wire in a rather elaborate timer system.

"Then the problems started. Just after we'd finished preparing the container, I got word from Teheran that several of my banking accounts were being monitored by the U.S. government. They apparently have a source — a spy might be a better word — within your Justice Department who keeps them informed of such things. The Americans seemed interested in some of the interactions I've had with various dissident groups in Africa and the Middle East.

Teheran was uneasy. They worried about someone tracing the connection back to them through me.

"They called an emergency meeting in Istanbul. We talked. They wanted to put distance between them and the bomb. They said my plans were too shallow, too obvious to fool the Americans. And there was a new problem. Your government had announced that it was increasing security at seaports. There was a fear that the container might be detected as it was being unloaded, or in customs. The higher-ups in Teheran were getting cold feet. They wanted to back out of the deal. I could keep the down payment, they said, but hinted they'd kill my family unless we called things off.

"Now, I didn't mind that especially. Nearly fifteen million dollars in profit for very little work. But it was the principle of the thing, and the rest of that hundred million was just out there, waiting for me. I made them a deal. I would come up with a new plan. Something that would meet their original objective of a spectacular act designed to cause chaos in America while pointing the unmistakable finger of blame to some domestic dissident group. They were reluctant, but eventually they agreed to it and gave me a month to come up with a workable plan. I mapped it out, presented it to them and they were back on board. Unfortunately, Clair, it involved your sister.

"I hated to bring Becky into it. I really did. But she was the logical choice. She had motive. Her business gave her opportunity. All I had to do was create sufficient evidence she was behind it all. That was easy. I stole her laptop. I used her computer to log on to racist chat rooms that were sure to be monitored by American security forces. I had her post threatening messages on various blogs. For all anyone might know, they were coming directly from her."

"So it was you!" Clair screamed. "The things I found on Becky's computer."

"Oh, that. In Atlanta, yes. I had a key to her condo. After what happened in Paris, I had someone upload a few files just to be sure. Icing on the cake, as I believe you'd say.

"But we're jumping ahead. What I'm most proud of, and what I think the Iranians liked the most, was the part of my plan designed to bypass port security while embarrassing American law enforcement. I needed one thing, though. I needed an inside source, and they came through for me. When you were in Paris at the US Embassy, do you remember the secretary? A dark headed woman with a large nose? She was in and out of your meeting that day when the FBI spoke with you two together for the first time, remember?"

I did. I remembered her clearly, but?

Ulbricht answered my question before I could ask it. "She's an Iranian agent. She's worked there for years. I know everything that was said in that room and I knew it almost as soon as it was said. How do you think I sounded so convincing when we first met at my flat in Paris? Why did you walk away suspicious of the FBI? Because I wanted you to. I wanted you to work with them, but I didn't want you to trust them completely. You see, they've become players in my little game.

"I had to make the FBI suspicious of Becky, but I wanted to draw their focus away from the container. I wanted them to see the trees, not the forest. So I arranged for Lavalle, the antiques dealer in Montmartre, to contact her about the paintings. They're —"

"They're forgeries!" Clair said. "Did you know that? Or were you tricked, too."

"Of course they're forgeries, but very good ones. I'm glad you figured that out. That in itself is an entire story. I bought them years ago thinking that I might pass them off one day at a private sale, but they're too well known. So they've sat a bank vault for the last ten years until I came up with the idea of using them as bait."

"Bait?" I said.

"Certainly. Did you never read the Iliad? This whole scheme, it's the Trojan Horse in reverse. Troy fell because the Trojans saw the horse, never considering what might be inside it. Your FBI in their zealous rush to charge me with a crime saw only the paintings, not the container that delivered them. You see, by drawing attention to the paintings, I was certain that the container would be unloaded and visually inspected. I'm in the import-export business. I know how these things work. Containers chosen for inspection bypass the 'routine' mass screening measures. If, for example, your Customs agents had x-rayed the shipment, they would have immediately detected the lead shielding. A random radiation check might have picked up some leaks in the shielding. They swallowed the bait, though. They inspected it by hand. They looked at it. It seemed all right, so why shouldn't it be? By this time next week every newspaper in this country and around the world will fly banner headlines screaming, '*TRAGEDY COULD HAVE BEEN AVERTED! PLUTONIUM BOMB BROUGHT IN WITH THE BLESSING OF THE FBI!*' I do suspect heads will roll."

CHAPTER
Forty-Seven

ULBRICHT'S PLANS WERE all too obvious. He was feeding us too much detail. Too many facts. We weren't going to be around to repeat them. From what he'd said, he was on some sort of time schedule. I needed to act rapidly if we were going to have any chance at all of escaping. Maybe if I made them mad. Maybe they'd get careless and drop their guard.

"You asshole!" I snarled. Mavik set down his magazine and started to stand up. Ulbricht stopped him with a wave of his hand. Clair stared, wide-eyed. "You said that you were falling in love with Becky and now you're telling us you had her killed. What kind of coward are you?"

"I'll soon be a very rich one, thank you. Life is full of compromises. I had to make a choice. She could have — she almost did — destroy the entire plan."

"But she loved you!" Clair screamed.

"Give me some credit, please! I hadn't planned to have her killed, but if you want an explanation of why it became necessary, I'll give you one." Ulbricht paused, thinking. "My original plan — to use another American expression — was that I'd have my cake and eat it, too. I'd fabricated overwhelming evidence to prove Becky was behind what is about to take place tonight. There would be others implicated, of course. She couldn't have done it alone. My strategy was to have the authorities believe she perished in the explosion. In fact though, I hoped to spirit her out of the country, give her a new identity and a new look, and in a few years, who knows? We might have gotten married. What choice would she have? Face America's wrath for a crime she didn't commit, or accept a new life of luxury in some remote part of the world? What if your father had been offered that choice? It would be an easy decision.

"Becky's mistake was that she insisted on inspecting the paintings. It was that Friday, just as I was leaving town. I really didn't see a problem with it, but of course I hadn't told her they were forgeries. She knew there was a question of ownership, but was willing to overlook that to save her business.

"To my surprise, she noticed something that everyone else had missed. When the Germans confiscated the Schloss paintings, these two works were picked for the collection of the planned *Führermuseum* in Lintz. The copies were made at the behest of Hermann Göring who — so I was told — planned to switch the forgeries for the originals, which he wanted for his estate at Karinhall. The forger was a Polish Jew named Kahn whom Göring snatched from a concentration camp. They were copied directly from the originals early in the winter of 1944, and were so perfect he even copied the classification tags fixed to the back by the Nazis. But — and now here's the catch — Kahn changed the date to read April 19, 1943, the anniversary of Warsaw Ghetto uprising. It was a minor thing, a passive act of protest, but the works weren't catalogued until August of that year. Becky had done her homework. She was the only one who caught the discrepancy.

"Of course, she didn't immediately recognize them as copies. She just knew something was wrong. She tried to call me. I was traveling and couldn't be reached. She went to my flat on Île St.Louis. Maria was there and let her in. She was going to leave me a note and went into the library looking for a bit of paper. As luck would have it, she just happened to open the very desk drawer where I had hidden her missing notebook computer. She took it out and began looking at it. She checked the email and the web browser and discovered what I'd been doing. According to Maria, she was quite calm and left without saying a word.

"I finally got her message and called her back that afternoon. She was furious. She demanded an explanation. I told her we needed to talk. I wanted to clarify things, put them in perspective. She said she never wanted to see me again. I would have dropped everything and been there in an instant, but I was in St.Petersburg. I begged her to meet with me. She refused at first, and then said she'd think about it. I pleaded with her and finally she said she'd meet me the next day at the Musée d'Orsay. I told her I couldn't be back by then but I'd send an emissary, someone to talk with her, to arrange a time and place where she'd feel comfortable meeting me. She had every reason to be angry but I wanted her to be more understanding. She'd be *sharing* the hundred million dollars.

"So I sent one of my associates — a man I knew I could trust — to the museum. Becky told him things were over between us. That she was afraid me. That if we were going to meet it would have to be in a public place. They agreed on the Eiffel Tower at five. I'd be back to Paris by that time.

"I was waiting for her on the third level of the Tower as agreed, but I'd made arrangements, just in case. Becky said I'd betrayed her and she would never trust me again. I explained to her what I was trying to accomplish, but she wouldn't listen. She said she was going to the police, and that for all she cared I could go to hell. She left me no choice. She had to die."

Ulbricht had been quite calm, as if the explanation of why he'd found it necessary to kill his fiancée was more of a complicated business transaction than a vicious act of murder. So much for my efforts to make him angry. It was probably a stupid idea anyway. I was still lashed to the chair. Maybe another tack. Pretending to look discouraged, I hung my head for a moment and took a quick look at my ankles. They were bound to the chair legs by plastic ties pulled firmly just above my shoes. I reasoned that if I could flex one foot to tilt the chair back I might be able to ease the other leg down far enough to slip the loop over the bottom of the chair leg. That would free one foot, and getting the other off would be easy. My arms would still be strapped to the chair, but at least I could use it as a battering ram.

Ulbricht was sitting at the table between Clair and me. That blocked his view of my feet. Mavik was the problem. He seemed engrossed in the magazine, but if he looked up I'd had it. To make this work, I needed to distract Ulbricht for a few minutes more. "So why hijack your own truck?" I asked.

"Good question," he said. "Two reasons, really. First, I knew the FBI would be watching it closely. I couldn't risk having them grab it once it reached Atlanta. The timer has to be activated. For maximum effect the explosion must take place in a certain spot. That sort of thing. I couldn't risk losing control."

I cast a sideways glance at Mavik. He was still reading. I began to ease back in the chair, pushing down with my left foot while working my right foot toward the bottom of the chair leg. Ulbricht didn't seem to notice and continued, "The other thing was the conspiracy issue. One of the first things the investigators will do after the bombing is trace the origin of the truck cab. They're going to find that it was purchased from a dealer in Greenville, South Carolina and was paid for by a wire transfer from a bank account in New York. That account is listed as belonging to Tate Interiors, LLC."

"Tate Interiors doesn't have a bank account in New York!" Clair interjected. Ulbricht was momentarily distracted. Mavik continued reading. I slipped the tie binding my foot over the bottom of the chair leg, freeing my right leg.

"But you do. You've had one for many months. When they trace that account, they'll find it was opened by your sister. On my advice, of course. I told her I wanted to use it as an escrow account for the down payment made on the paintings. Her name and handwriting is on the signature card, and the instructions for wire transfers have all come from her computer using her own private password. All part of the background."

"How could you tell her you loved her and do that to her? How? Why!" Clair demanded. I pressed down with my right foot, tilting the chair back slowly.

"Business. Money. I don't know. You're a woman, Clair. You get emotional about these things. This has been a very complex undertaking, and I don't like to leave any little thing to chance." I slipped the tie binding my left foot over the end of the chair leg. Now only my hands were tied.

Ulbricht continued, "Henri flew into Washington, took the train. What was its name, Henri?"

Mavik looked up., "*Pardon?*"

Ulbricht spoke in French. "The train you took to Greenville. Its name?"

"Oh. *Le Crescent Limité.*"

"That's right, The Crescent Limited." Mavik resumed reading. Ulbricht continued, "All he had to do was take delivery of the truck, spend a few days going from truck stop to truck stop where he'd blend in with the crowds, and then grab the container as it was leaving the port. I'd arranged for some local help, but that's another story." Ulbricht looked at his watch again. Time must be getting short. I needed to make a move.

Mavik was the biggest threat. I needed to take care of him first. "So, your lapdog hijacks the truck and kills the driver. Seems like he would have had enough of that kind of fun in Bosnia." At the mention of the familiar name, Mavik's head jerked up. "I hear his specialty was women and children. Isn't an ordinary trucker a little out of character for him?" Mavik flung down the magazine and was on his feet. He stalked toward me, fists clenched.

Clair gasped. Ulbricht was on his feet, "Henri!"

I braced my legs, waiting for the exact moment. Mavik inched closer, drawing back his right hand as he prepared to strike. He was now within range. He lifted his hand higher, his face twisted in a sardonic smile. "You shouldn't have said that." Kicking off with all my strength, I launched the chair with me tied to it toward him. My shoulder hit his chest with a sickening thud, propelling him back across the room into a shelf displaying a dinner set of English ironstone.

Mavik lay on a bed of smashed porcelain, stunned for an instant. Rapidly regaining his wits, he leapt up and rushed toward me, his arms outstretched. At the last second I swiveled, causing him to crash head on into the underside of the chair still strapped to my arms. It shattered as he fell to the floor clutching his belly. I jerked my hands free and started to turn toward Ulbricht.

I caught a movement in the periphery of my visual field. Clair screamed, "Nate! Look out!" A flash of cobalt blue and blood red and the impression of a large vase descending toward my head flickered through my consciousness just before the world went black.

CHAPTER
Forty-Eight

A STICKY FEELING ON MY FOREHEAD. A pounding pain in my left temple. The smell of wood and grease and something rough against my right cheek. I opened my eyes. Dim light. I couldn't focus. I tried to speak. My lips wouldn't move — they seemed to be stuck shut. My hands were numb, twisted behind me and bound tightly together. My legs the same way. I lay, right side down — somewhere?

I sensed a movement just behind me. Voices. Speaking French. Ulbricht. "So what I do is place this plug in this socket, here. See?"

"Yes." Mavik's voice.

"And then I enter the access code, like this." A series of six electronic beeps followed.

"Now it asks, 'Do you want to activate?' and I press '1' for 'Yes.' Another beep. "Then I enter the time delay. What does your watch read?"

"Eight-ten." I must have been unconscious for more than an hour.

"All right. We need about, say, thirty minutes to get there, and we'll allow an hour after that before it detonates, so we'll enter '90,' like this, for ninety minutes." Two more beeps. "Now I enter the arming code," six more beeps followed, "and it's done. The only way to disarm it is with this controller, and only then if someone knows both the access and arming codes. The Iranians are terribly ingenious. If someone tries to disarm it and one of the first three codes entered is not correct, then 'Boom!' Or if any one of the matrixes of wires that tie the detonators together is cut or broken, the same thing."

"What about them?" Mavik asked. "Shall I finish them?"

"I think you have a taste for killing, my friend. No. Let the blast do it. It will be quick and painless."

I heard a door creak shut, followed by the sound of a latch clicking into place. It was dark. We had to be inside the container. Inside the bomb. There was a scraping and another click just behind me. Someone was putting a lock on the latch. Silence, then a muffled sound of a door slamming and the throaty hum of a diesel engine starting.

I felt a movement near my feet and heard a muffled, "Mmmugh." I moved my legs slowly. They touched something soft. Clair! I felt her press against me and give another unintelligible "Mmmugh!" She seemed to moving her head back and forth in the darkness. Finally, "Nate, can you hear me?"

I tried to reply, but couldn't speak. Instead I made an "Uh-huh" sound in my throat.

"You've got tape over your lips. Scrape your cheek against the floor and you can peel it off."

I tried it. The floor was rough, wooden. The tape caught quickly and with a twist of my head it folded back. "Are you all right?"

"I'm alive." Clair's voice was weak.

"What happened? Where are we?"

"I thought you were dead. Ulbricht hit you on the head with a huge Imari vase. You've been bleeding. Mavik was going to kill you but he stopped him. They tied us up and threw us in the back of the truck. Just a minute ago, while you were still out, they were doing something. I couldn't see anything but I could hear them. They spoke French. I think they were programming the bomb."

"I was awake. I heard them. It's set to go off at nine-forty. Ulbricht said something about 'needing an hour' after they reach the spot. I guess they want to be as far away as possible."

"Did they say where they're going to leave it?"

"No. Only that it takes about half an hour. Somewhere downtown." I struggled against my bindings. "Can you work your hands loose?"

"No. Mavik made sure of that. You hurt him. You hurt him bad. He used those plastic ties and pulled them really tight."

I sensed I was lying on an object. My cell phone! "You didn't see them take the phone out of my pocket did you?"

"No. But I don't know what they did when they took you out to the truck. They left me tied up on the floor while they carried you back to the warehouse."

"I think my phone is still in my pocket. Is there any way you can wriggle up here and try to get at it?"

"I'm not sure. I'll try. My hands are tied behind my back like yours. I can't see anything." I could feel Clair twisting her body, trying to inch in my direction. She was beginning to make progress when there was a sudden hiss of air brakes releasing. The truck began to move forward, easing out from the loading dock. We must have moved

291

only a few yards to the end of the drive when Mavik applied the brakes again, causing Clair to roll forward.

"You okay?"

"I think so, but I can't brace myself. I'm going to be rolling back and forth every time he stops or makes a turn."

"Keep trying."

Slowly Clair worked her way up until she was nestled next to me. "God, I wish we were doing this at a different time and in another place."

"I know," I said. "I'm going to roll over on my back so you can reach my pocket." I could feel her hands on my thigh. "A little higher." She wriggled again and moved up a few inches.

"That's it. Now, can you feel the phone in my pocket?"

"Yeah. You want a Mae West line?"

"No, just reach in and get it." After another minute of effort she had the phone in her hands.

With a hiss of brakes the truck made a sudden stop and she rolled forward. "Almost dropped it! Do you have speed dial programmed? I can't see anything so I'll just have to hold a key down and hope it connects."

Then I remembered. "It's not turned on. I cut it off when Colette called this afternoon. I forget to turn it back on."

"That bitch! You know you never should have married her."

"I wish that mattered. Right now you've got to feel and see if you can turn it on. It'll ring a musical tone when it powers up." I could feel her fumbling with the phone in the darkness. We hit a bump and both rolled backward. The phone emitted a series of notes. I looked down and could see light as the display lit up. "You got it! Now see if you can hold it where I can see it. I think I can guide your fingers to nine-one-one."

I scrunched down until the lighted display was less than a foot from my face. Clair was holding the phone with both hands. "Okay," I instructed, "Try holding the phone with your left hand and pressing the keys with your right." She shifted it to her left hand and held open the display to face me. "Now move your right index finger down." Five minutes later the display read "911."

"Now you're going to need to hit the 'Send' button. Move your finger up —" There was a sudden sharp hiss of breaks. The force of deceleration rolled us both forward. The phone flew out of Clair's hand and skidded off toward the front of the truck. I caught a glimpse of the lighted keypad as it slid under a pallet, coming to rest no more than a foot from her head. It could have been a mile. There was no way either of us could reach it.

CHAPTER
Forty-Nine

"ANY OTHER IDEAS?" Clair asked.

"No, but once Mavik's parked the truck we should have more than an hour." I didn't want to say it. "We'll holler at the top of our lungs. Someone's got to hear us."

"What if he leaves it in a parking lot? Or on some deserted street?"

Before I could answer the brakes hissed again, rolling us forward as we came to a complete stop. Mavik killed the engine. "I think we're there, wherever 'there' is." The unmistakable sound of a vehicle passing filtered into the container, followed shortly by another. "We must be on a street somewhere." Another sound from the front of the truck. A door slamming. Mavik getting out.

"Let's give him five minutes or so to make his escape and then we start yelling," Clair whispered.

We lay still, not daring to move. My head throbbed. My hands and feet were painfully numb. We heard the sound of two more cars passing. Clair whispered again, "There's not too much traffic. We're on a side street somewhere. You *know* there's got to be a sidewalk. People can hear." The sharp whoop of a police siren pierced the container's walls. "Yes!" she said.

"Hold on a second. Let's see what's happening."

The sound of a door slamming, this time coming from behind the truck. A voice, southern accent. "This your truck?"

"Yes, officer." Mavik. They were standing just outside the container door. A few feet away.

"You can't park here. You gotta move yer rig."

"I'm sorry, officer. The engine died. I have turned on the flashers and I am putting out these warning signals."

"You talk funny, mister. Where you from? Mexico?"

Mavik laughed. "No. Canada. Montreal. I am French-Canadian." A pause. "I have called for assistance."

"Well, you can't leave your truck here. This is a restricted area. You gonna need to call a wrecker. Get it towed. I need to call this in. Lemme see your license and registration." Another pause. "This is a French driver's license. I thought you said you were from Canada."

"It's time," Clair said and yelled, "Help! Let us out! We've been kidnapped!"

The policeman's voice again, this time to us, "Hold on. We're going to open the door." Then to Mavik, "I don't know who you are, mister, but you better get that lock off that door real quick."

"Just a moment officer. I have the key right here." A sound of scraping, then a creak as the latch lifted. One of the panel doors eased open. Twilight mixed with the yellow glow of a streetlight rushed into the container. I caught a flash of Mavik's face as he pulled the door open and stepped back.

The officer peered in. Late twenties, close-cropped brown hair. Beyond him sat a white City of Atlanta patrol car, its blue light flashing rhythmically. My face, covered with dried blood, must have been the first thing he saw. "What the hell?" he started and was cut short as Mavik struck him on the back of his head with a heavy wrench. The policeman's eyes rolled back as he crumpled to the ground.

Mavik kicked him aside and glared at me. He spoke in French, "I should have killed you back there. Now I will." He raised the wrench. A horn sounded behind him. A red Ford Expedition came to a screeching halt next to the police car. The driver hit his horn a second time. I could just make out Ulbricht behind the wheel. Mavik glanced over his shoulder, then at me, then back at Ulbricht. With a snarl, he said, "You'll die soon enough," dropped the wrench and sprinted toward the passenger door of the Excursion, pushing the container door shut as he fled. The interior returned to darkness.

"We're going to be all right!" Clair said, as if to reassure herself.

"Not unless someone stops to help us. He didn't latch the door. I'm going to see if I can't push it open with my head." Like an oversized worm I began to inch toward the door. I placed my head against it and gave it a sudden thrust. It swung open a foot and stopped. It was out of reach.

"Can you see out? Where are we?"

Through the crack I could see we were parked on a small city street. It was almost dark now. Across the way there was a grove of mature oaks and beyond it a plaza with a small white monument. "I don't know. It looks like we may be near some sort of public building. I can't tell."

"Can you see a sidewalk? Any people?"

"No."

A car sped past, not slowing. "Why didn't they stop? They've got to see the cop on the ground and know something's wrong."

"That's just it. I don't think they can. The patrol car is too close to the back of the truck. He's laying between them. They'd have to slow up and look at exactly the right angle to see him." Another car cruised by more slowly. I could feel the thump-thump vibrations of rap music bouncing off the truck walls. Snatches of lyrics faded in and out. "*...slap the bitch's ass...*"

I craned my neck but couldn't see any more. "Don't worry. Another patrol car is bound to come along in a minute. They'll see what's going on and stop."

Two more cars whizzed past. I watched the reflections of the blue light reflect off the trees in the distance. The thump-thump sound reappeared, coming this time from the direction it had disappeared toward. The car crept by. It was a metallic blue Chevrolet Impala, a mid-sixties model sporting oversized chrome wheel covers. The driver, a youngish black male, wore a dark knit pullover watch cap. I caught a glint of blue light reflected from the gold chains around his neck. He came nearly to a dead stop, looked at the policeman lying on the pavement, then sped away.

"That's the second time that car has driven past. He slowed up, I know he saw the cop. Probably went to call somebody."

Four more cars, a taxi and a pickup drove past. No one stopped. Then I heard the thump-thump again. They were coming back!

The Impala pulled up slowly beside the front of the patrol car and the back of the truck, stopping so the passenger's window gave a clear view of the situation. Another young black male peered out the window. He studied the scene for a moment and said, "Yeah. He be down all right."

They couldn't see me watching from the darkness of the container.

From somewhere in the car I could hear, "Get it man! Grab his gun."

"Shit. I ain't gon' do that. They think' we done kilt the police."

"Shit, Tyrone!," came from inside the car. "Do it. And that door to the truck's open. See what's in there."

"Okay, but…" The passenger's door opened and the man got out. He was wearing a baseball cap turned backwards and a Miami Heat jersey. Looking around, he walked over and kicked at the cop. "Hey, man." No response. He reached down and grabbed the gun out of policeman's holster.

Tyrone started to open the container door as I yelled, "Hey! What the hell are you doing?" He stared me straight in the face. His eyes grew wide and he stumbled back, nearly sprawling over the hood of the patrol car. Still clutching the gun in his hand, he leaped back in the Impala and slammed the door. With a screech of tires, the blue car sped away, its chrome wheel covers spinning with the acceleration.

CHAPTER
Fifty

CLAIR, FROM HER POSITION behind me, hadn't been able to see the whole ugly picture. "What was that all about?"

I didn't want to try to explain it. "You don't want to know."

"Tell me, dammit!"

I took a deep breath. "I think they were more interested in ripping off the cop's gun than —" Tyrone had left the container door open. I stopped when I saw another patrol car turn the corner and enter the street. It slowed and then, turning on his blue lights, the driver pulled in behind the first car. I yelled at the top of my lungs. "Over here! Help!" Two officers approached the truck cautiously, drawing their guns when they saw the patrolman on the ground.

I yelled again. "Call for back-up. There's a bomb inside this truck. You've got to move quickly or it's going to explode."

One of the policemen peeked quickly in the truck and then stepped back out of view. "Who's in there?"

"There're two of us. We're both tied up. You've got to try to catch two men in a red Ford Expedition. It's the only way to disarm the bomb."

"Have you been drinking or using drugs?"

"No! Goddammit! The truck — this container — is a bomb. It's going to explode in less than an hour. You've got to-"

"How many of you are there in the truck?"

"I told you. There are two of us."

"Are you armed?"

"No! We're tied up. Open the door and look inside."

He did, holding his flashlight in one hand and his gun in the other. Satisfying himself that we represented no threat, he holstered his weapon and kneeled down to check on his fallen colleague. I could hear a moan and a weak, "I'll be okay."

His partner, who had been calling for backup, said, "I've got an ambulance on the way and I've alerted the bomb squad." He shined his flashlight in my eyes and said, "You look like you've been beat up. What do you two have to do with all this?"

"We were kidnapped, but that's not important right now. This truck is a bomb that is set to go off at about nine-forty. It's full of plutonium. It's a dirty bomb. There's only one way to disarm it. Untie us! We don't have much time."

The patrolman cut the ties that bound my arms and legs, then cut Clair's. My hands were numb, my feet in pain. I tried to push up to a sitting position but couldn't. "Don't worry," he said. "The bomb squad's on the way. I think you need to get to the Emergency Room. Grady Hospital's just down —"

"No!" I yelled. They didn't seem to understand. "The bomb can't be disarmed. If they try, it'll blow up." I looked around. "Where are we?"

"On Auburn Avenue where it runs through the Martin Luther King Center. That's the new Ebenezer Baptist Church behind you and Dr. King's tomb is over there." He pointed at the small white monument I'd seen. Suddenly Ulbricht's plan was clear. The ultimate race crime! The destruction of the one place most sacred to the American civil rights movement. The radioactive contamination of Atlanta's core. All neatly blamed on Rebecca Tate, the daughter of racist bomber. The ultimate revenge.

Clair had managed to sit up and was rubbing her wrists. "Nate, they've got to get Ulbricht! It's the only hope."

An unmarked police vehicle skidded to a stop next to the patrol cars. A man in a suit jumped out and sprinted over. "I'm Captain Marks. I'm in charge of the bomb squad. I heard the call on the radio and got here as soon as I could. You want to quickly fill me in?"

"What time is it?" I asked.

"Eight forty-eight."

"You want a quick answer. Here it is. This truck is a ticking bomb. It's filled with approximately a hundred kilograms of Plutonium-239 and enough plastic explosive to level every building within a hundred yards of here. In fifty-two minutes it's going to go off. If it does, most of downtown Atlanta will be uninhabitable for the next several thousand years. There's one man who can stop it, and right now he's on the run in a red Ford Expedition. I have no idea where he's going, but if I were him I'd be heading upwind. You don't have time to evacuate the city. If you can catch him and get him back here in time you have a chance to stop it. If not, thousands of people are going to die."

The officers stared, speechless. Marks whispered, "Holy shit."

TWENTY MINUTES LATER we were sitting in the Atlanta police's mobile command center parked in the middle of the street two blocks away from the bomb. An EMT had bandaged my head. Clair was still rubbing the red marks on her wrists. The first idea had been to move the truck. Mavik had left the keys in it, but it wouldn't start. He'd disabled it — part of the plan, no doubt. A team of mechanics was working on the problem. Bomb squad technicians were trying to come up with a way to disarm the device without setting it off. Orders had gone out to cordon off downtown Atlanta. The expressways leading into town were blocked at the perimeter beltway. Officers were rushing door to door for twenty blocks around the King Center, evacuating homes and businesses. An all-points-bulletin had gone out for a red Ford Expedition traveling away from town. The FBI and FEMA had been notified. The Governor had been requested to call for an emergency mobilization of the National Guard.

"All right," Marks said. "Here's what I've done: I've got three choppers in the air on call and waiting. I've set up a landing zone in the ball field on the other side of the Center. We'll pick up these guys, Ulbricht and Mavik, and fly them back here. They'll have the choice of disarming the bomb or getting blown up by it. The fallback plan is to get the truck started and move it somewhere to minimize the damage if we can't stop the explosion. The problem with that is there's nowhere we can drive in," he paused and looked at his watch, "...half an hour that won't be a heavily populated area. I've talked with the mayor. We don't have many options. At nine-thirty — that'll be ten minutes before it's set to go off — I'm going to have to pull everybody out."

"Captain Marks!" A clerk interrupted him. "We may have spotted them. The state patrol is shadowing a red Expedition traveling west on I-20 toward Birmingham. They're just past the Lithia Springs exit. They're running the tag number now, and I've got a chopper on the way."

"Great! It'll be close but we've got enough time to do it."

The clerk broke in again. "They've got 'em confirmed. The vehicle was rented from Avis at the airport this afternoon. The driver is a German national named Hans Dieter Ulbricht." He listened for a second on his headphones. "Georgia State Patrol's cut on their blue lights and is about to pull them over."

"Can you put that on the speaker?" Marks said. "I think we all want to hear it." The clerk flipped a switch and the crackle of a police radio band filled the small space.

"...*in pursuit. I'm at mile marker thirty-six. They see my lights and are signaling to pull over.*" The sound of a siren wailed in the background.

"*Roger. They are armed and dangerous. I repeat armed and dangerous. Do not exit your vehicle until backup arrives.*"

"*Ten-four.*"

"*GSP nine-oh-one. I'm passing mile marker thirty. I'll be at your twenty in four minutes.*"

"*Okay. They've stopped. I'm going to get on the speaker and... The passenger's getting out. What the hell is he doing? Sir, stay in your car. I repeat, stay in your-*"

The sharp crack of two quick gunshots exploded from the speakers.

"*GSP nine-oh-one. What happened?*"

There was no reply.

303

"*This is chopper four. I'll be over the area in twenty seconds.*"

"*Use your light. Look for the red Expedition. I'll be there shortly.*"

"*Chopper four. Got 'em spotted. They're moving fast. I estimate over a hundred.*"

"*I'm right behind them.*"

"*I'll stay over them.*" A pause, then, "*Who the hell is this nut? He's weaving in and out — he just ran a pickup off the road.*"

"*This is Ferry. I'm at the scene. We have an officer down.*" His voice broke. "*It looks bad. I need a medevac chopper quick.*"

"*Chopper four. You want me to divert?*"

"*No. Stay with them. I think it's too late. Don't lose the bastards!*"

"*Ten-four. I'm over him. The stupid fool is...Oh, shit! He lost it. Looks like he's hit a bridge abutment. I can see a fire... Damn! There's been an explosion. Gas tank must have gone up. I'm going to try to set down on the median.*"

Marks grabbed the microphone. "*Chopper four. This is Captain Richard Marks of the Atlanta police. Are there injuries?*"

No reply.

"*Chopper four. I repeat. Are there injuries?*"

"*Captain, a better question would be 'Are there survivors?' The answer is no. The place is a burning inferno. No one could survive that wreck.*"

Marks looked at his watch. "That bomb's going to explode in twenty-one minutes, unless someone here comes up with a miracle."

CHAPTER
Fifty-One

MARKS TURNED TO HIS LIEUTENANT. "I need a report from the bomb techs, now! And the mechanics. Find out if they're making any progress on getting the truck started." Turning toward us, he continued, "You two need to get out of here. If you hadn't been here we wouldn't have known where to start, but it looks like — "

"We can't let this happen," Clair said. "My sister, my family, will be blamed. If the King Center is destroyed the Tate name will go down in history with James Earl Ray..."

"But you had no part in it, Clair," I said.

"True, but everyone who could prove that is dead. All we've got left is the evidence Ulbricht planted to implicate Becky."

We were interrupted by the Lieutenant. "Here's where we are, Captain. The bomb techs say the control devices are welded into one of several steel boxes under the frame. They're all connected by metal conduit. They *think* one or more of them may be decoys, but they aren't sure and don't want to risk it. They tried using portable x-ray but the lead shielding totally blocks everything. It's too risky to start cutting into metal. I think they're pretty much ready to give up on this one. Oh, yeah, one other thing. They found a cell phone in the truck. Somebody named Colette calling…"

"Okay, okay, that's not important right now. How about the mechanics, they get anywhere on starting the truck?"

"I talked to the head guy. Whoever set this up planned it well. The truck has an electronic ignition. The guy jerked the circuit board when he left. They managed to find a replacement, but he must have had a backup plan — cut some wires or something. They'll keep trying until you give the order to pull out."

Another officer stuck his head in the room, "Captain Marks, I've got CNN, CBS and three TV stations on hold. We've got four news choppers hovering overhead. All the expressways out of town are gridlocked, and we're beginning to get reports of some looting on Peachtree near Five Points. The news is out. The CNN guy tells me they estimate that four hundred thousand people are trying to leave the city. If this thing blows, they're all going to be exposed to the radioactive dust cloud. What do you want me to do?"

Marks looked around the room, then at his watch one more time. "Any ideas? Anybody?" No response.

"Okay, that's it. We've got twelve minutes, and you know as well as I do that's a guess. We're cutting it too close as is. Get those choppers away from the area. Tell everyone to drop what they're doing and pull out. Tell 'em to get as far away as possible, and when they hear the blast, they need to get inside the nearest structure and stay there until the dust cloud settles."

"Captain, I'm getting word they got the truck started."

"Too late now. Tell 'em they need to get out — now!" He turned toward Clair and me. "You two wait for me in the car; it's right outside. I need to notify the Governor, and I guess he'll need to call the President."

Clair said, "You're just going to let it blow up? You're not going to try to move it? They said they got the truck started."

"Look, lady," Marks snapped, "I didn't write this script. For all we know the rig may be booby-trapped. We don't have the time to figure that, and at least we've done our best to evacuate this area. If we move it to —" He stopped suddenly. "Hell, I don't have to explain this to you. Get out! Wait for me in my car outside."

We half ran toward the door. The driver of the command center van fired up his motor, waiting for Marks to make his calls before leaving. The scene outside was one of chaos: an eerie light show of flashing blue and red and yellow lights, mingled with the sound of helicopters overhead and the wailing of Civil Defense sirens in the distance.

I limped toward the Captain's car. Clair said, "There's something I've got to do. It's just an idea but it may work. I'll catch up with you later." She sprinted off toward the King Center and the truck bomb.

"Clair! Where the hell are you going? Come back!" She didn't hear me, or chose to ignore me if she did. I set off running behind her, my progress slowed by the pain in my feet.

I rounded the corner onto Auburn Avenue. The street was deserted except for the truck, its flashers still blinking a warning message into the empty night. I was fifty yards behind her when she reached the cab and bounded up into the driver's seat. By the time I got there she was sitting staring at the instrument panel and gears. "Nate, I don't know how to start it. And these gears, how many are there?"

307

"Are you crazy? We've got to get out of here. This thing is about to explode."

"I've got an idea! I need your help. Can you drive this thing?"

I spent springs and summers during my high school years delivering loads of Vidalia Onions to farmers' markets and grocery store across the state. Driving an eighteen-wheeler is one of those bicycle-type skills. You rarely forget how. "Yes, but..."

"Then get in! We don't have much time."

"What?"

"Get in, dammit! Start the truck!"

Clair slid over while I climbed in the driver's seat. The key was in the ignition. I turned the key one click and waited for the glow plug light to go out. I pressed the clutch, put the gears in neutral and turned the key. The engine fired immediately. "Where to?"

"Straight ahead down Auburn. You'll need to take a left and then another left. I'll show you."

I released the air brakes with a hiss, pressed the clutch again and eased the gearshift lever into first. We began to move. "We've got eight minutes," Clair said. "Hit it."

"Where are we going?"

"The only place nearby that might limit the damage. Underground Atlanta."

CHAPTER
Fifty-Two

GAINING SPEED AND IGNORING traffic lights we barreled down the deserted street toward the city's center. The lighted towers of office buildings lining the ridge along Peachtree Street came into view as we passed under the I-75/I-85 connector. Two City of Atlanta patrol cars, abandoned by their drivers with blue lights flashing, were parked sideways across Auburn Avenue at Woodruff Park.

I downshifted and tapped the brakes, slowing the truck. "We're blocked! We can't get out this way."

"Ram them!" Clair screamed.

"Hang on then!" I pressed the accelerator. The tachometer swung toward the red zone. Shifting into a higher gear I aimed at the space between the two vehicles. We were doing forty as we struck, the mass of the truck sending the patrol cars spinning out of our path. The one on Clair's side smashed through the plate glass window of a restaurant featuring chicken wings. Its sign advertising that "Only a

Rooster Could Get a Better Piece of Chicken" landed askew across the cruiser's roof.

"Left here," Clair directed as Auburn dead-ended into Woodruff Park. "This street intersects Martin Luther King Drive three or four blocks from here. You're going to take another left there."

"Where the hell are we going?"

"I told you. Underground Atlanta. If we can get this truck inside, I think it might contain the explosion."

"Clair, there's no way! I've been there. We are going —"

"— are going to die, then." She finished my sentence. "Gotta make it work!"

We were doing fifty as we approached the stop light for MLK Drive. I tapped the brakes again, downshifted and made a wide swing to the left, clipping a fire hydrant in the process. A rooster tail of water erupted behind the truck as we turned. The illuminated gold dome of the Georgia capitol hovered ahead of us in the dark night. I wasn't familiar with the area. "How much further?" I yelled over the roar of the engine.

"Just one block and then left."

An intersection lay ahead of us. On the right a glass sheathed office tower disappeared above into the night. Beyond it stood an ornate brick church. Across the way and to our left I could see an open plaza dominated by a huge Coca-Cola logo. The sign over the next street read, "Central Ave. SW." I started to turn.

"Not here!" Clair screamed. "There!" She pointed at the plaza.

"There's no street!"

"I know. You have to drive across the plaza. There's a fountain in the middle. Steer to the left of it."

"Where are we going?"

"Drive, dammit! I don't have time to explain."

I pulled the wheel to the left, bumping over the side-walk and smashing through a granite monument that read "Steve Polk Plaza." The World of Coca-Cola building tow-ered straight ahead. Clair waived her arms frantically point-ing. "There! Go through there!"

Green traffic bollards snapped under the truck as I fol-lowed Clair's directions and accelerated across the deserted plaza. The Central Avenue viaduct rose to our left. We were headed toward what appeared to be a cul-de-sac. There was no way out. I hit the brakes, bringing us to a sharp halt.

"What are you doing? Why are you stopping?" Clair screamed.

"There's no where to go. No outlet. We're blocked in!"

"No! Look there — that's how you get to Underground Atlanta." She pointed ahead under the viaduct. I could see a neon sign advertising "Johnny Rocket's" and beyond it a glass-fronted entrance. "There's an old street there. It's a pedestrian walkway now, but I think we can get this truck down it. If it blows up in there it will be inside a protected space." She looked at her watch. "We've got three minutes. Drive!"

I revved the engine, pushed the gear lever into first and popped the clutch. With a lurch the truck leaped forward. I eased the accelerator to the floor and shifted to second gear. The entrance rushed toward us. "You'll need to steer to the left just inside. Try to keep in the center of the passage," Clair directed.

"We'll never make it in. There's not enough clearance for the top of the trailer."

"*Go!*" Clair screamed.

I hit the doorway doing thirty-five. The aluminum and glass-framed lattice that held the doors in place melted away under the force of the truck. With a screeching sound of metal against metal, the huge Kenworth plowed through hastily abandoned vendors' carts, past Johnny Rocket's and Orange Julius before wedging in a tangle of overhead pipes in front of a store selling quilts and "Southern Country Handicrafts" imported from China and the Far East. The motor groaned as it struggled to drag free.

"That's it. We're stuck."

"Then this is where we get off," Clair said, leaping out of her door. "Follow me. I know a quick way out." Grabbing my hand she pulled me down a smaller side street toward a sign pointing the way to Kenny's Alley. We ran past empty baby carriages and half-filled shopping bags, all evidence of a hurried evacuation. Coming to another entrance, Clair half-dragged me across a small open plaza and up three flights of steps into a multistory parking garage. We stopped to catch our breath and get our bearings. I was lost.

"I think the street's this way," she said and began running down a ramp toward a streetlight glowing in the distance.

I looked at my watch. It was exactly nine-forty. "We need to get out of this parking deck. If that bomb blows while we're here — "

There was a flash of light like summer lightening on a spring evening followed immediately by a force wave that was more felt than heard as it rumbled through the building. We were hurled to the floor. A cacophony of car alarms and flashing headlights exploded around us. A late model BMW sedan, evidently knocked out of gear by the jolt, drifted out of its parking slot and rolled backwards down the ramp toward us with increasing speed. I pushed Clair to one side as it zipped past, crunched through the barrier at the bottom of the ramp and landed on the street three stories below with a long metallic grinding.

One by one the car alarms cycled off. In the distance, Civil Defense sirens still wailed. I could hear the howl of an ambulance far away. Otherwise, silence. I looked out across the city. The buildings that lined the Peachtree Street ridge stood quietly undisturbed. In the opposite direction, the gold dome of the capitol still glimmered with reflected light. My feet and ankles still ached. I smiled. It was what I didn't see that made me happy. The sky was clear. There was no cloud of dust. And we were still alive.

CHAPTER
Fifty-Three

FOLLOWING THE END of the Civil War, a thriving complex of multi-storied commercial buildings sprang up from the ashes around Atlanta's central train depot. In the early twentieth century a series of iron viaducts and later concrete bridges effectively raised the street level to the second floor of these buildings. For decades the abandoned "underground" storefronts were used for storage and as service entrances, their ornate iron, marble and granite facades undisturbed by the flow of traffic on the streets above. The idea for an entertainment district known as Underground Atlanta originated in the late nineteen-sixties. By the late nineteen-eighties, the area had been restored and reopened as a downtown nightlife center, only to suffer from mismanagement, political cronyism, and a high crime rate that deterred the anticipated droves of free-spending conventioneers.

More than two hundred blocks of downtown Atlanta were cordoned off under martial law for two weeks following the explosion. Radiation suited members of the Georgia National Guard patrolled the area, while hoards of similarly garbed investigators from the FBI and other Federal agencies sifted for clues through the ruins of Underground. It soon became evident the plutonium had been secreted in the long sides of the container, yielding the fortunate, if unintended, result of blowing it into the storefronts that lined either side of the central pedestrian walkway. Radioactive material expelled from either end of the tunnel was minimal, and was rapidly contained and removed. After two weeks of exhaustive study the central city reopened to vehicular traffic, the exception being an immediate two block area around what was now referred to as "ground zero." Or Underground Zero in the hands of the pundits.

On a practical basis it was impossible to remove the plutonium dust that now made even a few minutes of unprotected exposure in the blast area a mortal danger. With a half-life of more than twenty-four thousand years, the ruins of the shops and restaurants were forever contaminated. After due consultation with local, state and federal authorities, work began on a stainless steel and lead-lined Chernobyl-style sarcophagus, designed to last at least a hundred years, constructed over the site of Underground Atlanta.

As for Clair and me, we spent the three days following the explosion in an isolation ward of Emory University Hospital. Neither of us had been severely injured. My head wound required eight staples and an oversized bandage. We both had bruises and scrapes here and there but nothing a few weeks wouldn't heal. We were told we were being observed for potential radiation poisoning, despite all evidence that the container had been well shielded and that our actual exposure was negligible.

The more obvious reason for our enforced segregation became clear when the familiar face of Agent Kelly appeared on television screens the day after the averted disaster to state unequivocally that Clair and I had been working with the FBI all along, describing us in glowing terms as "heroes who saved an American city from the threat of foreign terrorism." Vague references were made to al Qaeda and "sleeper cells." No mention was made of Becky, the Tate family or Ulbricht.

Kelly visited us in the hospital the following day to thank us for our help and to deliver checks for one million dollars to each of us from a "special anti-terrorism reward fund" established after the September Eleventh attacks. He also informed us that since our role in the events involved national security issues, we were prohibited by law from discussing anything with the press or any other public news outlet. He made it quite clear our acceptance of the "reward" funds was inextricably linked to this demand, and made us sign documents to that effect before handing us the checks.

Under Agent Kelly's watchful eye, Clair and I were the center of attraction at two stage-managed "press conferences" held at the hospital's media center. Questions were carefully screened. On several occasions Kelly cut off our answers, citing the "ongoing investigation." After our discharge we returned to Becky's old condo, not answering the phone and dining on gourmet take-out dutifully delivered twice a day by Kelly or Harriet, Becky's interior designer. The media vehicles that had set up camp outside gradually lost interest and drifted away one by one.

Life gradually returned to normal in Atlanta. The two-week hiatus that had, for practical purposes, shut down city and state government was deemed by most observers not to have been such a bad thing. Over the ensuing months, the Atlanta City Council squabbled over which politician the sarcophagus should be named for, finally settling for

The Heroes Memorial when someone reached the conclusion that its presence represented a greater potential tourist attraction than the former Underground ever did.

Publicly, the American government continued to search for the "masterminds" behind the bomb, vaguely assigning blame to several little-known Islamic extremist groups. Privately, Kelly assured us that the planned series of arrests in Europe and the Middle East had taken place, and that the suspects were being held and questioned in a nameless foreign country whose government was known to turn a blind eye toward more coercive methods of interrogation.

One night in late May a series of bombings in northern Teheran destroyed three apartment blocks and four government ministry buildings. The death toll was reputed to be in the hundreds, including a number of influential members of the Iranian government. International press reports attributed the attacks to well-funded dissident groups seeking a democratic government for Iran. Reports of two American stealth bombers dropping a series of precision-guided thousand pound bombs were widely discounted as false.

It was more than three weeks before I heard from Colette. It may have been that she didn't realize my cell phone had been destroyed in the blast; I wasn't about to give her my new number. She tracked me down by finding Becky's old number and then calling repeatedly until I got tired of seeing her name on Caller ID and picked up the phone.

Carl had moved back in, Colette said, and she needed my advice. It seems that the nurse with whom he'd been involved was also married, and her husband was one of Atlanta's more notorious and aggressive trial lawyers. Having discovered his wife's infidelity and observing that Carl was chairman of the Orthopedic Department at the hospital where she worked, he presented him with the unpleasant choice of a very public and very messy sexual harassment lawsuit or a large cash settlement to replace his wife's salary after her anticipated resignation from the nursing staff. Carl chose the latter, and with his tail between his legs came home to Colette and Carl, Jr. Unfortunately, Colette explained, his financial obligations from his previous marriage had left him with limited disposable cash. She offered to sell me the flat in Paris with all its furnishings to buy his way out of the situation. I paid for it out of my reward money.

Clair used half of her reward to set up a trust fund to ensure her mother's continued care in the nursing home and the other half to retire the outstanding debt of Tate Interiors. Harriet, in partnership with another interior designer, offered to purchase the business for a mid-range six-figure sum. Clair accepted.

Shortly after the first of June, I returned to Paris to attend to my long-neglected duties as manager of Madeleine Tour's European office. Clair came with me, intending to stay a few weeks while deciding what to do. Four months later she was still here and had taken over my home office which she was furnishing with baby things.

Author's Note

I hope that my readers have enjoyed this novel. Although it is a work of fiction, I like to believe that the story is one that could have taken place, even if it did not. One reviewer of the completed manuscript said that he found the novel most believable, except for the opening scene at the Eiffel Tower. For the record, that event, with some minor literary liberties, happened exactly as I describe it. I was in Paris in late March 1989 attending a scientific meeting. A friend and I were waiting in line for the lift at the Eiffel Tower when a blotch of red suddenly appeared on the white kid leather jacket of a French girl standing next to me. I thought at the time, *if I ever write a novel...*

For those interested in art history, the systematic looting of European Art by the conquering German armies in World War II is a fascinating tale. Even today, some sixty years after the end of the war, paintings missing since the early 1940's still occasionally turn up at auctions and in museum collections. The Schloss Collection did in fact exist, but the two paintings that I created for this novel are fictional. More information is available on the Internet at http://www.diplomatie.gouv.fr/archives/dossiers/schloss/index_ang.html. For additional reading I recommend highly Lynn Nicholas's work, *The Rape of Europa* (Alfred A.Knopf, Inc., 1994), and *The Lost Museum* by Hector Feliciano (in English translation from Basic Books, 1997).

The scenes that take place in Paris, Savannah and Atlanta should be accurate. I took only minimal literary liberties in changing a few things, but I did personally trace the steps of Nate and Clair through all three cities.

I highly recommend the Jules Verne restaurant, but make reservations far in advance. Unfortunately for the "foodies" amongst my readers, Chez Maurice and others are figments of my imagination.

I welcome readers' comments and feedback. Feel free to contact me via email at: rawlings@pascuamanagement. com, or visit my Web site at www.williamrawlings.com.

William Rawlings, Jr.
Sandersville, Georgia
April 2005